MURDER OF A POST OFFICE MANAGER

A CRIME NOVEL

By Paul Felton

HARDBALL PRESS

Published by Hard Ball Press. Release date: March 15, 2013

To contact the author or publisher: info@hardballpress.com, or
www.hardballpress.com

Cover art by Patty G. Henderson:
www.boulevardphotografica.blogspot.com

ISBN 978-0-9814518-8-6

Dedication

This book is dedicated to the hard working stewards in many different unions who fight for justice every day on the workroom floor.

Acknowledgements

The author would like to acknowledge and thank the following people (and one building):

Timothy Sheard and Dave Bass of Hardball Press for giving me the opportunity to publish this novel and for helping me every step of the way.

Donna Ratkos-Mercier for mentoring me when I was a new steward.

Nancy Felton, my older sister, for being a positive influence when I was a young adult, and throughout my life.

The Forbes Library in Northampton, Massachusetts, upon whose tables many of these chapters were drafted while I visited my sister.

Rhonda Greene, who helped to kick start the kickstarter fundraising effort to get this project off the ground.

The author also thanks all of the pioneers of the labor movement, upon whose shoulders I stand.

Finally, thanks to all the kickstarter contributors:
Dee Burton, Grover Furr, Miriam Pickens, Mary Ellen Howard, Kevin Smith, Lis and Stuart Bass, Chris Sheard, Roy Murphy, Thomas Lothamer, John Dick, Joe Berry, Nancy Vogt, Pam Sporn, James Phillips, Beth Morrison, Vince Tarducci, Bill Manley, David Greene, Sue Doro, David C. Yao, Kimberly Shuller, Jody Spencer, Laura Lee Dominguese, Brent Garren, Joann Hertel, John Rummel, Carl Bunin, Benjamin Obecny, Jon Bekken, Jane Duggan, Glenna Green, Nancy Felton, Katie Elsila, John Merritt, Michael Flora,

Brenda R. Moon, Georgiana Hart, Suzanne Nash, Nagaraj, Leo Parascondola, Amy Bromsen and Bill Parker, Andrew Wentink, and John Jaros

Introduction

I have a unique story to tell. I was a steward at the Post Office in a union local that experienced two workplace shootings in an 18-month period. As Editor of the union newspaper, I reported on those shootings. As a steward, I dealt with the same management team that created so much tension in the months leading up to the Royal Oak shooting.

I also like reading mystery novels, especially those that involve courtroom scenes. So I wrote a mystery novel loosely based on my experience as a steward that ends with a courtroom drama.

I have three goals in publishing this story.

The first goal is to entertain with a murder mystery/courtroom drama.

The second goal is to dramatize the role of a union steward; fighting for justice, defending employees' rights, and putting a check on unbridled managerial authority.

The third goal is to provide some background for the series of postal shootings that gave rise to the expression "going postal" in the early 1990s.

None of the characters in this novel are real. The closest one is Paul Farley, who in some respects resembles me. But this is not an autobiography. The Paul Farley character is part fantasy, part nightmare, and part reality.

None of the managers represent a real person in any fashion.

I hope reading this novel gives the reader some insight into the daily life on the workroom floor at the post office, at the same time as it keeps you guessing about who killed James Newton.

Enjoy,
Paul

One: THE RENDEZVOUS

November 18, 1998

Prosecutor: Was the defendant home at the time of the murder?
Witness: No.
Prosecutor: How do you know this?
Witness: We called him three times and got his answering
machine.

James Newton spent the last day of his life the way he spent every day – flexing his muscles as the man in charge of the midnight shift at the Plant. He was more than a boss at a large postal facility, he was the king of the midnight shift, also known as Tour One. His empire included three buildings, the Plant, the Building on Big Beaver (the BOBB) and the Stephenson Highway Operation (the SHO). Machines that sorted mail rapidly and efficiently filled these buildings. Machines that gave Newton the best production numbers in the state of Michigan.

Newton arrived shortly after midnight and sat back in his plush executive chair. A round of phone calls to his subordinates prepared him for his 1:00 meeting with Elliott Drummond.

Technically, Drummond was Newton's equal; they both had the title of MDO (Manager, Distribution Operations). But as the elderly Drummond made his way into Newton's office, dragging his left leg, the power relationship was clear.

"We're going to start a new sick leave policy," Newton told Drummond. "Three absences in 90 days and you get discipline. I'm sending a memo to all the supervisors."

"Okay with me."

"Show me today's sick call list."

Drummond handed Newton the list. "Jim, you know who called in sick today? Paul Farley."

Farley was a steward whose confrontations with Newton were

1

legendary. As was his temper. Farley mocked Newton in the union newspaper, calling him "Fig Newton" and distorting the facts in his libelous articles. The latest one was called "Fig Newton Must Go." Newton had been making his life hell ever since.

"Elliott, did you ever notice how ugly Farley is? I mean, with that ridiculous mustache, the unruly hair, the pasty complexion, the bald spot in back of his head? How can anyone stand to look at him?"

Drummond shrugged his shoulders. Newton continued, "But of course, it's the ugliness of his soul that's most important. We're going to step up the pressure on Farley when he comes back to work."

"We're already disrupting his union time," Drummond said. "What else do you plan to do?"

"Elliott, you don't want to know."

At 1:30 (or 0150 in postal lingo) Angela Roberts knocked on the door, interrupting the MDOs' conversation. Angela was a steward who stood firmly behind her coworkers, but didn't disrespect management like Farley did. She drove a hard bargain, even when she compromised. She kept her cool and was intelligent. Newton didn't know a black girl could be that intelligent. But today Newton had the upper hand.

"You owe five people back pay on my overtime grievance," Angela said.

"Don't waste your breath and don't waste my time. You're not getting back pay on your grievance. Send it to Step Two."

Angela spoke slowly as she wrote "Don't waste your breath and don't waste my time. You're not getting back pay, send it to Step Two." She added, "That's going in my Step Two appeal."

After Angela walked out, Newton told Drummond, "I've talked to the manager who's handling the Step Two. He's denying it. It'll take *years* for them to get their money."

Newton walked through the automation area. He loved the sound of the Optical Character Readers (OCRs) and Delivery Bar Code Sorters (DBCSs). Years ago you'd walk through the building and hear people's voices. Now the dominant sound was the whoosh-whoosh of mail being drawn into the machines and the clackety-clackety-clack of mail rushing through and landing in bins along the side of the machine. The feeder and sweeper were too far away from each other to talk – as long as they were doing their job. On those occasions when his numbers fell, it was because of lazy employees, the union that defended them, and the wimpy supervisors who were afraid to confront them. Newton stared at a young man who was supposed to be sweeping OCR #3; the employee cut short his conversation and scurried to the other end of the machine.

Back in his office, Newton looked in the mirror behind his desk. Others might call him a little overweight at 5' 7" and 190 pounds. But in the mirror Newton saw a man who was solidly built. At the age of 50 he still had a full head of brown hair, carefully combed to one side, a little bit long but very neat. His tan skin and long hair added to his youthful appearance; he could easily be mistaken for 40. With his almost baby face features, your first impression would be of a pleasant, mild-mannered guy. But his dark eyes could look right through you; he could intimidate his foes and get what he wanted most of the time. It was his personality and good looks that attracted the women.

Or, one woman in particular. Stacey Kline was a supervisor at the 110 belt. In her mid-thirties, she worked out three times a week, and you could see the results. She had straight blond hair down almost to her shoulders, sparkling blue eyes, smooth skin, and a figure like a model.

Stacey's tour ended at 0500. Wednesday was the day Stacey's husband went to his job early, leaving their Bloomfield Hills home at 5:00. Harold Kline used to supervise at the Post Office and then had gone successfully into the business world. He earned $90,000 a year, worked 60 hours a week, had a beautiful home and a lovely wife. He had everything he wanted, but he didn't have a life.

Stacey and Jim Newton met for breakfast shortly after five every Wednesday. Newton's shift didn't end until 0850, but nobody would question his absence. Drummond would assume Newton went to the BOBB or the SHO. Newton would still be home at the usual time so his wife wouldn't suspect a thing either.

When Harold Kline was out of town on a business trip, Newton would arrive home late. That's when Newton and Stacey did a lot more than breakfast together. He would tell his wife he had to take care of a minor crisis at work. Mrs. Newton understood that her husband was dedicated and conscientious, while the other MDO was old and useless.

Newton's musings were pleasantly interrupted at 0300 when Stacey Kline dropped by his office. She wore a low cut blouse underneath a sweater. "I'm glad you denied that overtime grievance," she said as she unbuttoned the top button of her sweater.

"I've already made a phone call, it'll be denied at Step Two," he said, as Stacey unbuttoned two more buttons.

"Here are the clock rings you need," she said as she slowly leaned over to lay the stack of papers on his desk. Newton's pulse quickened as he watched this beautiful, sexy woman. Stacey then buttoned her sweater, said "See you later, boss, you know today is Wednesday," and headed back to the workroom floor.

He was thinking about her for the next two hours. He never thought about his wife like that anymore. Of course there were other well built ladies in the Plant. But there was something about the sparkle in her eyes, the warmth in her smile, even the crispness of her speech that excited him. And naturally, she was loyal to him. Yes, she would make an excellent MDO when old man Drummond retired. Newton would see to it that she got the job.

Newton walked out to the dock to watch the 0500 dispatch. It was a sight to behold. Mail rolling out to 20 different truck stalls, workers loading the trucks headed to communities throughout Oakland and Macomb counties, delivering every letter with a 480 or 483 zip code, everything running like clockwork. All because of Newton's management skill.

After 0500 you could feel the building exhale. Oh, there was still more work to be done: clerks with scheme knowledge sorting Troy, Royal Oak, Birmingham, Rochester and Warren mail down to the carrier, and DBCSs placing mail in the order the carriers walk their routes. But the 0500 dispatch was the hectic one. Today it was finished early. And that was fine with Newton, because it was time for a delicious breakfast.

The Chef's Hat Diner, a 24 hour place on Rochester Road, had a private back room with a separate entrance. Stacey ate there every Wednesday. When Newton had suggested a weekly breakfast back in May, Stacey knew the perfect place. They had their routine. Stacey came in the front door and chatted briefly with Fred Stone, who ran the diner. Newton came in the back entrance five minutes later. The slight risk of being seen together just added to the excitement for Newton. But they were confident nobody knew of their arrangement.

Stacey entered the diner and waited for Fred to finish serving a couple of groggy, middle-aged men in business attire. He spotted her and said, "Hi sweetie! What's up with you?"

"I think I'm getting a promotion soon. I expect it'll be some time next year."

"I'm sure you deserve it, honey."

Meanwhile, Newton parked his Cadillac in the Chef's Hat parking lot. He pressed the button for his remote car alarm. The car chirped twice. With a satisfied smile he turned toward the diner, his feet crunching on the gravel. Newton was almost to the door when he heard a loud *crack* and felt a sudden blaze of pain in the back of his head. He stumbled forward. Two more bullets struck him in the back. He felt no more pain and heard no more sounds as his lifeless body crumpled to the ground a few feet from the diner's door.

Hearing what sounded like shots, Stacey and Fred went out the back door together. She nearly fainted at the sight of blood flowing from Newton's head.

Fred helped her to a chair in the back room and called 911. Then he sat down with Stacey, in the chair Newton usually occupied.

"It must've been Farley," she muttered.

"What's that?"

"Paul Farley. He hates Jimmy, and he wasn't at work today. We've got to nail his ass! Let me get his number from the Plant, I'll bet he's not home."

She called Farley's number, then asked Fred to do the same. Ten minutes later the police called the same number. "You've reached 881-1730. Please leave a message and I'll get back to you as soon as I can."

By 6:30 the police were gone. Stacey rested her head on the table and quietly sobbed. Fred was serving the breakfast crowd in the front. She was hardly aware of the dishes' clatter and the customers' chatter. Her mind was focused on a nightmarish image – Newton's lifeless body next to a red puddle. Her anger at Farley was pushed aside by an overwhelming sense of despair. Her mentor, her boss, her lover was gone. James Newton was dead.

Two: THE BEGINNING

Prosecutor: Did Mr. Newton try to get you removed as a steward over a claim for Shelley Hart's jacket?
Defendant: Yes.
Prosecutor: How did that make you feel?

It was just before midnight, November 11th, 1983. Shelley Hart was in a foul mood as she came through the turnstile to begin a new workday on Tour One. Shelley was an Army veteran, and her husband was an ex-Marine. Veterans Day meant a lot to her. Even though she was a new employee, barely off probation, she should not have had to work her holiday.

But seniority had prevailed, and Shelley Hart was one of a handful of names placed on the holiday schedule. The arguments had taken place when the holiday schedule was posted the week before. Supervisor Jim Newton blew her off. Then she approached Paul Farley, the new steward. He said, "You can ask for official union time to see me later, but I really won't be able to help you." She gave him a dirty look and walked away. She hadn't joined the union yet, and she didn't know if she ever would.

Shelley complained to her coworkers at lunch that day. "It's crazy, the holiday isn't even on November eleventh. It's the night before."

"That's still the eleventh on our Tour," Celia Derringer said. It's the *morning* of the eleventh."

"But that's my point. No mail is delivered that day. Why make a veteran like me come in to sort mail that's just going to sit there twenty-four hours?"

"We all went through it honey when we first hired in," Emma Friedman chimed in. "It's not the end of the world."

<><><><><>

7

Shelley replayed last week's conversations in her mind as she entered the building. The lanky, long-legged 25-year-old woman turned left and headed for the women's locker room, her new winter jacket unzipped but still on her shoulders. It was the first day almost cold enough to wear it. She loved this jacket. For weeks she'd been looking forward to putting it on for the first time. And now, all she could think about was the damn holiday schedule. She could understand seniority. But really, there was no need for *anybody* to work this holiday. The building had been dead as Shelley and a dozen coworkers sorted mail that was going nowhere.

Now Oliver Simms was coming towards her with a hamper of mail. The hamper had a bad wheel and a metal rod protruding through the dirty off-white canvas. Oliver was in a hurry; Shelley's mind was on the holiday schedule. Her train of thought was broken when she felt a sudden jerk on her left side and heard the sound of cloth tearing. *"Simms, you idiot!"* she shouted. Her favorite jacket was ripped apart, so her evening was complete.

Shelley held back tears as she told Supervisor Jim Newton about it. He said, "That's too bad. Now report to the letter hand case section."

"He didn't give a shit," she said, telling her story to a Rochester scheme clerk. The clerk suggested she talk to the union.

<><><><><>

Paul Farley was listening to a J Geils tune on his Walkman radio while keying on the LSM (Letter Sorting Machine), when Jim Newton pulled back his mail and said that Shelley Hart needs to see him on union business. Newton told Farley he could see her from 3:00 to 3:15, then they both had to report to the 044 hand cases. If they needed more time they could get it tomorrow.

Paul repressed an impulse to argue. Newton was being a jerk. Since the day after the holiday was always light on Tour One, he should get as much time as he needed. And 0300 was the worst time to do it. Union business was conducted in the break room (which everyone referred to as the "swing room" for some reason), and another LSM crew would be on break at 0300. Their conversation would periodically be interrupted by a group of black women card players yelling "Boston!" and slapping high fives. But Paul didn't complain. Maybe he could handle Shelley's complaint in fifteen minutes. Once he became more established as a steward, he could demand respect.

Paul hummed the J Geils tune to calm his nerves as he headed to the locker room to put away his radio. He looked forward to the day he could aggressively take on management; when he knew the contract backward and forward; when he knew how to back a supervisor down. He reminded himself to act confident when he talked to Shelley, whom he barely knew. Every new grievance would affect his reputation, for better or worse, and with it, the strength of the union on Tour One.

Paul was relatively new in the Plant, and very new on the Tour. He had volunteered to be a steward in September, after Ron Davidson bid to day shift (Tour 2). The union was permitted five stewards on Tour One (which included the 8:30 PM shift as well as midnights). But Ron's departure left just one alternate steward on the 8:30 shift and nobody on midnights. So Paul stepped up to do the job.

Paul thought back to the two cases he'd handled in October. They were attendance discipline cases, the most common grievance in the Post Office. In the case of Tawanna Chambers, Supervisor Butch Hobson tried to take advantage of him. Before issuing a Letter of Warning, the supervisor is supposed to talk individually to the employee about their attendance, and give the employee a chance to improve. Hobson issued Tawanna a letter without going through this preliminary step. He claimed when he gave a stand-up talk to the entire Pay Location about attendance, that constituted Tawanna's "Discussion." Paul had learned about attendance grievances in his steward training, and he stood his ground on this

9

case. Tawanna's Letter of Warning was expunged. Now Tawanna smiled and said a friendly hello whenever she saw Paul.

Bob Saunders' settlement was a compromise: "Letter of Warning will be removed from grievant's record six months from date of issuance, provided there is no further discipline of a same or similar nature." Bob was polite but reserved when he saw Paul. How would Shelley feel after Paul handled her issue?

At 0300, Paul met Shelley Hart in the swing room. There were four long tables, each with room for 20 people or so. There were vending machines along one wall, with pop, coffee, candy, pastry, and sandwiches. Two microwaves sat on a counter at one end of the room. And unlike the rest of the building, there were windows along the north wall. They looked out on the employee parking lot, which was shaped like a slightly rounded triangle. At night you could see nothing but blackness out the windows. Still, the mere presence of windows gave the room a more relaxed feeling than the workroom floor.

Paul and Shelley sat near the window in the northeast corner of the room. Nobody was sitting immediately next to them, but a group of card players sat a few chairs down. They could smell the chili one of the card players had just heated up. The other tables were about three-quarters occupied. They could overhear an argument two tables away about whether the Beatles or Stones were the best rock and roll performers of all time. Paul would've joined the debate and argued for Bob Dylan, but he was on union business, not break. At the very next table a slightly overweight clerk put his head down to catch a 15 minute nap, while his female companion read a day-old newspaper she found lying there.

Paul handed Shelley an 1187 (the form to join the union) and she filled it out. She realized if she was going to ask the union for help, maybe she should join.

"Okay, I'm in the union. Now I want Simms to buy me a new jacket. Look at what he did to it!"

Paul examined the torn cloth. He looked into Shelley's eyes and saw anger, hurt, and self-pity. He knew he couldn't get Simms to pay for the jacket; he really wasn't sure what he could do other than lend a sympathetic ear.

"That sure is a nice looking jacket, apart from the tear," he said. Looks brand new too."

He let her talk about the jacket. She'd fallen in love with it when she saw it at a store in Oakland Mall, but they only had it in one size. Her bad luck had turned to good when she found the same jacket, on sale, at another store in the mall. Now her good luck had turned bad again. She looked at the jacket, willing the tear to disappear and the jacket to look like new again. *Oh why was Oliver so damn reckless?*

Paul said he would find out what could be done and get back to her tomorrow. Now he was glad for the fifteen minute time limit, because this subject hadn't been covered in steward training. If he had more time with Shelley today, she'd see he didn't know what he was doing.

Paul dropped by the headquarters for his Local Union in Ferndale after work. His American Postal Workers Union (APWU) Local covered more than 50 Post Offices, and had one full-time Officer (the President). There was usually another Officer around to write up grievance appeals and help answer questions.

Vice President Harry Parsons snapped his suspenders and looked Paul in the eye. "What did I tell you at steward's training?"

"I don't know, what?"

"You don't need to memorize every provision of the contract, but you need to know what every article is about. You need to know where to look when a situation like this comes up."

'Okay, where do I look?"

Harry opened the contract to Article 27. Paul saw the following language: "Subject to a $10 minimum, an employee may file a claim within 14 days of the date of loss or damage and be reimbursed for loss or damage to his/her personal property except for motor vehicles and the contents thereof taking into consideration depreciation where the loss or damage was suffered in connection with or incident to the employee's employment while on duty or while on postal premises. The possession of the property must have been reasonable or proper under the circumstances and the damage or loss must not have been caused in whole or in part by the negligent or wrongful act of the employee…"

Paul thanked the VP and headed home.

The next day Farley asked for more time with Shelley Hart. He gave her a claim form and assured her she had a good case. The possession of the jacket was "reasonable and proper" and the damage had been caused by defective equipment.

Shelley had a receipt for the jacket, but this raised a question. The receipt indicated a price of $140, with a $45 discount, so she actually paid $95 when she purchased it. The sale was now over, so it would cost $140 to replace it. Should she file a claim for $140 or just the $95 she had paid? Paul wasn't sure, but figured they should ask for the full amount.

"They can always bargain it down later to ninety-five dollars. In fact, that's what usually happens with these claims. Management denies them at first. They go through a different procedure than grievances. After it is denied, the next step will be arbitration. That could be six to nine months from now, or it could be a few years. A day or two before the arbitration, management might make an offer to split the difference. Sometimes they'll offer half, sometimes a third, depending on various factors. In this case,

12

there's no depreciation, since it was brand new. So let's ask for one-forty, and maybe they'll settle for ninety-five. Just don't expect to get the money anytime soon."

Paul felt competent and confident. He thought he was handling Shelley's case with professionalism and skill. He didn't let it show, but he felt a sense of exhilaration. In 24 hours, he had become a knowledgeable steward on the subject of employee claims.

Shelley thanked Paul for his effort. Yesterday, she had no idea whether Paul knew what he was doing, or even whether he cared. Today, she felt much better.

On December 1st Shelley heard her name over the PA system. *"Shelley Hart, report to the manager's office!"* The voice was Jim Newton's and it didn't sound friendly. What could this be about? She was past probation so she wasn't going to be fired. Or was she? She couldn't think of any reason why she would be in trouble. Halfway to the office she heard the loudspeaker again: *"Shelley Hart, report to the manager's office. Now!!* With trembling hands she opened the door to the office and walked inside.

"Close the door!" Supervisor Newton yelled at Shelley. His lower lip quivered and he glared at her as he gestured for her to take a seat.

"This is your signature, is it not?" he asked, showing her the claim form. She nodded. "You know what you did? You falsified a government document! You submitted a claim for a hundred-forty dollars when the receipt plainly shows the coat only cost you ninety-five. We'll have to call the Postal Inspectors in to investigate."

"Can't I just fill out a new form for ninety-five dollars?"

"It's not that simple. This is a matter of *ethics*. It's a matter of *honesty*. Postal employees must have good character. We can't keep someone who tries to steal from us, and that, young lady, is exactly what you did. How can we let a thief keep working here? You might get a window job at one of the stations, where you'll handle money every day. No, Shelley, I have to recommend termination."

"I'm sorry, Mr. Newton. I was just confused about how it works. I thought I could put down the entire amount, because that's what it would cost to replace it now. I wasn't trying to get anything I wasn't entitled to." She started crying. She used the back of her hand to wipe her eyes. "Please, Mr. Newton, I really can't afford to lose this job."

James Newton handed her a tissue. "Did that steward Farley advise you to ask for a hundred-forty dollars?"

"Yes, he did."

"Well, Shelley, there may be a way out of this. Just write a statement renouncing your claim. Explain it was Farley's idea to use the inflated figure of one-forty. We may be able to save your job yet. If you were following bad advice, it wasn't all your fault."

"I have to drop the claim completely?"

"Yes, that's the best way. It isn't worth losing your job over a claim for a jacket. With your salary, you can buy a new one. And you wouldn't have won the claim anyway, Farley should have told you that. We would have denied it because of your negligence. You didn't look where you were going, otherwise you'd still have the jacket in one piece."

Five minutes later Newton paged Farley over the PA system. Newton was grinning from ear to ear. He had Farley right where he wanted him.

When Farley entered the office, Newton's grin turned into a growl. "You advised an employee to cheat the Post Office out of forty-five dollars. A steward who tells people to steal from the Post Office won't be a steward for long!"

Paul saw Newton's mouth moving but he couldn't concentrate on the words. As the supervisor ranted and raved, Paul heard the menacing tone, saw the piercing eyes, and had a sinking feeling in the pit of his stomach. As Newton's angry voice reverberated in the room, Farley started doubting himself. For a moment, he thought he might actually be guilty. But he played it over again in his mind, and his advice to Shelley Hart seemed reasonable. So why was this supervisor badgering him? Still, he didn't argue. He just said, "I'll talk to my Local President about this."

Newton shot back: "You do that!"

Paul trudged out of the office and headed for the men's room. A heavyset man at the next urinal said: "You alright man? You look kinda pale."

Paul just nodded. He felt worse than he looked. Gone was that feeling of exhilaration. He felt whipped, confused, uncertain, angry, and even a little guilty. And his confidence was gone. He wondered if he was the right person for this steward's job.

Leslie Loder was a quietly effective, efficient, well organized union official. Now in her second term as Local President, she had originally been elected in a close race over an incumbent who was her complete opposite: militant rhetoric, a flashy style, and no substance. Nobody had opposed her when Loder ran for a second term. She was not a leader who inspired anyone, but she was a good judge of people, got along well with everyone and got tough when she had to. She would never make any dramatic innovations in the Local, but she was a good problem solver. And on the morning of December 2nd, she had a problem.

Management was demanding she remove Paul Farley from the position of steward on Tour One. Labor-management relations required mutual trust, and management should not have to deal with someone who advises employees to falsify documents. Jim Newton had talked to the Tour Superintendent, who in turn had talked to Doug Asner. Doug was just under the Postmaster. It was Asner who wanted Farley removed.

Leslie sat behind her large desk and put a pile of grievances off to one side. She put out a cigarette, then ran her hand over her short brown hair as Paul took a seat in a comfortable armchair facing her. He explained the situation. Leslie was shocked, but not at Paul. "It's ridiculous for management to charge a violation of ethics here. At most, it's a matter of interpretation. She paid ninety-five dollars, but the jacket is worth a hundred-forty, and that's what it would cost to replace it. But I've never seen a receipt like this before. Usually, if you buy something on sale for ninety-five dollars, the receipt just says ninety-five dollars. This one gives both the regular price and the sale price. If I were the steward, I would have done the same thing, Paul."

"Well, I just figured if there was any doubt, ask for the higher amount. They can always bargain down from there. The receipt was included, so anyone could see what she actually paid for it. We weren't trying to fool anyone."

"You know I got a call from Doug Asner. He's going crazy over this thing. Of course, Asner only heard Newton's version, but he demanded I remove you as a steward." Seeing the instant fury in Paul's face, she spoke quickly. "Look Paul, I support you. They can't make me remove you. I'm going to have a meeting with Asner. I'll show him the person causing the problem here is not you, it's Newton. He manufactured a crisis over what should be a simple disagreement appealed through the normal channels."

"Why would Newton make such a big deal out of this? He scared that young lady half-to-death. And I'll admit it, he had me on the defensive too."

"It's not about saving the Post Office a little money. It's a power play, Paul. You're a new steward, and he wants to intimidate you and limit your effectiveness. Maybe employees on the Tour would lose confidence in you if he gets the claim dropped. It's not unusual for managers to give stewards the 'rookie treatment,' but this is going way too far. He used to deal with Ron Davidson, and Davidson would compromise with him quite a bit. Perhaps, too much. Newton had it pretty good, but now he wants it better. He wants to destroy the union on Tour One by destroying you. I'm not going to let him get away with it."

Paul breathed a huge sigh of relief. Hearing his Local President say he had done nothing wrong confirmed what he believed all along, but he needed to hear it. At the same time, his resentment grew as he came to understand Newton's cynical power play. Newton had been around long enough to know most stewards would've asked for $140 and then bargained down. But he made a show of righteous anger and his play acting was superb. He'd put the fear of God into Shelley and intimidated the steward – just to weaken the union. He probably wouldn't get away with it. But even with his Local President's reassurances, Paul was still on edge.

On December 9th, Loder and Asner reached an agreement. The original claim form would be denied at the local level, but it would be processed and sent up to the next level. An explanatory note would be signed by both parties, explaining the jacket had only cost the employee $95 when she bought it on sale, but it normally sells for $140. They could decide higher up what amount, if any, should be paid.

Farley was not satisfied. He had been put through an emotional wringer by a supervisor who gave employees lectures about "ethics" but didn't know the meaning of the word.

Loder warned him not to confront Newton about it again. "You and Newton will be dealing with each other for some time to come. You have to establish a working relationship, and another confrontation won't help. I'll convey our position to management behind the scenes."

Farley followed this advice, but it left him with a seething resentment. As a new steward, he had expected to run into hard-nosed managers. But he didn't expect dishonest power games. He did not express his feelings. But he would never forget the man who put him through this week of hell.

Three: THE WRONG ZIP

Prosecutor: In your opinion, did Mr. Newton deliberately provoke the defendant?
Witness: Yes, he enjoyed it when he got the defendant to slam the door or raise his voice. It was like a game with him.

By the summer of '86, the Union Office at the Plant was a busy place on Tour One. Gone were the days when union business was conducted in the swing room. The new office wasn't huge, but it had room for the necessities: two tables, some chairs, file cabinets, bookshelves, etc. The plaster walls, painted off-white, were not much to look at, and the unfinished wood door had a large window, allowing supervisors and employees alike to peek in. Still, there was more privacy than in the old days.

Also gone were the days when stewards spent most of their time distributing mail, interrupted only occasionally for a grievance. Since Jim Newton was appointed Tour One General Supervisor, the tension had been rising. A constant stream of mistreated employees kept all three stewards busy.

Paul Farley had basically handled Tour One by himself for a couple of years. He was now a seasoned veteran. Angela Roberts, a slim, dark-skinned woman, had joined Paul in the union office in 1985. Angela wore her hair extremely short; Paul was still getting used to hair that short on women. Her face was rather plain, but not unattractive. She wasn't sexy, but she had a sort of elegance in the way she moved that Paul noticed when she first hired in as a Troy clerk.

Angela had graduated from Wayne State University and taken classes in Labor Studies while majoring in English. When she took the test to get on the postal hiring roster, she didn't really expect to work here. Now she was finding out whether the theories she learned in Labor Studies classes apply in the real world of grievance handling.

The other Tour One steward was Ron Davidson. After a few years on day shift, he bid back on midnights for the ten percent night differential. His experience and knowledge helped Paul and Angela. And Ron seemed to know everyone, on all tours, in management and in the craft. He could find out what was going on behind the scenes, even when management was stonewalling the other stewards.

The funny thing was, you could never tell whether Ron gave a damn about anything that happened at the Post Office. He hid his feelings behind a sense of humor that, well, let's just say it took some getting used to. Like when a day shift steward suffered a death in the family, Ron had actually wondered aloud whether the union newspaper should run a headline: "Steward Grieves Mother's Death."

Where the other stewards seemed to carry a spirit of idealism with them as they went about their work, Ron was totally cynical. Yet he was surprisingly effective for someone who didn't seem to care.

On a Thursday morning over a bag of microwave popcorn that filled the room with its buttery aroma, the three stewards discussed Jim Newton's recent promotion. Paul said: "I was hoping Reggie Green would get the position, instead of that vicious character with the pretty boy face."

"You know," Angela said, "most women would find Green unattractive, especially compared to Newton. He's a little chubby, he's bald, he's got that funny crease above his nose that runs straight up to where his hairline should be. His skin is even darker than mine, if that matters. Yet when I look at him, I see a kind, decent human being, and that makes him more attractive in a way. I mean, that's what counts, isn't it?"

"That's why he didn't get the promotion," Paul said. "He's too good. Not that he's a pushover. Everyone respects him. When you think about it, he never has to raise his voice – people just listen to him. But he's fair. You show him a contract violation and he'll correct it. He goes by the book."

"I'll tell you what happened with the promotion," Ron said. "They had a screening committee to interview the top three candidates, Newton, Reggie, and Rose Bancroft from Tour Two. They summarized their findings in a report to Doug Asner. Then Asner ignored the report and picked the guy he wanted all along. He likes Newton's intensity. He thinks Newton gets things done, and he knows he's better off not knowing exactly how Newton goes about it. But the interview process was a sham. The winner was chosen before the interviews began."

"Does Reggie have any appeal rights?" Angela asked.

"No. On paper, all the proper procedures were followed," Ron said. "The criteria are left a little vague, so the appointing official can take into account what they call intangible leadership qualities."

"You mean, they can pick the one who's really going to stick it to us," Paul said glumly.

"That reminds me," said Angela. "Have you guys dealt with the new eight-thirty-to-five LSM supervisor, Red Collier? He's like a Jim Newton clone. He even combs his hair the same way, except it's red."

Davidson looked puzzled.

"You know what a clone is, don't you Ron?"

"Yeah, that's like a perfume, only men wear it.'

"Not a cologne, Ron, a *clone*."

"Oh yeah, that's a funny guy in the circus."

"No Ron, I'm not talking about a clown. *You're* the clown. I'm talking about a clone!"

"Okay, okay. It's like someone put Newton through the copying machine, pushed one wrong button and the hair came out red, but everything else came out the same."

"Yeah, he's got the same personality, the same temper, the same lack of principles, the same vicious streak," Angela added. "On my way in here I saw him arguing with Tawanna Chambers. Paul, your girl might be coming in to see you again."

Tawanna Chambers was not Paul's girl, but she was what he called his "number one grievant." Tawanna was a light-skinned woman in her twenties, with an infectious laugh and a beautiful smile. Paul had been attracted to her instantly. Reading his intentions, Tawanna let him know she was happily married before he made a fool out of himself. Paul had won her respect when he got her Letter of Warning thrown out in 1983, and had handled about a dozen cases for her since. Even when she was in the wrong, contractually speaking, she took that news well if it came from Paul. They had grown to like and trust each other, in a very comfortable steward-grievant relationship. She had also taught him the card game many of the black women at work played (bid whist, or "bid" as they called it) and she kept him informed of whatever was going on among her work crew. They never saw each other outside of work, but it was hard for two people who weren't friends outside work to have a closer relationship. There was just a nice chemistry between them.

Ron picked up the ringing phone just as Tawanna entered the union office. It was Butch Hobson, who was now the Warren supervisor. "I've got a problem with Candace Brown," he barked into the phone. "Ron, you can set her straight."Hobson went on to explain that Candace had reported two hours late, at 0225. It had been scheduled in advance, so that wasn't the problem. But 0275 was her crew's first break, and Hobson wasn't going to let her take a break after working only half-an-hour. Candace wanted to see a steward.

"This isn't a complicated issue Davidson. I'll let you see Miss Brown for fifteen minutes."

Ron had a clever idea. He smiled as he stepped out of the room.

Candace walked towards him at a brisk pace, a grim expression on her face. "Candace, the union office is kind of crowded right now. Why don't we sit in the swing room and talk for fifteen minutes, like we did before we had a union office. I'll buy you a coffee if you like." Candace broke out laughing. She was going to get her break after all, no matter what Hobson said. Davidson really didn't know if he was pulling a fast one on Hobson or whether this was exactly what Hobson intended when he let her go for fifteen minutes. In any event, no grievance was filed.

While Ron and Candace were drinking coffee in the swing room, Paul was giving Tawanna a friendly teasing. "Hey T, how come you haven't been in to see me lately? I was beginning to think you forgot about me."

Tawanna wasn't smiling. "If they keep that Collier on the LSM, I'll be coming back here every day. And half the crew will be back here, too. You'll need a bigger office and you'll have to hire more stewards."

"Are you volunteering for the job, T? I'd love to work with you back here. We could have some fun with management."

"No, just take care of my edit, Paul."

On the LSM, 12 people sat in front of keyboards typing address codes as letters moved in front of them at a speed of 60 per minute. With an edit, a printout of your keystrokes for 25 letters was compared with the addresses on the letters. If your keying average fell below 95%, you could be disciplined.

"How many errors does Collier say you made, T? And what's your average?

"Just one error. And my average is ninety-nine point six. But that's not the point. Collier is so petty about everything. I want to fight him on this. He enforces all the silly rules that nobody else bothers with. Three seconds to relieve another employee for sweep, no radios on the console – every other LSM crew puts their radios on the console, you get better reception that way. He makes us attach the radio to our belt or keep it in our pocket. What difference does *that* make?"

"I guess it makes Collier look good in Newton's eyes," said Paul. "You ever notice he looks just as ugly as Newton? Even has the same hairstyle."

"Okay, let me tell you what that ugly motherfucker did." The language was strong, but Tawanna was smiling now. "He counted one error against me, but the letter had a wrong zip."

"Did you key it to the zip like they say you're supposed to? It's Newton's new rule, you know. They posted it in the Order Book and by all the LSMs. Always key to the zip."

"No, I keyed it to where it's really supposed to go. The letter was addressed to Detroit, Michigan four-eight-oh-two-three. The zip code is Fair Haven. But the street address was on Seven Mile Road. Everyone knows that's in Detroit, and that's where I sent it. I live around there. The zip code should be four-eight-*two-oh-three*."

"So following Newton's rule would send the letter to Fair Haven and delay it at least a day."

"You got it. You know, some supervisors will give you the benefit of the doubt on an edit if the letter is confusing. Collier won't give anyone a break. But I didn't make a mistake and I'm not asking for a break. I'm right, he's wrong, case closed. Go out there and look at the letter, Collier said he'd save it for half-an-hour in case you want to see it."

The letter was addressed to Morris Office Supply, 414 W. 7 Mile Road, Detroit, MI, 48023. Farley tried to convince Collier it should be a zero-wrong edit, but the supervisor wouldn't budge. Paul made a Xerox copy of the letter and put it back in the mail stream to be miskeyed by someone who follows all the rules.

"We're going to have to challenge Newton's rules, T," Paul said back in the office. He looked at the address again, and a mischievous smile appeared on his face. "You ever been in this office supply store?" Tawanna shook her head. "Tell you what. I need a small box of envelopes, T. Here's a dollar. Buy me a box, and while you're there, get a business card from Morris Office

Supplies. Tell them your boss might want to order a special type of brief case or something."

Tawanna's eyes lit up. "You want proof I keyed the right zip for Morris Office Supply."

Paul winked and let her go back to work.

Paul and Tawanna met with Supervisor Red Collier at Step One the following week. Before the Step One meeting, Paul told Tawanna to stay calm. "We both know we're right on this one. We have the business card that makes our case. But if he wants to act stupid and deny it, he can't hurt you. You still have an excellent average. So either we get what we want at Step One, or we'll sit back, watch him act stupid, and send it to Step Two."

They started the Step One Meeting with some generalities. Collier stated that the rule of keying to the zip code made perfect sense.

Paul quietly laid two documents on the table. The Xerox copy of the letter and the business card with the correct address and zip code. He said, "Here's the proof Tawanna was right."

Collier refused to look at the business card. "You're not telling me how to run the Post Office, are you Farley? Rules are rules. Nine times out of ten the zip is right. She could have missent mail keying the way she did. We've got to prevent that."

"But Red, if she keyed by the rules, she would have missent it."

"Did she key to the zip code, Farley?"

"No, but the—"

"No buts!" Collier interrupted. "This grievance is denied."

"But you haven't even listened to us. At a Step One Meeting, management is supposed to give the union a full opportunity to present its case."

"You presented your case, Farley. Tawanna, here, chose not to key to the zip code. You're lucky she's not getting a Letter of Warning for failure to follow instructions. Grievance denied."

Farley said, "Come on T," and slammed the door on the way out. "What an asshole," he muttered.

Now it was Tawanna's turn to tease Farley. "You forgot to enjoy the meeting, sugar. I enjoyed watching you fight for me, but it didn't look like you were having any fun."

Paul had a scowl on his face.

Tawanna could see what was really upsetting Paul. He had a crush on her and really wanted to please her. He pretended his attraction to her played no role in his emotional reaction to Collier's denial of her grievance. It was amusing, and kind of endearing at the same time.

"You did what you could, Paul," Tawanna said. "Collier wasn't going to listen whatever you said. I'm sure you'll write up a Step Two grievance that'll convince whatever moron you meet with that I keyed the right zip."

Paul wasn't ready to go to Step 2 yet. His next stop was Mr. Newton's office. This wasn't an official part of the grievance procedure, but he hoped he could show Newton the business card and get Tawanna's error thrown out. And maybe there would be a little more flexibility in enforcing the "key to the zip" rule.

Paul saw a sign on Newton's desk that read "The Buck Stops Here." It was pretentious, given that Tour Superintendent Drummond was Newton's boss on the tour, but it was probably accurate. Paul sensed that Newton's power exceeded his position. That's why he came to Newton rather than Drummond.

"You gave Collier quite a scare, there, Farley," were the first words to greet him when he sat down opposite Newton. "You can't be slamming doors every time you have a little disagreement. And over what? An edit that had one error?"

Newton was enjoying the moment. Farley knew the story would be repeated and exaggerated to make him look bad. He decided to let Newton have his fun. Hopefully Newton would listen to reason after he was through.

But Farley had no such luck. Newton said, "The issue here isn't whether the zip code is correct. The issue is whether employees follow the rules. If employees can make their own rules we'll have chaos around here."

Paul opened his mouth to object but Newton held up his hand as a stop sign and shook his head. Turning his eyes to a memo on his desk, he muttered, "Close the door gently on your way out, please."

Paul felt a churning mixture of anger and frustration as he left Newton's office. Newton knew Tawanna was just being conscientious when she keyed the letter to 48203. And he knew that was really the right zip. He would say no to Paul regardless of the facts. Paul wanted so badly to win this case for Tawanna. But the worst part – the thing that made Newton so vile – was that he enjoyed twisting facts and enjoyed getting Paul upset. In fact, that was the main point. Newton had been smiling as Paul closed the door, gently, on his way out.

When he got back to the union office, Angela Roberts was seeing another employee on Collier's crew. Emma Friedman had encountered a letter addressed to "Clawson, MI, 48077." Clawson's correct zip was 48017; the 48077 zip would be Sterling Heights. The address on Crooks Road had to be in Clawson. Farley wished Friedman and Roberts good luck.

Paul held a Step Two meeting two weeks later at the Main Post Office, several miles away from the Plant, where the Employee & Labor Relations Department was located. The Postmaster's office was also at the Main. Paul sometimes felt the physical distance was helpful. There was a different atmosphere, and sometimes a different outlook in this building.

Nancy Barber was far from the worst E&LR rep to meet with, but Newton had called her about this case. Farley felt he was in a scene from "Alice in Wonderland." Or maybe "1984," where War is Peace and Freedom is Slavery. Barber said it was better to have the mail keyed to the zip even if the zip was wrong. That way, the customers who got their mail late would tell whoever sent them the letter to make sure they use the right zip code next time. Ms. Barber said all of this with a straight face. From her tone and demeanor, you would think she was making a serious, intelligent argument. And the bottom line was she didn't see any contractual violation in the way the edit was conducted. Grievance denied.

"What bothers me," Farley told his fellow stewards the next day, "is they don't want employees to *think*. You know those new OCRs they have now? They scan an address, and if it doesn't make sense, they look for something that does. If a letter is addressed to Warren, MI, but the street address doesn't exist in Warren, it searches its computerized memory bank. If the street address exists in Warren, Ohio or Warren, Pennsylvania, the OCR sprays the appropriate bar code on it, and that's where the letter goes. They let the machines think, but we're supposed to be unthinking robots."

"Don't sweat the small stuff, partner," Ron said.

"But they're punishing people for caring about the customer."

"I know, I know," Ron said. "I'm not saying to drop the grievance. Just don't let it get to you. After all we're talking about a one-wrong edit."

Ron could see it was still bothering Paul, so he added, "Maybe you'll get it straightened out at Step Three."

The Step Three Meeting two months later in Chicago was a high-speed trade-a-thon. A Business Agent for the union and his management equivalent went through 30 cases in an hour. The management rep said, "On this edit, I'll give you language that if the error causes grievant to go below ninety-five per cent it will be thrown out. If she never goes below ninety-five, no harm was done. Right?"

The Business Agent didn't read the explanatory note Farley included in the grievance package. Farley wanted to challenge the policy of keying to the zip. He wanted employees to be able to use their best judgment. But the Business Agent signed off on management's offer.

The settlement really did Tawanna no good. It was unlikely that this error would throw her under 95%, even if she had a few bad edits in the future. Paul thought he had prepared a good case to take to arbitration and win. But at Step Three, the union reps tried to get as many cases out of the system as possible, because there was already a long backlog of cases waiting to be arbitrated.

Farley didn't look forward to breaking the news to Tawanna. For weeks he had anticipated the smile on her face when he handed her a Step Three settlement allowing LSM operators to use their knowledge and common sense. Now he was apprehensive.

"The Business Agent thinks we won the grievance," he told Tawanna. "I think we lost. There was a principle here. They let that asshole Newton off the hook."

"Oh well, you did your best, Paul. It's not the end of the world, losing this grievance. It just shows we're smarter than management, and that's never going to change."

29

Four: SONYA

Prosecutor: What did the defendant say about Mr. Newton?
Witness: He said he's a rotten excuse for a human being and
I'm going to make him pay big time!"

Paul woke up about three on a sultry August afternoon. He was not in his own bed. Lying next to him, sound asleep, was a gorgeous black woman. She had a very dark complexion, shapely legs, and breasts that were big enough. She was a little bit plump, but attractively so. He watched her chest rise and fall with her breathing. He gazed at her pretty face, peaceful and content. When she was awake she had sparkling eyes and a smile that could light up any room.

Paul was very much attracted to Sonya Wells. Nevertheless, he wondered how he had ended up in bed with this woman whom he really didn't know very well.

Sonya was a new employee at the Post Office. She was 29 years old, though she looked more like 23. She was fighting for custody of her seven year old son as part of a nasty divorce proceeding. At work, she was assigned to learn a Royal Oak scheme. That meant she had to learn every street in certain zip codes of Royal Oak and the carrier who delivered to each address. Then she had to learn to key this mail on the LSM.

Paul had started playing bid whist at lunch with Sonya, Tawanna Chambers and Selena Thomas. Paul and Sonya were partners. She was always smiling at him. For a time Paul had thought about asking her out, maybe for dinner and a movie, but hadn't gotten up the nerve.

But that day, just after punching out at quarter to nine in the *morning*, Sonya went to the locker room to change into a short mini skirt; the kind that attracts attention from men and causes talk among the women. She waited by the employee exit for Paul to make his way out. When Paul saw Sonya's outfit, he was practically drooling.

"Hey sexy," he called out. Sonya smiled. She asked if he was in a hurry to get home or if he had a little time to kill. When Paul asked what she had in mind, she said she had half a bottle of wine in her fridge and maybe he'd like to help her finish it.

He followed her along Interstate 696 to the house she rented in Oak Park. He played WJLB, the r & b station, on his car radio. He didn't listen to 'JLB too often, but today he had it on with the volume cranked up. When they reached her place, they didn't bother with music or wine, they got right into bed. She was the first black woman he'd ever had sex with (he'd gone out with some black women but never got this far).

Was it different, having sex with a black woman? As he sat up in bed thinking back on it, that was a hard question to answer. For the most part, the difference is just what you made it in your head. Because, really, *every* woman is different. Sonya hadn't wasted time with foreplay. Before he knew it, she was guiding him right in. She was pretty loud: moaning, squealing, shouting his name.

Paul had been satisfied. Yet there was not the closeness, the intimacy, he sometimes felt during sex. Maybe that's because they rushed it so much. Maybe that closeness would come as he got to know her better. Sonya said it was great for her, but how could he know that was true? She seemed anxious to have him believe she had enjoyed sex with him.

Now he felt conflicted. Who was this woman sleeping next to him? If he decided to pull back from the relationship, would she think it was because of her race? He'd had "quickies" before. He never felt good about hurting the woman by dropping the relationship. When he hurt someone else, he hurt himself too; he was a pretty sensitive guy. That's why he had promised himself to take it slow next time, take the woman out to dinner, get to know her awhile before jumping into bed. But those good intentions were swept away by this beautiful woman, who was more than willing.

Then again, maybe he should stick with her. All he needed was to go a little slower. They could just go out, not sleep together again right away, get to know each other better, then maybe try again. Sure, that resolve would last until next time Sonya tried to get him into bed. Hey, she was gorgeous, fun to be with. So why was he having second thoughts?

Sonya woke up, kissed him, and put on a pair of shorts and a T-shirt. She poured two glasses of wine and sat on a wooden chair at her kitchen table. Paul sat facing the screen door, through which he could see the rear of the neighbor's brick house. The smell of fresh cut grass wafted in with the warm breeze. The noise of a lawn mower stopped abruptly, and Paul heard the competing sounds of the Isley Brothers and Eric Clapton blasting from open windows down the block.

Sonya started talking about the attendance problems she was having at work. It was odd; all of a sudden he was a steward again.

"Harold Kline called me into the office. He gave me a lecture about my absences."

"Did he give you any paperwork?"

"No. he just told me I'll be in trouble if I don't improve."

"Sounds like what they call a Documented Discussion."

"Was I supposed to tell him why I missed?"

"That's up to you."

"My father's dying of cancer. I flew down to New Orleans to see him last month. My mother was falling apart. I had to be the strong one. I hardly got any sleep and I got sick when I got back to Detroit. I went back to visit last week and I didn't recognize him. Paul, you can't imagine what that felt like. Just to see him like that. I'm afraid I'll have to go back for his funeral before too long."

Paul was stunned. He had no idea the burden Sonya was carrying. Her family was all in the south, her marriage was dead, she might lose custody of her son, her father was dying, and she had no family in Michigan. Paul looked down and noticed he was holding Sonya's hand. Tight.

"But Sonya, you always seem so cheerful!"

"Maybe that's just when I see you, Paul."

All of this added a new layer of guilt to Paul's misgivings about their relationship. This would not be a good time to give Sonya another emotional shock. He should stick around, be supportive, just take it slow. He liked Sonya. It would all work out.

Two weeks later, Sonya received an emotional shock of a different kind. It was a Notice of Removal. It had nothing to do with attendance. She was getting fired for failing her scheme training on the LSM. She had needed a 98% accuracy rate to pass the training, and on her final hour of training she reached 96.8%.

The Removal was issued by Harold Kline. Paul found him by the supervisor's desk in his work area while the employees were on break.

"Do you really think Sonya should lose her job?" said Paul.

"I don't want to fire her, she's not a bad kid, but that's what the rules say."

"I'll see if I can come up with another solution we can both live with."

"I'm open to suggestions. But I'll also have to consult with my boss if we do something out of the ordinary."

Later that day, Paul talked it over with Ron and Angela. Angela described how she settled a similar case for Naomi Nadeau. "The settlement gave her five more hours of training, and if she passed in that time she kept her job. Unfortunately she failed." Angela figured management might not want to try that type of settlement again for Sonya.

"Shit on a stick!" said Ron. Angela and Paul turned to him. "Now I know what they meant. I heard Newton talking to Harold

Kline. I just caught a little piece of it, something about not doing anything to help Farley's whore."

Paul felt like he had been punched in the gut. "How would Newton know about me and Sonya? That's none of his damn business!" Paul's thoughts raced back and forth. Newton was racist to disrespect Sonya that way. But that's not even the most important thing. Newton was playing hardball just to hurt Paul. Newton knew that, to Paul, this was more than just another grievance.

Angela had a different perspective on Newton's remark. "Why is it that the men who fool around the most make the crudest judgments about women? Newton just remarried, what, six months ago? And already he's having an affair with a supervisor over at the Main. Everyone knows about it, except his wife. But he can say something like that about Sonya. What a pig! If only we could prove what he said."

On September 11th, Paul met with Harold Kline at Step One. Sonya was in New Orleans for her father's funeral. Paul had considered postponing the meeting, but changed his mind. If Sonya was going to get any sympathy, this would be the only time.

Although Harold Kline didn't speak with much conviction, he upheld the company line. "I'm going to have to go by the book. If you fail the training, you're fired. Those are the rules."

"But the handbooks allow you some leeway. And this is a young lady who's had a lot on her mind lately. You can give her a break. If there's ever been a situation that called for it, this is the one. Between her divorce, her custody battle, and her father dying, it's been hard for her to concentrate."

"I'm sorry, Paul. I'm going to go by the book. I'm just glad I'll soon be supervising a manual operation where I won't have to deal with this type of removal case. I don't enjoy it, believe me. If you want to try to get my decision overturned, talk to Newton."

"Yeah, okay." Paul rose slowly from his chair. "Say, uh, Newton didn't make any personal remarks about this case, did he?"

Kline seemed to flinch, or maybe it was Paul's imagination. "What do you mean?" he answered, with a poker face. "All I know is, Newton's making the call on this one. I'll have no hard feelings if the decision is overturned."

Paul was in Newton's office ten minutes later. The General Supervisor was wearing a white shirt, a red tie, and a smug expression on his face.

"We're not bending the rules Farley, we tried it once and it didn't work."

"But Sonya's case is different. She was training while her loved one was dying and she was involved in a really bitter custody dispute. It was hard to concentrate. I think she did well to reach 96.8 under the circumstances. With a few more hours she could pass."

"If your girl had concentrated, she could have learned it."

"What do you mean, 'my girl'?"

"The girl you're representing, Farley. What do you think I mean?" Newton was barely able to suppress a grin, but he managed.

"The handbook says you're supposed to consider reassignment to another position and not automatically remove her."

"I followed the handbook, Farley. I considered reassignment. I decided against it. Her attendance is poor, she can't learn a scheme, and we've got no need to keep her. Nadeau had perfect attendance – *that's* why I gave her a break."

"Sonya had attendance problems because of her dying father, the same reason she couldn't concentrate. I think she did better than many people would have done in a similar situation."

"She didn't do well enough. You see this sign, Farley. It says 'The Buck Stops Here.' I decide, I live with the consequences. The union always defends the worst employees. People who drink on the job, people who fake injuries to get off work, people who never come to work, people who can't learn their scheme. The union wants me to give everyone a break. I've learned my lesson about bending the rules with Nadeau. If I give Sonya Wells more time, next month the union will want me to give someone else more time. And that person will have a heartbreaking story too. From now on, either you pass or we'll replace you with someone who can do the job."

"Fuck you." The words were almost whispered as Paul left the room. And he really didn't care whether Newton heard him.

It was amazing how Newton's behavior changed Paul's attitude towards Sonya. Suddenly there was no conflict, no ambiguity. He cared about her more deeply than he had realized. He would do whatever it took to protect her job. He'd ask the Local President to go over Newton's head. He'd represent Sonya in an EEO appeal; since Nadeau was white, this was a blatant case of discrimination (especially considering the remark about "Farley's whore"). He'd call the media if necessary.

And now he wanted to see her again, to hold and comfort her. Maybe this would be the girl he finally got serious with. He had trouble understanding the rapid changes in his emotions.

Sonya called from New Orleans that afternoon. Paul said he really missed her. Then he told her about the Step One Meeting. "James Newton is a miserable excuse for a human being. He enjoys seeing you suffer, and he enjoys seeing me suffer. I'm going to see that he pays for this, big time!"

Sonya told him she was staying in New Orleans for another week. Her mother needed her. She would think about the grievance when she got back.

As it turned out, Paul never saw Sonya again. She moved to New Orleans with her son, whose custody she had won. She phoned Paul when she got back to Oak Park to clean up her house and make all the arrangements. She told Paul to drop the grievance as long as management would agree to change the firing to a voluntary resignation for personal reasons.

"Paul, I really like you, and I won't forget the time we spent together. I appreciate how hard you tried to help me. Nobody outside my immediate family has ever done that for me. But I need to leave Michigan behind. My ex-husband who brought me here, Mr. Newton, all the rotten memories. I've decided to do this, and if you and I got together, it would only weaken my resolve. I still care about you, more than you know, but I've got to start over somewhere else."

Paul hung up, made a fist, and punched the wall. His hand stung. He went downstairs to his basement bar and poured himself a drink. Then he started thinking. He couldn't help but wonder what would have happened if Newton had granted the five hours. Would Sonya have stayed? Would they have gotten closer and closer? He really wanted to see her again, to hold her in his arms, to touch her, hear her laugh, to see her smile.

But it was not to be.

It was not to be because of the sadistic General Supervisor who instructed Harold Kline to deny the grievance. Just to rub it in Paul's face. Just to show Paul that he had the power and could use it as he pleased, and that Paul was helpless to do anything about it. Just because Sonya was Paul's girl. Just because he had a chance to stick it to Paul where it really hurt.

Paul's strong feelings for Sonya would eventually fade, and other women would come and go in his life. But his hatred of James Newton would only grow more intense as the years went on.

Five: BLAMING THE VICTIM

February, 1991

Prosecutor: What was the defendant's reaction to the letter putting Martha Huntington off work for safety reasons?
Witness: The defendant threatened Mr. Newton's life.

It was a bleak, wintry day, as Paul Farley drove to work in the darkness. The starting time on his new bid was 8:30 PM, but it was just as dark then as at midnight this time of year. It hadn't been very bright during the day either. In fact, the sun hadn't made an appearance all week.

Paul had to tell Martha Huntington that she was needed as a witness at an Arbitration hearing, but Martha hadn't made an appearance this week, either. After determining that she was absent again, Paul got the phone number from her friend Celia Derringer, and made the call.

A male voice answered and called Martha to the phone. Martha explained she was dealing with some family problems, but she told Paul not to worry. This was Thursday, the hearing was next Tuesday, and everything should be straightened out by then. She wrote down the time and place of the Arbitration and promised to be at the hearing.

Paul went back to his bid job in the manual flat cases. While he threw magazines, newspapers, and large envelopes to their proper destination, a storm that had been brewing in Martha Huntington's household finally erupted.

Philip Knapp, Martha's boyfriend, was a muscular, 27-year-old man with tattoos on his arms and chest. He and Martha had met at the Plant, and had been living together for six months. It started out great for both of them. They laughed together, they talked about their dreams, their insecurities, their fears, and some of their secrets. And although he wouldn't admit this, she was the first woman with whom sex had been enjoyable for him. With other women either he hadn't been able to get it up, or he had been barely able to come (and to validate his manhood to himself). But with Martha he had discovered what an exciting and joyful experience sex could be. There was some talk of marriage, but Martha wasn't real sure. Her ambivalence about marriage was eating away at him. And lately she wasn't as eager for sex as she used to be. He didn't understand what was happening.

When Martha hung up the phone, Phil asked her who had called. "Oh, it was nothing important," she said.

"Who was that man on the phone," he demanded.

All of a sudden his questioning seemed invasive. Why couldn't he just trust her? "It was just something about work," she told him.

Phil slapped her in the face – a forceful blow.

"You're cheating on me," he snarled, with fury in his eyes.

"No, no, it was just the union steward. They want me to testify about a grievance."

Martha saw the punch coming but couldn't react. She was frozen with fear. The next punch sent her reeling backwards. She tripped over the coffee table and landed on the couch. He went to get a can of beer. He drank a little. Martha was still on the couch, sobbing quietly. He slapped her again, then grabbed her on both shoulders and shouted "Tell me the truth, tell me the truth!"

"Okay, just get off me," she said, tasting her own blood as she spoke. Her entire head was throbbing with pain.

As soon as Phil got off the couch, Martha ran to phone and dialed 911. Phil cut the phone cord with a pocket knife, then slashed her with the knife, ripping her blouse. The blade barely nicked her body, but something changed inside her. She realized she had been living a lie for the last six months. The person she thought she knew was gone. And his face that used to look handsome had turned into the ugly face of evil. But she didn't have time to think of her love turning to hatred, of the sense of betrayal, of her own bad judgment in letting this monster into her life. All that mattered was survival. He expected her to shatter like a fragile piece of china. But her adrenaline was kicking in.

Phil glared at Martha menacingly. Martha looked him right in the eye. He focused on her stare. She gave him a swift kick in the crotch, he bent over in pain, and she fled to a neighbor's house to call the police.

Paul went on union business again after midnight. Ron's jokes were worse than usual. "Do you know which kind of criminal uses a spoon for a weapon?" After Paul and Angela gave up, he said: "A cereal killer." Angela gave him a dirty look. "Okay," Ron said, "How about this one? A man left his wallet in his pants pocket when he put them in the washing machine. The police came into the Laundromat and arrested him. You know what the charge was?" The other stewards shook their heads. "Money laundering!" The other stewards shook their heads again.

"Hey Ron," Paul said. "Did you put that shit up there?" Paul pointed to an 8½ x 11 inch sheet of white paper with a drawing of an unclothed, smiling toddler sitting on a toilet. Next to the youngster, larger than scale, was a roll of toilet paper, and underneath that were the words "The job is never finished until the paperwork is done." Ron said, "Somebody's got a fine sense of humor."

Angela turned the discussion to more serious matters. "They're going crazy with discipline around here. The other day Arnold Foster was using a hand jack to lower a pallet of magazines to be worked on the belt. He lowered it right on Andre Martin's foot. Andre had to go to the clinic, he thought it was broken, it was so painful. Turned out not to be that serious, though. You know

41

what that new supervisor Mary What's-her-name did? She gave them *both* Letters of Warning for unsafe practices. Arnold for lowering the pallet and Andre for having his foot in the way!"

"Wait a minute," Ron said. "You mean if your careless actions cause me to be injured, I get discipline too?"

"Mary said she didn't know which one was really at fault. If I, as the steward, could tell her, she would expunge one of the Letters of Warning. But I'd have to accept a year on the record for the other one. I get to pick who gets stuck with the discipline! I told her to visit a very warm place underneath the earth's surface. The grievances are going to Step Two."

Paul started thinking about Mary. "She's just a 204-B, isn't she? She works as a clerk in that area three days a week, and supervises on Reggie Green's off days. Some people forget where they come from real quick. How can she look Arnold and Andre in the eye?"

"You know it's all coming from higher up," Angela said. "Ever since that new management team came in from Illinois, it's been hell around here. When the Region sent in Ben Herman as Postmaster at the Main and Joe Borelli took Doug Asner's job, they thought their numbers would improve. But nothing's improving, unless management is graded on the number of disciplines being issued."

"I never liked Doug Asner," said Paul. "But I kind of miss him now. What's he doing these days, anyway?"

"I think he's got some job shuffling papers at the Main. Same salary, less stress, so don't feel sorry for him."

"You know," Ron added. "I've heard a lot of the managers aren't happy with the new regime. Labor Relations doesn't like the added work. They've got to type up suspensions that they know aren't going to stand up, and they have to deny a lot of our grievances. They'll catch hell if they don't go along with the program. There is one manager who really likes Borelli and Herman, though. That's Paul's buddy, Jim Newton."

<><><><><>

42

Paul took Monday night off to prepare for the Arbitration hearing. So when Martha Huntington called the Plant Union Office, Angela Roberts answered.

"You can tell Paul I won't be at the hearing," Martha said, and then started sobbing. She started to speak but broke down in tears again. Angela listened patiently.

After Martha composed herself, she told Angela of being beaten by her boyfriend and cut with a knife. She told of Philip Knapp's arrest by the Ferndale police. But that was last week; that's not why she was crying now.

Martha read from a letter she got earlier in the day from the United States Postal Service: "You are hereby notified that you are being placed in an off-duty status (without pay) effective immediately upon receipt of this notice, and will continue in this status until you are advised otherwise. The reasons for this action are: Information received from the Postal Inspection Service indicates that coworker Philip Knapp was arrested on or about February 21, 1991 by the Ferndale Police Department and charged with Felonious Assault after you filed a complaint that he assaulted you and threatened you with a weapon. Retaining you on duty may be injurious to yourself and to others. Based upon the above, your retention in a duty status would not be in the best interests of the Postal Service."

Angela couldn't believe her ears. The victim of a vicious attack was being told not to come to work because management was afraid of a bloody scene at the Post Office. As if it were Martha's fault that her boyfriend attacked her. "Who signed the letter?" Angela asked.

"James Newton."

"That son of a bitch," Angela said in a voice that was barely audible.

"I need to come back to work," Martha pleaded. "I need the money, but mostly I need to get out of this house. Right now,

Philip's in jail, so why do they think he'll attack me at work?"

"They have no reason, Martha. Even if he *wasn't* in jail, they should help and protect you, not punish you."

"Angela, what if Philip attacks me again? If I file another complaint with the police, will the Post Office fire me?"

The question was absurd. Yet given management's response to Philip's arrest, it was not so ridiculous. Angela's heart went out to this young woman who had been abused by her boyfriend and betrayed by her employer. They talked for another half-hour. Angela was not trained as a counselor but she had good instincts. She knew the most important things were to comfort Martha, to build up her shattered self-esteem, to alleviate any misplaced guilt and shame. And to let her know she would do everything in her power to get James Newton's letter rescinded.

Angela headed straight for the Tour Superintendent's office. She was stopped by a tall black man, in his early thirties. Tyrone Wheeler, a Royal Oak scheme clerk, wanted her to go back to the union office with him. He said the 8:30 - 5:00 shift had worked overtime the day before, including even the non-list employees who didn't want the overtime. But the midnight clerks who wanted the overtime, like himself, had not been permitted to work.

Angela listened impatiently, then resumed walking towards Newton's office. "You've got no grievance!" she called back over her shoulder. She didn't take the time to explain the overtime rules to Tyrone. She wondered why a steward's job never flows smoothly. There are always pesky interruptions, even idiotic ones, when you have urgent business at hand.

She found Newton and Elliott Drummond together in the office. "I just got off the phone with Martha Huntington," she said. "She needs to be at work." She stared at Newton, then Drummond, and then back at Newton. She continued, "The last thing we should do is add to the ordeal she's going through. Can't we show a little compassion? Philip is in jail, he can't cause any trouble here."

"He won't be in jail forever," said Newton. "There's still a threat to the facility."

"If you're really concerned about that, we could detail her to another Post Office. Philip won't know where she's working."

Drummond snickered. "We don't have to detail her anywhere. She should take care of her own personal problems."

Newton defended his letter. "We believe in following the contract. Article Fourteen says we have to provide a safe working environment for the employees. We're doing just that. We don't know when her boyfriend will get out of jail, he could be out on bail any time. We can't endanger our employees. The decision stands."

For Angela, this was the most frustrating situation she had ever encountered as a steward. She barely kept her composure as she left the managers' office. For the rest of the day she thought about nothing else.

At nine in the morning Angela was in Ferndale talking to the new Local APWU President, Donald Humphrey. Humphrey had replaced Leslie Loder, who now had a staff position at APWU headquarters in Washington. Humphrey called the Labor Relations Department expecting to get Martha back to work. But Labor Relations stood behind Newton's decision, citing Article 14. "I've never seen you guys take Article Fourteen seriously before," Humphrey said bitterly. "Why start now?"

It was hard to tell if Labor Relations believed what they were saying, or were just doing what was expected of them by the Herman/Borelli team. Hanging up the phone in disgust, Humphrey said, "You'll just have to file a grievance."

Paul Farley arrived at the Local Union Office around 11:00 AM. The Arbitration hearing had been short. "Our star witness didn't show up," Paul said.

Humphrey and Roberts filled Farley in on Martha Huntington's situation. The two stewards continued talking while Humphrey took a phone call. They were not satisfied with the suggestion that they file a grievance. Something drastic was called for. They agreed to think about it.

Shortly after midnight, Farley was in Elliott Drummond's office. Newton was nowhere to be seen. Farley was furious. "If I came in here and told you I was going to shoot and kill James Newton, would you put *him* off work without pay like you did with Martha? Is that how you would protect the safety of the workforce?"

Drummond slowly ran his fingers through what was left of the gray hair on his head. A slight upturn of the lips appeared momentarily. Then he spoke softly but firmly.

"Are you threatening Mr. Newton's life? I think the police should be notified."

"No, I'm not threatening anyone, I'm just making a point."

"I think I heard you threaten to kill Mr. Newton," Drummond repeated.

Farley knew Drummond was just pretending he didn't understand the point and was having some fun at Farley's expense. Farley left the room fuming.

A few minutes later, Paul recounted the conversation to Angela. She appreciated Paul's energy but didn't agree with the approach.

"It almost sounds like you were trying to out-macho management. That's not what we need."

"Well we damn sure need something! And it's not about being macho, it's about being...emphatic. We can't let Martha suffer while Newton and Drummond play their cruel games."

"Look, I agree with you. I despise Newton and Drummond for tormenting her like this. But we have to be smart."

"Newton and Drummond are scum! Worse than scum." Paul slammed a pad of paper down on the table. "There's no excuse for it. We've got to make them back off, and fast."

Angela bit her upper lip and closed her eyes. Paul knew to keep quiet; when she did this an important thought was struggling to get out.

"We need two things right now," she finally said. "We need compassion for the victim. And we need allies."

Angela got busy the next morning. She called some friends in the National Organization for Women (NOW) and the Coalition of Labor Union Women (CLUW). She asked them to mobilize support for Martha.

She also called a reporter for the *Detroit Free Press*. Louise Henderson was an old friend of Angela's from her days at Wayne State University. Louise was shocked.

Louise said, "This could be a *big* news story, Angela. I can't believe your managers are so cruel."

"I know they'd be embarrassed if you wrote the story, but my first priority is helping Martha. I hope the fact that you're *investigating* their behavior will back them off."

"I hear you. I'll call and let them know they could be the subject of a big exposé. But if they let your employee come back to work, the story loses its news value. My editor won't approve of me using my influence like this, but if they back off my boss will never have to know. If they don't budge, I'll have my big story."

CLUW and NOW took similar approaches. There would be mass pickets if Martha stayed off work. If management settled, no pickets and no adverse publicity.

Management had no idea what kind of numbers these organizations could muster in a protest demonstration, but they didn't want to find out. They saw the light and returned Martha to her regular job assignment. She had missed two working days since receiving the letter, and the union processed a grievance for back pay. Management argued that Martha had not come to work from the time of the attack until she received the letter, so there was no reason to believe she would have been at work on the days being grieved. In any event, the threat of publicity helped management see the logic of the arguments that had gone unheeded when presented by the union.

When Martha returned, she stopped by the Plant Union Office and gave Angela Roberts a great big hug. Ignoring the bruises on Martha's face, Angela said, "You look great!"

"You're a liar," Martha said, then she hugged Angela again.

Meanwhile, Drummond and Newton were talking in the managers' office. Newton wanted discipline issued to Farley for threatening to kill him. "That's a removable offense, if not a criminal one."

"No sir," said Drummond. "I've talked it over with Borelli. We do that, and all the circumstances will go public. That Henderson reporter lady will write her story after all. We have a better way to handle it. I've written a statement of exactly what Farley said. It might have been a real threat, but we decided not to take action, to give him the benefit of the doubt. But if Farley makes any aggressive move towards you in the future, as we both know he will, we'll have the statement on file. We'll use it against him long after this Huntington business dies down."

Six: GRIN AND BEER IT

Prosecutor: Who did Mr. Newton blame for the stunt that was pulled to defend Ellen Rudny?
Witness: He blamed the defendant.

The Optical Character Reader (OCR) is a truly remarkable piece of equipment. You can't tell by watching it how much this machine really does. You see letters being fed to the machine at one end and rapidly deposited into bins along the length of the machine. What you don't see is that within a fraction of a second a computer reads the zip code and street address, and a bar code is sprayed on each letter. This bar code prepares letters for the BCS (Bar Code Sorter).

With an OCR, a crew of two people (a feeder and a sweeper) can sort mail a lot quicker than an LSM crew of 18.

It was early morning on a cool spring day, and a large drink in a plastic container from Burger King was sitting on top of OCR #2. The official policy prohibiting food and drink on the workroom floor was enforced sporadically, at best.

But Ellen Rudny was giggling a lot, her speech was unclear, and she stumbled and almost fell a couple of times as she fed mail onto OCR #2.

Lawrence Harris, a young 204-B who supervised the OCRs, watched her closely. Lawrence, a black man of 33 with a boyish face that made him look under 25, was brand new in the management program. He looked like a kid, but he had the self assurance of a man who'd been supervising for decades.

Lawrence walked over to the OCR and took the lid off the Burger King drink container. There was Coke or Pepsi, along with the smell of alcohol. Probably rum, he thought.

"Ellen, I'm going to have to remove your drink. You know it's not permitted on the floor."

Ellen started to protest that everybody brings drinks on the floor, then stopped in mid-sentence. "It's not my drink anyway," she said.

"Sorry, honey, I don't believe you."

"No, somebody must have put it there while I was at lunch. It isn't mine, honest," Ellen said. Then she giggled again.

Lawrence took the drink into the Tour Superintendent's Office and explained the situation to James Newton and Elliott Drummond. Newton's lips curled into a wicked smile. He had a plan of action. "We'll have the drink analyzed. And let's get a couple of supervisors to talk to Ellen. Once they confirm she's drunk, she's out of the building. Her boyfriend can take emergency leave and drive her home."

The other supervisors came over and talked to Ellen. Between the smell of alcohol and her out of character giggling, they knew she was drunk. Charles Valmont took three hours of emergency annual leave and drove Ellen home. Management wrote witness statements to pave the way for discipline.

Fred Turner was in the Union Office talking to Angela about his suspension for attendance. Fred looked like a hippie from the sixties, although he was only in his late thirties. He was kind of a loner. Every day at lunch he went to his car, which he parked by the back fence, and smoked a joint by himself. Paul, who was in the Union Office doing some paperwork, was not altogether surprised that Fred was in trouble for his attendance.

Just then Ron Davidson practically ran in the door. "They printed it, they printed it!" he said.

"Calm down, Ron," said Angela. "What did they print?"

"You know the Question of the Month they put in our union paper? I didn't think they would print my answer. But they did!

They were asking, 'Do you favor drug testing for postal employees?' They expected answers like 'Yes, because postal employees shouldn't use drugs,' or 'No, because it's an invasion of privacy.' They got a couple of answers like that from other members. But I threw them a curve ball."

"Okay, Ron," said Paul. "What did you say – do you favor drug testing for postal employees?"

"Yes! I think all drugs should be thoroughly tested before they're distributed to postal employees."

Fred broke out laughing. "Yeah, man, that's a good idea," he said.

Paul smirked and shook his head. Angela looked annoyed.

"Hey, it's just a joke," Ron said. "I'm not a druggie. But I don't sit in judgment of what people do in their spare time, either. I didn't realize you were such a crusader against drugs, Angie."

"Oh, it's not that," she said. "In fact, I tried snorting coke once. Didn't like it. The ice cubes kept getting stuck in my nostrils."

Paul laughed, while the other two guys just stared at her.

There was a knock on the door. Harold Kline, Paul's supervisor, motioned for Paul to come to the door.

"You don't need me to throw flats, do you?" Paul asked. "Is the big boss on your back to cut my union time?"

"No, I just want to give you a heads up on a discipline you'll be handling. They took Ellen Rudny out of the building today. Apparently she was quite intoxicated. I understand they're talking removal."

Paul left the office to continue the conversation out of earshot of Fred Turner.

As Paul stepped out, Tyrone Wheeler entered the office and announced, "I'd like to see Angela." Technically speaking Ron was Tyrone's steward. Ron was also unoccupied at the moment, while Angela was with Fred Turner. But Angela graciously said: "Fred, we're through for now, I'll get back to you," and motioned for Tyrone to sit down.

In spite of the relatively cool weather, Tyrone was dressed in a red muscle T-shirt, which showed off his well-developed biceps. Other than that, his build could best be described as lanky. He smiled at Angela, and speaking in a deep voice, he told a long rambling story. But when he was done it boiled down to a simple scheduling question. Tyrone was a Royal Oak scheme clerk. Every day some people in his section were scheduled to key on the LSM, some were assigned to throw manual letters in a hand case, and some were assigned to throw flats. There was supposed to be an equitable rotation, but Tyrone hadn't thrown letters in over a week. He wanted to know why.

This sounded like the kind of petty complaint stewards hate to handle. These situations seldom result in a grievance you can win. Angela wanted to say "Leave me alone and let me help someone who really has a problem." Instead she said, "Let me check into it, and I'll get back to you."

"You'll bring me back here to tell me what you find out, won't you?"

When Angela said okay, he seemed satisfied.

About an hour later, Angela and Tyrone were back in the union office. "The rotation is alphabetical," she explained. "Your part of the alphabet fell in manual letters on your off days. It'll even out over time."

Tyrone smiled and said, "Thank you for taking the time to check it out. You seem like a real nice person."

Angela's mind raced ahead to the next item on her list. She paged supervisor Red Collier and said "Bye" to Tyrone, who smiled at her again as he left the room.

On May 10th, 1991, Ellen Rudny got a Notice of Removal. Management had prepared well. The drink was analyzed, and there was no doubt it contained alcohol. Witness statements from

Lawrence Harris, Red Collier, Butch Hobson, and James Newton stated she was drunk. It looked solid.

Paul bounced some ideas past Ron. "We've got a case where Nate got a suspension for being drunk. Didn't you handle that case?"

"Their proof wasn't so strong with Nate. They didn't have whatever he was drinking as evidence, just his behavior. And the smell of alcohol. And they liked Nate, that's the main reason they gave him another chance. That, and he was already seeing the Employee Assistance Program counselor."

"Well, they don't have proof the drink was hers."

"Paul, is there really any doubt? I wish you good luck on this one. If she's got a good record maybe you can work something out – if you get on your knees and beg."

James Newton issued the removal himself. Normally, the supervisor in the work area would issue the discipline, but they didn't want a 204-B handling a removal grievance.

Paul talked to Newton off the record. "Look, Nate Ramsey got two weeks off for the same offense. Ellen's a good kid. She's got no prior discipline. Can't we work something out?"

"So, you're admitting she's guilty?"

"No, I'm just trying to settle this case, if possible. She says it wasn't her drink. Maybe we can prove that to an Arbitrator, maybe we can't. But going to Arbitration means she sits home for nine months or more, hoping for back pay in the end. That's hard on you even if you win. If you give me the same offer as Ramsey, we can settle this thing."

"I'm sure you will, Farley. But intoxication on the job is a removable offense, you know that. We gave Ramsey a break because he was a long term employee – 18 years with an excellent work record. Rudny's removal stands."

Paul looked at the sign on Newton's desk: "The Buck Stops Here." Then he said, "Look, you have some discretion here. We could offer to enroll her in EAP and you give her a two week suspension. That should correct the problem. And that's all discipline is supposed to be for, to correct a problem, not punish people. Why not give her another chance?"

"No dice, Farley. Unless you come up with some extraordinary proof that the drink was not hers, the removal stands."

Paul didn't hold a formal Step One meeting that day. He knew it looked pretty grim. Newton would deny the grievance and Labor Relations would rubber stamp the denial at Step Two. The removal would take effect June 12th (the contract required at least a month's notice for removals). He hated Newton's arrogant attitude. Newton enjoyed firing people. And it looked like he was going to make this one stick.

Paul talked to Ellen's young coworkers. They didn't think she should lose her job over this. She wasn't a habitual drinker, and she was a good worker. Mail Processors worked in teams of two. Nobody felt they had to carry her slack when they worked with Ellen. But nobody wanted to put that in writing. They were afraid of Newton.

Just before he went home at 0500, Paul took a written statement from Charles Valmont, who said he knows Ellen well and can tell when she is or isn't drunk, and that she was sober on the day in question. Charles hung around after 0500 talking to Ron Davidson. "If they didn't do a blood test, they can't prove she was drinking," he said.

Ron shook his head. "I'd hate to go before an Arbitrator and stake her career on that argument. If Paul can get her a two week suspension, she should take it in a heartbeat. Of course, if she had insisted on a blood test and management had refused, that might have helped. But if she had asked for it, management probably would have readily agreed. And that might not have helped her case one bit, you know what I mean?"

Charles shrugged his shoulders. "We'll never know for sure," he said. "That's why the removal shouldn't stand."

On May 14th, Charles Valmont was working on OCR #4. He went out to his car for lunch at 0300. Acting Supervisor (204-B) Claudia Stinson noticed the smell of beer as soon as he returned at 0350. He must've spilled some on his shirt while he was drinking; the odor was so powerful.

Claudia was in the 204-B program just to earn a little more money. She had no plans to become a regular supervisor. She wasn't out to get anyone. She would've ignored Charles' problem that night if possible. He didn't let her.

He was feeding mail onto the machine all right, but his motions were a little clumsy. He was loud and boisterous. He started singing "One Bourbon, One Scotch, One Beer" (a George Thorogood song) at the top of his lungs. Then he stopped and called out, "Hey Claudia, this machine's running too fast." It was a ridiculous complaint. In fact, he was keeping up pretty well, which was surprising, considering his condition.

"C'mere, Claudia, look at the mail they gave me to run. Is this the right mail? I think this belongs on OCR #2!"

Claudia came over and told him to keep his voice down. She also told him that this was the same type of mail he runs every night. The odor of beer was still strong.

"I think you're cute," Charles said. *"Hey, isn't she cute?"* he yelled for his coworkers to hear.

Claudia was not a bad looking woman, but she did not enjoy this type of attention. And she was not enjoying supervising Charles tonight. While Ellen was a giggly drunk, Charles was apparently a loud and obnoxious one.

"Don't make any more personal remarks to me, Mr. Valmont," she said. "Just concentrate on your job."

"What's the matter, you didn't get laid last night? I can fix you up with somebody."

Claudia decided she'd had enough. As she left the area, Charles laughed loudly. Mail still ran smoothly through the OCR, and a young woman named Aretha Simmons swept. Aretha tried to ignore the antics of her partner.

Claudia Stinson returned with another Mail Processor. "Carolyn will take your place, Charles," she said. "Mr. Newton wants to see you in the office."

Newton, Elliott Drummond, Red Collier, and dock supervisor Gwendolyn Rogers were seated in the office. They smelled beer on his breath and on his shirt. A short argumentative conversation convinced them he was quite drunk.

"You're drunk, Valmont," Newton said while glaring at the employee. "Today, Ellen can take *you* home. I don't know why you're doing this. You and your girlfriend will both be out of a job soon."

"You can't prove I'm drunk," Valmont replied.

"We've got four witnesses. That's enough proof. And it smells like a brewery in here right now."

"Send me to the clinic for a blood test. If you're going to fire me, you've got to prove I'm drunk."

Newton smiled. "That's a good idea," he replied. "But after you go to the clinic, you will go straight home. When we get the results of the blood test, you'll be history."

On May 17th, Newton and Drummond were sitting in the office. Valmont's test results had come back negative. Newton was beside himself. He slammed a fist onto his desk.

"That asshole Farley! *He* put Valmont up to this."

"I don't think so Jim. Claudia has it from a pretty good source, the whole thing was Valmont's idea. He was trying to help his girlfriend out of a jam. I don't like the way he did it one bit. But it was his idea."

"Believe me, Farley had something to do with it."

"You don't know that, Jim. But it really doesn't matter. The question is what do we do with Ellen Rudny. Everyone's been talking about it. And from what I hear, none of her coworkers want her fired. A suspension, yes, but not removal. She's normally a good worker."

"Why should we reduce it to a suspension? She's guilty as sin. That prank with the O' Doul's beer doesn't prove a damn thing."

"I don't know if an Arbitrator will say we should've sent her for a blood test. But even if we can make it stick, we really don't have to. She doesn't have a bad work record. We can make mandatory EAP part of the settlement. And you can issue Valmont discipline even though he wasn't drunk. Conduct unbecoming a postal employee. Make it a seven day suspension, Jim. The way he treated Claudia on the workroom floor is unacceptable."

Newton didn't want to go along with Drummond, but this time Drummond pulled rank. He had talked to Claudia Stinson at some length. Stinson was a 204-B who had the respect of the employees, and who also knew how to listen and learn from what employees were saying. Earlier in the week, employees were shocked at Valmont's behavior, and had told her so. Now that they knew the whole story, including that Charles had apologized to Claudia, their sympathy returned to Ellen Rudny. In fact, Drummond's decision was entirely based on Claudia Stinson's idea. He wasn't going to tell Newton that. But in Drummond's view, it was a sensible way to resolve the situation.

After the Step One grievance meetings, Ellen Rudny's removal was reduced to a two week suspension, to remain on her record for two years, and Charles Valmont's seven day suspension was reduced to five days, to remain on his record for one year. Newton was frustrated. He was still convinced it was the devious mind of Paul Farley that thwarted his efforts to give Rudny the level of discipline she really deserved.

Seven: STICKER SHOCK

July, 1991

Prosecutor: What discipline was issued to the defendant for this incident?
Witness: A seven day suspension.

It was almost five a.m., the sun had not yet risen, but the sky was already brightening a bit. It had been a very warm night and was just now cooling down to the lower seventies. It was a nice time of day to be outdoors, but that's not why seven supervisors and 204-Bs, plus James Newton, were standing in the parking lot.

Inside the building there was a mad rush to get the 0500 dispatch out. Reggie Green saw to it that the 110 belt finished in plenty of time, but the LSM ran a little late. This delayed the 112 Area, where direct trays from the LSM had to be loaded into APCs (All Purpose Containers) to be dispatched to the dock. As on any typical day, about 70 employees ended their tour at 0500, and they straggled out of the building, one or two at a time over a ten minute period, heading for their cars.

Paul Farley was among the first to leave the building. He walked out the front door and was shocked to see so many supervisors. Jim Newton was in the center aisle of the parking lot. One aisle over to the left was Butch Hobson. One aisle over to the right was the 204-B Lawrence Harris. The other supervisors were strategically deployed throughout the lot.

As Paul headed for his car, Butch Hobson walked alongside him. "I'm following you to your car to make sure you have a parking sticker on the windshield," Hobson informed him.

"What's the big deal about a parking sticker?"

"It's a regulation, Farley. As a steward, you should know that."

"And you're going to follow me to my car? That's a little extreme, don't you think?"

"It's important that we know who doesn't have stickers. We want everyone to be in compliance. You have one, don't you?"

"I'm off the clock. I don't even have to talk to you. You're going to look anyway. But I don't appreciate you following me to my car."

Paul kept his calm. He saw a couple of LSM operators leaving the building and being followed to their car by James Newton and Gwendolyn Rogers. Paul had a sticker on his car. He also knew that since management paid close attention to him, they already knew he drove a blue Plymouth Horizon. It still seemed like an invasion of privacy. He knew his coworkers would be steaming.

Two hours earlier, Newton had called a meeting of all Tour One supervisors. "We've got to have a parking sticker on every car in that employee lot. We made announcements on the loudspeaker last week. Nobody listened. We put a notice in the Order Book. Nobody read it. Last week we had Lawrence and Gwen put fliers on the windshields of the cars without stickers. All they had to do is show us their car registration and we'd give them a sticker. But they're defying us. So here's what we're going to do…"

After Newton laid out the plan, Reggie Green spoke up. "That's idiotic. There are other ways to find out who's got a sticker and who doesn't. I can take care of my Pay Location without following them to their car."

For a moment there was a stunned silence. Gwen Rogers and Butch Hobson stared at the floor. Elliott Drummond suppressed a grin.

"Are you afraid of your own employees, Mister Green? We don't need chicken-shits directing our employees. When they defy us, we've got to set them straight." Newton glared at Reggie as he spoke.

"I'm not afraid of *you*," Green replied. "Following employees to their car is the wrong way to go about it. I'm not taking part in the great parking lot escapade!"

Then Drummond spoke up. "We're going to need a few supervisors inside anyway. Reggie, why don't you start your dispatch a bit early so you can go cover Gwen on the dock, she can go outside."

Now Newton glared at Drummond, but the compromise was adopted.

On their 2200 break the following day, Tawanna Chambers and Emma Friedman took a stroll through the supervisors' parking area. They found two supervisors' cars without stickers. They wrote down the license numbers and description of the two vehicles. They were in the union office with Paul minutes later.

"What hypocrites," Emma said. "I'm going to give this info to Newton. Do you think he'll do anything about it? *No!*"

"What does it matter?" asked Tawanna. "We all got a sticker when we hired in. When we bought a new car we didn't get a new sticker. Why should we? Is there a guard who checks for stickers when we drive into the lot? No! Is there any security out there at all? No! Does it matter whether we have a sticker? No! It's just an excuse to harass us when we're off the clock."

"Maybe you should file a grievance, Paul. Management should restrict employee harassment to times when they are on the clock." Emma smiled as she made this suggestion.

<><><><><>

Shortly after midnight Emma and Tawanna gave the supervisors' license plate numbers to Newton. "How dare you go into the supervisors' lot," he thundered. "If there's any damage to their vehicles, we'll know who to blame, now won't we?"

At lunch time, the discussion in the women's locker room was animated. Emma and Tawanna told their story. Then Celia Derringer spoke out: "I don't want a male supervisor following me to my car. How do I know what his intentions are?"

Selena Thomas said, "I've got a parking sticker on my car, but I drove my husband's car to work today, just to make a point. They can't intimidate me. If they leave me alone, I get along with everyone, but now I'm *mad!*"

Word had already leaked out that management was planning the same type of operation at 0500 that morning. The women talked strategy. After rejecting some of the more extreme suggestions, as well as some of the humorous ones, a plan of action emerged. Nobody would say who came up with the idea, but it was a good one.

As word spread of this plan, people got excited. Paul couldn't wait to see this show of solidarity.

Emma and Tawanna were the first to exit the building at 0500. Newton and Lawrence Harris stood nearby, waiting to accompany the first employees to their cars. They were kept waiting. Emma and Tawanna stood on the sidewalk just outside the door, whispering to each other. Selena Thomas came out next and said, "Hey girlfriends. Ready to flip the script?"

By the time Paul came outside, about 15-20 people were standing on the sidewalk. Their numbers more than doubled in the next ten minutes. There was a festive atmosphere. People were joking and laughing. It felt good to turn the tables on management. A buzz went through the gathering as people realized what their solidarity was accomplishing.

Some of the bolder employees started heckling the managers. Paul said: "Hey Newton, did anyone ever tell you you'd make a great parking lot monitor? You should be out here eight hours a day!"

Newton just glared at Farley.

Tawanna called out: "Why don't you stand out in the *supervisor's* lot and catch the lawbreaking fiends who don't have stickers?"

Selena jabbed Tawanna and said, "Look at Lawrence, he looks like he's about to blow."

"Yeah, his Pay Location is running without a supervisor. They probably work better that way."

Inside the crowd, an unidentified voice called out: "You know it's still pretty dark out, you guys could get run over."

Finally at 5:20 AM someone said "Let's go!" Everyone went to their cars at once. There was no way the bosses could follow everyone. The employees caravanned out of the lot, using the back aisle. Horns were honking loudly. It was a celebration, a show of solidarity, and a protest all rolled into one.

Newton called the supervisors together right there in the lot. "This cannot be tolerated. *Insubordination! Disrespect!* I want names! Who did you see out there? Give me names!!

Later that morning Drummond and Newton were alone in the office. Drummond pointed out what the supervisors had been afraid to mention. The employees hadn't broken any rules. There was no basis for discipline.

But Newton raised a finger pointing to the ceiling. "I know they violated something. The parking lot has a posted speed limit of five miles per hour. Do you think anyone obeyed the speed limit?"

Drummond knew it was almost impossible to drive that slowly, but he didn't dispute Newton. He stood aside as Newton collected witness statements from all the supervisors that the employees were driving above the speed limit. They issued seven day suspensions for six of the employees, including Paul Farley, Tawanna Chambers, Emma Friedman, and Sharon Spencer, who was a steward for the

Mail Handlers Union (the union representing the people who load and unload trucks, among other duties). The suspensions charged the employees with driving dangerously, ignoring the posted speed limit, and creating a disturbance by honking their horns.

Newton called Supervisor Reggie Green into his office for some unfinished business. "You see this sign, Green? It says 'The Buck Stops Here.' I'm the boss of this operation Green, you get that straight! If you'd gotten the position, I'd take orders from you. As it is, you must follow *my* instructions. And don't undermine me either. Some manager told those employees we were going out into the parking lot again last night. Was it you?"

"I had nothing to do with it," Reggie replied.

"I don't believe you. I don't believe a word you say! Watch yourself."

In the grievance procedure, management offered to reduce the week-long suspensions to three calendar days, including two off days, so each employee would only miss one day's pay. They just wanted to keep some discipline on each employee's record to make a point.

All six employees defiantly rejected the offer. They went out on their one week suspensions while the grievances were appealed up the chain, asking for the suspensions to be expunged with full back pay. Resolution of the issue would take nearly a year, during which time there would be changes in some management positions, but these employees would eventually get their back pay.

Paul Farley wrote a blistering attack on James Newton in the Local Union newspaper, *The Commentator*. His article was entitled "Sticker Shock." It ridiculed management's exaggerated concern over a trivial issue. It railed against the heavy-handed tactics of management, both in following people to their cars and in issuing suspensions for a legal protest. The article ended with these lines: "I hope Tour One employees will not cave in to these bullies. We must continue to stick together and resist any further attempts at intimidation in a manner that is creative, legal, and effective."

Eight: ADDING INSULT TO INJURY

October, 1991

Prosecutor: What did the defendant say about Mr. Newton?
Witness: I don't remember.
Prosecutor: Let me remind you that you're under oath.
Witness: He said, "I can't tell you how much I hate that man.
He enjoys seeing people suffer."

Barry Sanders took the handoff and tried running around the right side of the Tampa Bay Bucs' defense. Finding no running room, he reversed direction and went around the left side. Ten yards downfield he cut back, left a defensive back grasping at air, got a block from a wide receiver to get by another defender, faked the free safety out of his shoes, and trotted into the end zone. After this spectacular 37 yard run, Barry quietly handed the ball to the official. The Detroit Lions had a 17 point lead midway through the second quarter. The Tampa Bay home crowd was booing their team.

Paul Farley was watching the game on television at Ron Davidson's home in Sterling Heights. It was a comfortable two story, three bedroom house, about 5 miles from the Plant. Ron's wife Pam had a roast in the oven. It was a cool but pleasant October day, and Ron and Pam's two children were playing across the street in a neighbor's yard.

Angela had also been invited for dinner, but declined. "She's probably home reading one of her mysteries," Ron said. "I don't see what she gets out of them."

"Hey, I started her on those books," Paul said. "I love reading them, especially the ones written by lawyers. John Grisham, Scott Turow, Steve Martini – all of them. Whenever I see one in a drug store, I grab it. But that's not why she's not here. She knew we'd be watching football all day."

"Well, it's no mystery what the Lions are going to do today. They'll blow this lead by the fourth quarter. They always tease us. You think they're really going somewhere, then they flop."

After running for a first down, Tampa Bay threw three straight incomplete passes, leaving fourth and ten. "It's a punning situation," Ron quipped.

"That's right," said Paul. "The Bucs stop here." Ron the punster howled at Paul's joke and gave him a high five.

Tampa's punter kicked the ball way over Mel Gray's head and the ball rolled dead at the eleven yard line.

"There's no turning back now," Ron said. "It's the punt of no return."

Paul didn't react to this last pun, as Ron headed for the kitchen during the commercial and returned with two more beers.

"No thank you," said Paul. "I've got to make a phone call at half time and I want to be halfway sober. Emma Friedman called and left a message on my answering machine while I was sleeping this morning. I had the ringer on the phone turned off. I slept until noon and didn't have a chance to return it. It seems they're giving her a hard time at work."

"How'd she get your home number?"

"I used to go out with her. It ended like most of my relationships. We weren't right for each other, but we're still friends."

"Did you ever go out with a Jewish girl before?"

"My mother's Jewish. I guess you didn't know that. She was really hoping it would work out with Emma."

"Well you ought to settle down with somebody pretty soon."

"Now you're starting to sound like my mother."

"So how was it growing up with a Jewish mother and a Christian father?"

"Fine. Neither one was very religious. They both figured if you try to be a good person and treat other people well, that's really all that matters. He never went to church, she never went to synagogue, so they didn't argue over where to go pray."

"Well the Lions better pray their defense holds up." After a Lions fumble, Tampa was inside Detroit's ten yard line. Two plays later, they scored their first touchdown.

The score was 17-10 at halftime when Paul went into Ron's bedroom to make his phone call. When Paul emerged almost an hour later, the third quarter was history, and so was the Lions' lead. Paul and Ron ate their dinner quietly in front of the television as the Bucs began the fourth quarter with a time consuming drive down the field. Pam and the kids ate in the dining room.

"I told Emma I'd be coming over right after we ate dinner," Paul said. "They wouldn't let her see a steward on Saturday, so I'm going to take her statement off the clock and grieve for both of us to be paid for the time."

"If you ask me, you're mixing business with pleasure."

Paul smiled but said nothing.

"Hey, go for it Paul, she's not a bad looking woman. And it'll make your mother happy. What more could you want?"

Paul wasn't sure what his intentions were. He knew it would take a long time for Emma to write a detailed statement of everything she had told him on the phone. He knew it might be difficult to get her off the workroom floor long enough to write this statement at work. He also knew he didn't mind spending time at her house. Beyond that, he'd just play it by ear.

"Paul, we're short-staffed on our machine," Emma said, "so we never get a day off the LSM, and we've been doing ten hours most days. Keying every day, my neck and shoulder started hurting. I ignored the pain for awhile, but it kept getting worse. So I called in. That 204-B Elisha Ellison took the call. You know, the one they call 'Double E.' I made the mistake of saying it was job related. I should've waited to tell them later. Elisha took my number and said she'd call me back. That was at 8:30. By 11:00 I hadn't heard anything so I went to sleep.

"The phone woke me up, she must've waited 'til Newton came in. She demanded I come in right away so they could send me to Metro Hospital for a Fitness for Duty exam. You know what she told me? If I don't come right away they'll mark me AWOL and give me a suspension!"

"Newton's an asshole."

"Yes Paul, we know that. He wanted Double E to intimidate me. And I was scared. But I told her I was on muscle relaxers that make me drowsy, so I couldn't drive."

"Good thinking!"

"It was true! Anyway, I asked if I could come in the morning. She said she'd call me back."

Elisha told Emma she could report to Rose Bancroft on day shift at 10:00. What happened from that point on was unbelievable, and Paul had Emma write it all down.

When she reported to the Plant in the morning, Rose Bancroft gave Emma some paperwork and directions to Metro Hospital. At the hospital, a nurse led Emma to the examining room and told Dr. Gregory Tankarow, "This is the person they called about."

The doctor was very rude. Emma told him her neck was sore from keying at work, but he kept throwing suspicious questions at her. He asked if she lifts up her children at home, and she replied she doesn't have any children. So he asked if she does any housework, like lifting full garbage bags or scrubbing floors. Emma responded that she knew the soreness was caused by work. "It's really easy to figure out, doctor. At the beginning of the day I don't hurt too much, but after keying all day the pain is intolerable. I already feel a little better after taking a night off work."

Dr. Tankarow took some x-rays and told her to sit in another waiting area until he got the results. It was uncomfortably cold in the gown they had given her to wear. She wondered if the doctor forgot about her, because she had to wait over an hour.

Finally, the nurse gave Emma some paperwork. It said she was able to return to work immediately, with a restriction against lifting anything more than 20 pounds. There was no keying restriction. Emma knew if she followed the good doctor's advice she would be in severe pain again. Her own doctor had put her off work for a week, and she was following that advice, regardless of what this quack had to say.

There was something else on the paperwork that caught her eye. In a space on the form for comments, Doctor Tankarow had written in his sloppy but legible handwriting the following words: "No Injury At Work. Overuse of Muscle." Emma demanded to speak to the doctor about this notation.

Dr. Tankarow explained he simply meant to say there was no accident at work, like dropping something on your foot. The injury was progressive, from overuse of the muscle over a period of time.

"But the way this is worded could give someone the wrong impression. It's important for my claim that it be worded clearly."

"Don't worry, sweetie, it will be okay. I've done this before."

Emma left the hospital worried and upset. But she decided not to talk to anyone from the Post Office until she returned to work.

She had gone back to work Friday night (or "Friday night for Saturday" as the Tour One clerks say). She had asked to see a steward when she reported in at 8:30 P.M. She told Elisha she wanted to be paid for the time she spent at the hospital (a total of three hours), and she wanted a steward's help in processing her OWCP claim. She didn't think she should have to use 40 hours of her own sick leave for her absence – Workman's Comp should pay her.

Elisha said they could not spare her from the LSM to see a steward that day. Monday night would be better. Then, at 4:45 A.M. when the crew stopped keying to do the final pull down and dispatch, Elisha told Emma that she had talked to Mr. Newton.

Her next words were quite a shock.

"Since you were not injured on the job, you will have to pay for the x-rays and hospital visit at Metro."

"But you made me go! I had already been treated by my own doctor. I didn't need those x-rays."

"You can talk to Mr. Newton while we dispatch."

"I don't want to talk to Mr. Newton. I want a steward!"

"I suggest you see Mr. Newton. He can explain everything. He's waiting for you in the manager's office."

Emma sat on a molded plastic chair, looking up at Newton on his executive chair on the other side of the desk. Her thumb and forefinger ran up and down her purse strap as she listened to him.

"You were in pain and called in. You asked to be treated at Metro Hospital. You couldn't come in right away but we accommodated the request. Now you have to pay the bills, it's as simple as that."

Emma's mouth was wide open. At first her brain had trouble processing the information her ears were inputting. Then she responded, "Mr. Newton, that's simply not true. I don't know who gave you wrong information, but I never asked to go to the hospital."

"We have witness statements that you did."

"How can you have witness statements? I only talked to Elisha, and she knows the truth."

"She wrote one of the statements. You've simply got to accept responsibility for your actions."

Newton paused, leaned forward, and continued in his most sincere, compassionate tone.

"Look, I know you don't like paying for this, nobody would. The important thing is that your neck is better now. You needed to see the doctor, and we helped you. Now you have a hospital bill, but you're paid a good salary, you can afford it. I'm sure they'll let you pay it in installments. It will be okay. Really, it will."

As Emma turned to leave the office, he said, "Have a nice weekend."

Emma was in tears. She didn't understand what was happening. She didn't know what a hospital would charge for x-rays, but she was sure it was expensive. Somebody was being very dishonest, and she couldn't understand why.

Emma confronted Elisha Ellison and asked, "What are you trying to do to me?" Elisha didn't look her in the eye. She just said, "You can discuss it with a steward on Monday."

Emma had been miserable all day Saturday. She decided to call Paul Sunday morning. Now he was in her living room, reading her statement. He placed it on the coffee table and quietly regarded Emma, who was lost in thought. Her legs were curled under her as she sat in a large olive-green armchair, with a painting on the wall above her. The painting was an abstract landscape, with green smudges for trees and blue and white swirls for the sky. Paul remembered the playful argument they'd had when he pretended he thought the painting could've been done by a seventh grader. The aroma of cookies baking grabbed his attention. She'd also been baking something the day they argued about the painting.

He was struck by her simple beauty, with the dimple in her cheek, her pretty brown eyes that seemed to express kindness and warmth, and her straight black hair that rested now on her green sweater (which almost matched the armchair). You could admire her beauty and at the same time you could be comfortable talking to her in a girl-next-door kind of way. Right now, it was Paul's job to defend and protect this innocent girl against the evil manager.

"Like I said, Newton's an asshole. I can't tell you how much I hate that man. You know why he's doing this? It's not even to save the Post Office money or improve their on-the-job injury statistics.

At least, those aren't the main reasons. That man simply enjoys seeing people suffer. When he made you cry, that brought a smile to his face. And he's looking forward to watching me struggle trying to help you. But he made some mistakes, and we're going to set things right. That's what the union is for."

Paul told Emma she ought to be paid for the time spent at the doctor's office, and there was no way she had to pay the hospital bill for a Fitness for Duty exam. "And we'll file another grievance about the denial of a steward. You're supposed to see a steward in most instances within two hours of your request. In no case should the delay go beyond the end of your tour when you ask at the beginning of the day. We'll ask to be paid at the overtime rate for the hour it took us to discuss your situation."

Emma was still upset. "How could anyone believe I *asked* to go to Metro Hospital when I already saw my own doctor? My doctor is covered by insurance if my OWCP doesn't go through. Why would I have more tests taken at my own expense? My doctor was handling the situation, and I was beginning to feel a little better."

"Nobody believes you asked to go to Metro. This is just Mr. Newton's reaction to your request to see a steward. He plays dirty. Real dirty."

"I can't even believe this is happening. I'm a good worker. Why are they doing this to me?"

"The way they treated you Emma is unconscionable. We'll file a separate harassment grievance. It's not enough to straighten out all the paperwork, make sure your claim is processed, you are paid for your time, and management pays the hospital bills. Newton tried to frighten you, and punish you, from the time you started to stand up for your rights. He wanted to teach you a lesson. We've got to teach him one."

Emma still looked miserable. Paul put his arms around her and gave her a big hug. He held her tight. He realized his job was not just to prepare the paperwork but to help Emma feel more relaxed and confident. He also realized that he still really liked this young woman.

She invited him to stay and watch a movie she had rented. It was a sentimental love story, and that suited him just fine.

Monday morning, Paul went to the Union Office in Ferndale. He typed a letter on official union stationery, addressed to Dr. Tankarow at Metro Hospital. He asked for a further explanation of the words "No Injury At Work. Overuse of Muscle." He sent the letter by certified mail.

Monday evening they let Emma see Paul on union business. He filed grievances with Elisha for payment for the time spent at the hospital (three hours) and for the time spent writing the statement. Elisha said she would give management's response within five days. Paul wasn't ready to file the harassment grievance yet. He submitted a Request For Information for all relevant witness statements and documents.

After midnight Ron Davidson joined Paul in the union office with a mischievous smile on his face.

"I guess things went pretty well with Emma, and I'm not talking about the grievance, either."

"What do you mean?"

"I tried to call you at 11:30 last night. You still weren't home. Did you spend the night?"

Paul said nothing, but the grin on his face gave him away. When the phone rang Ron answered, and soon after he was leaving the room to hold a Step One Meeting with Butch Hobson.

While Ron was doing that, a young lady named Stacy Kline came to the union office. She was blond, she was sexy, and she wore clothes that showed her wonderful figure without crossing the lines of good taste (or the Post Office dress code). Ron always referred to her as the most beautiful woman at the Post Office. He sometimes compared her to Marilyn Monroe. Paul looked forward to teasing Ron about not being around when Stacey dropped by.

"I like that sign you've got on the wall," she said. It was a No Whining sign (the word "whining" with a line through it, like a No Smoking sign). Paul had mixed feelings about the poster.

In any event, Stacey wasn't whining. She needed to grieve a Letter of Warning for irregular attendance issued by Reggie Green. From the looks of it, her attendance was far from perfect, and they would probably have to accept six months on the record. But Stacey wanted none of that.

"You see, I want to go into the 204-B program, but they won't let me with any discipline on file."

Stacey's eyes flirted with Paul as she talked. He was going to be loyal to Emma, but it was hard to be completely unaffected by the breathtaking beauty in front of him.

"What do you think I can do?" Paul asked.

"I'm willing to make a deal, where I have to be absolutely perfect for three months. I won't be sick, I won't miss a day for any reason, and I won't even be late a few minutes. The Letter of Warning will stay out of my file for the time being. If I meet my end of the bargain, it will be expunged completely in three months. If not, it stays in my file for a year, which is longer than the six months you were probably thinking of. I get my opportunity to go into the 204-B program sooner, and if I mess up, management is protected."

"Why are you so anxious to go into the program? Management is really awful around here. They'll make you discipline and harass your friends. Are you sure you want that?"

"I think I can make things better," she said, and smiled at him. He tried to picture this beautiful woman as a supervisor who would treat people well and settle grievances fairly with him at Step One. It was a pleasant thought. But he had trouble believing it. Nevertheless, he decided to go ahead and try her approach to this grievance.

"Well, it isn't my job to help you get into management, but we are supposed to give you the best representation possible. If you want me to try out your proposal, I'll go ahead and run it by Reggie."

"Why don't you go over his head to James Newton? He knows I want to go into management, and he'll understand why I'm asking. You can tell him this proposal is 'corrective rather than punitive.' Isn't that the language you use? If I promise to be perfect for three months, why do you need discipline anyway?"

Within an hour, Paul Farley and James Newton were signing the settlement Stacey had suggested. The issuing supervisor, Reggie Green, was not even consulted. Newton shook Paul's hand and said: "See, if you approach me with the right attitude, I really can be quite reasonable."

Paul went to the men's room and washed his hands.

While Paul was in Newton's office, Tyrone Wheeler found Angela alone in the union office. He'd been back there half-a-dozen times in the past several months, and every time he had asked for Angela. She was getting sick of his frivolous complaints.

"I'm not here to file a grievance, Angela. I just want to ask you something."

Angela didn't look up from the case file she was reading.

"Will you have dinner with me?"

"I'm busy that night."

"But I didn't even say which night."

Now Angela looked up at Tyrone. She understood why he'd been coming back to ask her about overtime, job assignments and every other complaint he could come up with.

She blurted out: "Look, I'm not going out with you, and I'm sick and tired of handling your bullshit complaints. Next time you need a steward, see Ron or Paul!"

Tyrone was hurt. Angela could see it in his eyes. He left the room without saying another word.

Angela felt bad. Tyrone hadn't deserved all that. In fact, he really wasn't bad looking and he was kind of a nice person. It's just that either you were attracted to someone or you weren't, and Angela felt absolutely nothing for Tyrone.

Tyrone told Lawrence Harris what had happened with Angela. He couldn't understand why she had disrespected him. He asked if Lawrence knew whether she had a boyfriend.

Lawrence said: "That sister is a hard one to get a handle on. She's not married, I know that. But I haven't seen her with anyone and I've never heard of any boyfriend either. Her personal life is a complete mystery to me."

On Thursday, Elisha denied both of Emma Friedman's grievances, and also gave Paul the witness statements he had requested. The key document was a statement signed by Elisha Ellison. Paul studied the third paragraph:

"Ms. Friedman called in to report her absence from work due to a sore neck that may have been caused by keying on the LSM. I called her back at 0100. Ms. Ellison used the speaker phone, and General Supervisor Newton and Supervisor Gwendolyn Rogers heard the conversation. Ms. Freidman requested to be sent for treatment by a hospital that we would recommend. I told her we would not be able to pay for anything, and she said it wouldn't be a problem about the money…"

The statement concluded that the union's request for payment was unreasonable because Emma had asked to be sent to Metro Hospital. It was accompanied by a statement from James Newton that told the same story. Newton quoted Emma as saying, "I can afford to pay the hospital bill." Gwen Rogers' statement was only three sentences long and did not contain enough detail to either help or harm the grievance.

Paul stared at the third paragraph of Elisha's statement again. It was a lie of course, but something else was bothering him. He read the paragraph a couple more times. Then it struck him. The key phrase was "Ms. Ellison used the speaker phone." If Elisha had written this statement herself, it would read "I used the speaker phone." Somebody else had composed this statement, and then changed "Ms. Ellison" to "I" wherever it appeared – except they missed one. This grievance was getting very interesting.

Paul showed the statements to Emma. She stared in disbelief.

"But this isn't true. How could they say this happened?"

Emma already knew this was management's version, but seeing the signed statements was quite a shock. It was hard to believe people would blatantly lie like this. And for what purpose? Just to make her suffer, it seemed.

Paul pointed out the key phrase in the third paragraph. At 0300, Paul and Emma confronted Elisha, with Paul doing the talking.

"I can prove you did not write the statement you signed. I'm not going to tell you how I know. I just want to know who wrote it, and who made you sign it?"

"I can't say," said Elisha. "I mean that's not...I mean, what makes you think I didn't write it?"

"Your reaction just gave it away again. What's worse, we both know Emma didn't ask to go to the hospital. You told her she would be AWOL if she didn't go. You said it was a Fitness for Duty exam."

Elisha said nothing, but the pained expression on her face spoke volumes.

Paul wanted to nail Elisha in her lies, and get the person (Newton) who put her up to it. But his first priority was straightening out Emma's situation. He would go light on Elisha if necessary.

"Here's what I'm willing to do. If you write up a new statement that management instructed Emma to go to the hospital, I'll pretend the first statement you signed was a misunderstanding.I won't try to get you in any trouble for it. You can still deny the grievances as long as you put the facts in writing. I can straighten everything out for Emma at Step Two."

"Let me get back to you."

Before the end of the day, Elisha Ellison talked to Paul again. She looked relieved.

"I'll have the statement you requested tomorrow. And you can tell Emma the Postal Service will authorize payment for the x-rays and hospital bill, so she can stop worrying about that. The other grievances are still going to Step Two."

Back in the union office Paul could hardly contain himself when he told the other stewards about the grievances and Elisha's false statement.

"That sister was under a lot of pressure," Angela said. "Either sign the statement Newton gave her or, who knows, maybe get kicked out of the program. I'm glad they let her recant."

"Never mind Double E," Ron said. "Paul's going after Newton now, full steam ahead. Paul lives for these moments."

The harassment grievance was filed directly with James Newton. Normally the employee would be present at the Step One Meeting, but Paul didn't want to upset Emma any more. Nor did he expect to resolve anything at the Step One level. He didn't even want to resolve it here. The Step One was a mere formality. It would give him a chance to put the entire story of harassment and dishonesty in a written Step Two appeal. Newton could deny any personal involvement in Elisha's decisions, or tell any lie he wanted. Nobody would believe him when Paul took it to Step Two. At the Step One meeting Paul presented a brief summary of what had occurred and didn't even argue when Newton proceeded to tell him a bunch of new lies. He simply wrote down what Newton said.

In order to make sure he got a chance to write up a Step Two appeal, he requested a corrective action that would be unacceptable to Newton. It read as follows:

"Management will cease the practice of harassing employees

who are injured on the job. A complete investigation into the mistreatment of grievant Emma Friedman will be conducted by an Upper Management official, who will come on Tour One and interview all parties concerned with a union official present. Management will then take whatever corrective action is necessary to ensure this type of incident is never repeated."

A week later Paul received a letter from Dr. Tankarow which acknowledged that the "overuse of muscle" he referred to had occurred at the workplace. With this statement Emma's OWCP claim could proceed smoothly.

Paul met at Step Two on all of his grievances with Nancy Barber the first week in November. Nancy agreed to pay Emma three hours at the overtime rate for the time spent at Metro Hospital. She denied the grievance for compensation for the union time. She offered language about prompt release for union time in the future, depending on service conditions. Paul felt that wasn't good enough. Nancy Barber's argument was even if Emma should have been allowed to see a steward on the day in question, management's action did not necessitate conducting this business off the clock. No grievance would have been rendered untimely by waiting until the following Monday night. Paul knew he might have trouble winning the remedy he requested higher up, but he was stubborn on this one. He sent it to Step Three in Chicago.

Although Nancy Barber did not accept the strong language Paul had proposed for the harassment grievance, she seemed to be genuinely disturbed by Newton's behavior. She offered settlement language stating that the Labor Relations Rep. (herself) would set up a meeting with Joe Borelli at the Plant to discuss procedures for handling on the job injuries. Paul had mixed feelings but signed off on this language.

Back at the union office, Ron and Angela questioned Paul's

decision. Paul explained that Nancy Barber seemed really to be upset with Newton's behavior. "She's not going to put in writing that he harassed an employee and falsified evidence, but she understands exactly what went down. She doesn't like Newton, Borelli, or Ben Herman, but she only gets involved if there is a clear contract violation or some type of behavior that is inappropriate in the extreme. I think she wants to raise hell about this one, but she wants to do it behind closed doors, without the union's involvement. We'll never know what goes on in those discussions, but I decided this had a better chance of doing some good than appealing the grievance up. We all know what we'd probably get from Step Three: some general language about how management will treat employees with respect and follow all of the OWCP rules and regulations. They won't put it in writing that management lied and harassed anyone. So what would I accomplish?"

"Yeah, you're right I guess," Ron said. "But you know, when you told me about Emma being reduced to tears, it occurred to me she's not the only one. I can feel the tension all over this building. If people aren't crying, they're cursing or just muttering to themselves. I usually don't let this place get to me, but I'm starting to really hate those bastards."

Angela simply said: "Paul, I know it's been a rough couple of weeks for you trying to get this issue resolved. You did pretty well by Emma, as far as I can tell. But this stuff wears you out. I'll bet you could use a break. At least from these heavy duty cases."

Paul smiled. "As a matter of fact, I scheduled my vacation late this year. I'll be gone the next two weeks, visiting my folks in New York. Though I might come back a little early and spend some time with Emma."

Nine: A SHATTERING EXPERIENCE

November, 1991

Prosecutor: What did the defendant say about the 1991 shooting in his article in the union newspaper?
Defense Lawyer: Objection!

"They can't blame it on me. I was in New York."

Paul was in the union office talking with Angela and Ron about the shooting at the Main. Of course, there was no question about the identity of the shooter. A fired letter carrier brought a rifle into the building after learning of the arbitration ruling upholding management's decision to remove him. Several managers were killed, and a few craft employees were wounded or injured trying to escape. Then he shot himself.

Angela had business at the Main a few days after shooting. "You can't imagine what a terrifying experience it was. Everybody was still in shock when I visited, both for the people who were killed and for the entire incident. Just think about it. You hear a rifle shot in another part of the building. Then a man comes through your work area waving his rifle around. Even if it's not pointed at you, you have no way of knowing what's going to happen next. People jumped out of windows – even jumping out of a first floor window and landing on concrete isn't that easy. Other people dove behind desks. Then they heard another shot. A manager was helping another employee get out the window when he was killed. He wasn't a bad guy from what people tell me. Another one that was killed was Bob Sterns. He was one of Ben Herman's sidekicks and everyone hated him. Nobody would say they were glad he was dead, but nobody had anything good to say about him either. That part was eerie."

"I can't imagine what that was like," said Ron, for once not making a joke of the situation.

Angela nodded. "It was god awful. There were some people still in shock. Some of them are still out on stress leave. There was a Personnel clerk who started for work the day after the shooting but never made it. She got into the car and immediately felt sick at the thought of going back to the site of the blood and violence she witnessed the previous day. So she went back in the house and called in. She still wasn't talking about it. A friend of hers told me the story."

Ron Davidson filled Paul in about reaction at the Plant. "It's several miles away, but it still hit home here pretty hard. Most people who work at the Main started out here. Some of their managers were craft employees here at one time. So anyone who's been around as long as I have knows a lot of the people there. And we all know the building. That's where we went to apply for the job, and most of us have been back to the Personnel Office again for one reason or another."

"All the window clerks at the Main started here," Paul said. "People here don't know the Labor Reps like we do, but they know *somebody* over there. I guess it really struck a raw nerve."

"But there's more to it than that," Ron continued. "The mood was pretty somber at the Plant because people realized it could've happened here. Management pushed that guy over the edge. The way Borelli and Newton have been acting, we could've just as easily had that bloody scene right here."

Ron got up and locked the union office door. He lowered his voice and said, "You know, Charlie Valmont told me the shooter should've come over here and nailed some of our asshole managers. He thought I'd appreciate the sentiment. I just glared back at him. People say I make some insensitive remarks, but that one was too much, even for me."

Ron shook his head in sadness and wonder at the tragedy.

"And you know Candace Brown?" he added. "A friend of hers decorates T-shirts. Candace was selling shirts in here for six bucks that said 'Don't Upset Me – I'm a Postal Worker!' Some people thought it was clever. Management didn't. They ordered people not to wear the shirts at work. I guess I can see why they were a little touchy about it."

"And they made us take down one of our posters," Angela added. "The one that said 'WARNING: Due to a Shortage of Robots, This Worker is a Human Being and May React Unpredictably If Abused.' They said they won't stop us from putting up adversarial posters, as long as it can't be interpreted as a reference to the shooting. We had it posted before the shooting, and that's really not what we meant by it. But we agreed to take it down. We can find something better if we want. But maybe we'll wait and see how management behaves first."

"Are Herman and Borelli keeping their jobs?" Paul asked.

"No, they're out of here," Ron said. "Asner's temporarily back in his old job, and they detailed somebody from Detroit as Acting Postmaster at the Main for a few months. They're going to appoint a whole new management team."

"How were the news reports? Did they get it right?" Paul asked.

"The press was pretty hard on management," Angela said. "Of course, they also sensationalized whatever personality problems the shooter had. Management gave out details of every conflict with a manager or coworker, his discipline record, and so on. If the spin on the story was a deranged individual who went out of control, then management would appear blameless. The media bought it, but only to a degree."

Ron added, "They also interviewed letter carriers and clerks and got a different story. There was a lot of tension at the Main, just like here. People told stories about a guy who was sent home just for whistling when he sorted his mail, about managers screaming at employees over really trivial stuff, about the military style regimentation. The Main used to be a nice place to work; the atmosphere was much better than here. Then the Herman management team came in and people started hating their jobs."

Angela broke in and said, "I saw an interview with a steward for the carriers' union. He said management had picked on the guy that did the shooting. They nitpicked and poked away at him until he lost his temper. Then they nailed him with discipline. Yeah, the guy might have had a few personal problems, but if they'd have left him alone, this would've never happened."

"So are we going to see any changes around here?" Paul asked.

"They're sending supervisors to some kind of sensitivity training. The interim managers had a bunch of meetings with our top Local officials. They say they want to work with the unions to create a better atmosphere. I talked to Humphrey, and he says it's too early to tell."

Angela added: "I guess one of the biggest tests will be if we see any changes in your buddy, James Newton. I kind of doubt there's any way to change someone with a rotten character like his, but he's going to at least have to pretend to be nice for a while."

"I'm going to write an article saying we have to change the culture in this place," Paul said, "starting with changing the behavior of you-know-who."

Ten: JUMP SUITS AND JUMP SHOTS

January, 1992

Prosecutor: How seriously did the defendant take his grievances?
Witness: Sometimes it seemed like he was on a holy crusade.

"It's a good time to be a new steward," Ron was telling Shirley Jones. Shirley and her three kids were over for dinner on a Sunday afternoon in February, along with Paul and Angela. Pam's cooking was delicious, as usual. The menu of roast chicken, homemade mashed potatoes and broccoli was unremarkable. But Paul, who often cooked roast chicken for himself, knew his cooking wasn't nearly this flavorful.

After dinner the five kids (Shirley's, and Pam and Ron's) were huddled over a Monopoly game upstairs, Pam was doing the dishes, and the stewards talked shop in the living room. Ron was drinking a scotch and soda, Paul had a Budweiser, and Angela a glass of white wine. Shirley sipped on a Pepsi.

The three veteran stewards were listening to Shirley's account of her first grievance situations. Shirley Jones was in her late thirties, with cocoa-colored skin and short hair. She had a trim figure, but the wrinkles on her face reflected the hard times she'd seen. A single mother, she had left a lower paying job in a hospital to work for the Post Office a couple of years ago. As a junior employee, she had to work on the weekends, when the other Tour One stewards were off.

"Last night," Shirley was saying, "Selena Thomas got a Letter of Warning for being out of the area for twenty-five minutes. Reggie Green says he was at the belt the whole time and didn't see her. Selena says she went to Flats to get some mail to weigh over. Then she went to the restroom. It sounds all right to me, but Reggie isn't buying it."

Angela responded, "Let me tell you something about Selena. She spends more time in the ladies room adjusting her make-up than anyone I know. She's a married woman, for God' sake. I don't know who she's trying to look pretty for, but that's none of my business."

"You think she's in the wrong?"

"That's my hunch. I wasn't there, of course."

Shirley looked puzzled. "How do you feel about defending someone who's in the wrong? Shouldn't she get what's coming to her?"

Paul responded: "The people we defend aren't always angels, but you'd be surprised how little problem that causes. I almost never feel guilty about what I'm doing. More often, I feel like I'm on the right side. Management mistreats people and we stand up for them. Management issues unfair discipline and we try to get it expunged. Or management disciplines someone who really committed an infraction. Usually they go overboard, and we try to get it down to something reasonable."

"Take this case", Angela said. "If Selena doesn't grieve it, the Letter is on her record for two years. Any similar infraction in two years and she could be suspended. That's pretty harsh. Reggie doesn't even want that. You file a grievance, and you might get him to reduce it to three months, or six months, tops. He might even reduce it to a Documented Discussion. And that's *assuming* she's guilty."

Ron added: "You don't have to worry about defending people who are guilty. If the person is guilty, management knows it, and no amount of fancy footwork by a union steward is going to change that. The person won't go scot-free. You just want to get the discipline down to something reasonable, like Paul says. Management expects to have to bargain on discipline. When they issue a suspension, they issue it for more days than they intend to settle for – they build in their bargaining room. It's the way the system works."

"I know one person you didn't want to defend was Danny Vellarmo," Paul said.

"What did Danny do?" Shirley asked.

"He got a fourteen day suspension for choking people." Paul saw the shocked look on Shirley's face and continued. "He didn't try to kill them, of course. He said he was just playing around. He'd come up from behind on you, put his hands around your neck, and say 'I've got you.' Or sometimes it was 'I've got you motherfucker.' You wouldn't actually be unable to breathe, but his grip was strong and fairly tight. He'd let you struggle a little, then release you."

"It happened about a year-and-a-half ago," Ron added. "Vellarmo was nothing but a bully. Still is. Even though he says he's just playing, people are afraid of him. If he wants to sit on console number four on the LSM, people let him place his card there. He can intimidate just by glaring at you. You know how big he is, Shirley. With his temper, his unpredictability, he scares the rest of the crew half-to-death."

"I can believe it," said Shirley.

"Anyway, in the case I handled, four coworkers reported choking incidents to management. Newton interviewed Vellarmo, who said it was harmless horseplay. Labor Relations considered everything from removal down to a Letter of Warning. They decided on a 14 day suspension."

"How did you handle it?"

"I wanted to compromise on a seven day suspension, one year on record. But Vellarmo insisted on fighting it all the way. He said he was innocent. I looked at the four witness statements and I knew Vellarmo was wrong. Of course I knew that anyway. That's one of the few times I didn't show my grievant the witness statements. I was afraid he'd go after the people who wrote the statements. They were union members too. So I asked Danny what he wanted me to say on his Step Two grievance appeal, and I wrote down what he said, word for word. I figured he was getting exactly the kind of representation he wanted, and he'd hang himself. I knew he'd get what he deserved higher up."

Ron looked up as he heard his son and daughter arguing about the Monopoly game and told them to play nice. When their voices died down he continued.

"As I was saying, Danny served the fourteen days, and then last August his grievance went to arbitration. He was bragging all week about the back pay he was going to get. At the hearing, all four witnesses testified. They came across sincere and believable. It was tense, even though two of them had bid over to the BOBB and didn't see Danny anymore. By the time the ruling came out, the other two witnesses bid onto day shift. But we've still got Danny on our tour. Of course, the arbitrator ruled against Danny."

"That's an unusual example, Shirley," Paul said. "But even there, Ron wouldn't have had a problem if Danny had let him do his job. He'd have had a seven day suspension, which would've been better for Danny. And Ron's conscience would be clear because Danny would have had a suspension on record for a year, which would have offered some protection to his coworkers."

"Getting back to Selena, you shouldn't assume she's guilty off my reaction," Angela said. "Find out if anyone saw her weighing the mail over. I'm guessing she made that up, but I could be wrong. If you can't prove her innocence, don't tell Selena you don't believe her. Just say you can't prove her case and you think you should make the best deal you can."

Shirley's other grievance involved Supervisor Red Collier and a new PTF named Rachel Parker. "Over a period of time, Rachel noticed Collier paying especially close attention to her, singling her out if she was a minute late from break, and things like that. Last night he really tore into her. She went to use the restroom while she was on her sweep, which is no problem. But Collier said that when she returned to key, she left the sweep side in terrible shape for the person behind her. He raised his voice, called her a 'lazy, no good, bimbo' and said she ought to be collecting a welfare check instead of pretending to work for the Post Office. He was real loud, too. I talked to the person who followed her on sweep, and he says it wasn't all that bad. And she's generally not a bad worker. Collier ought to get in some trouble for this, don't you think?"

"He ought to but he ain't," Ron said. "You should still file a grievance on it though."

"And what kind of settlement can I get? I think 'management will stop harassing the grievant' would be appropriate."

"Shirley, you won't get that either," Angela said. ""In harassment grievances they never admit they did anything wrong. They offer neutral language, like 'management and employees will treat each other with mutual respect.' It's ridiculous. You can't get them disciplined and you can't even get them to put in writing that they need to improve their behavior. It's not the same for clerks. If one of our people has bad attendance, they get discipline. They don't get language like 'management and employees will both be regular in attendance.' That would be equitable treatment. But nothing's like that around here."

Shirley looked totally confused. "So what's the point of filing a grievance?" she asked.

"You might do some good," Paul answered. "First, you get Rachel and Collier in a room together. You explain Rachel's concerns. Red will deny he did anything wrong. But chances are he'll lighten up now that he knows the union's watching, especially with the new management team we've got. I think he'll be careful. You can settle at Step One for the meaningless 'mutual respect' language if the discussion goes okay. If not, if Red is belligerent, you might take it to Step Two. You ask Labor Relations to talk to Red. That part is off the record. The settlement will still be the same meaningless language, but Labor Relations will tell Red to back off. They're pretty careful about this type of thing, since the shooting. You just won't get anyone to admit in writing that Red did anything wrong. It would have to be much more extreme for that to happen."

"Yeah, I get it," said Shirley. "At least I think I do."

"You know Shirley, sometimes being a steward is frustrating," Paul said. "You're trying to prove management did something wrong, and they're playing games with semantics to deny it. Or you're fighting a discipline case you know you can't win. And sometimes you're just pleading with management to let someone take a day of annual that's closed in the book, because they have tickets to a concert or something. You have to maintain a professional relationship with management to keep those channels open. Even then, sometimes their response is 'tough luck, the day is closed, there's nothing I can do.'

"But then, once in awhile, I get really passionate about a case. I'm not just correcting a contract violation, I'm fighting for justice. Management has really wronged someone, and I feel their pain. More than that, I have the power to correct it – or at least I'm going to fight like hell to try. In these cases, sometimes there's a special bond formed between you and the person you're trying to help – even if you're fighting an uphill battle.

"I guess I've always been one to support the underdog. Maybe it started when I was in grade school – I was always the shortest kid in the class. I grew taller as a teenager, but I remembered what it meant to be smaller than everyone else, to have the bullies push you around. In sports, if the Lions or Pistons aren't playing, I root against the team that's favored.

"Now I'm in the union for the same reasons. I'm trying to protect a friend or coworker against a manager who likes to throw his weight around. Or, on a larger scale, unions defend working people against the rich bastards and their corporations who want to keep us down."

"Not every steward is like Paul," Ron chimed in. "He takes his work home with him. When I punch out, I'm happy to leave the Post Office behind and enjoy my family. But Paul, he never leaves it behind. Sometimes it's not like he's filing a grievance, it's more like a holy crusade."

"I'm not sure I understand," Shirley said. "Isn't our job just to enforce the contract?"

"Our job is a lot more than mechanically applying contract provisions," said Angela. "The contract is our starting point, of course. But we also have to understand people. Sometimes the best we can do is talk to them and make them feel better. We have to really hear what they're trying to tell us. Sometimes the fact that we file a grievance, even if it's not resolved right away, makes someone feel better than sitting back and taking it. We also have to understand when it's best to compromise, when it's best to hold our ground. When to confront management, when to sweet-talk them into a compromise. It depends on the people almost as much as on the technical language of the contract. And we've got some new people to learn about now."

The discussion then turned to the recent changes in management. The new Postmaster was Marty Potter, a soft-spoken seemingly intelligent man who used to manage in St. Louis. He brought his right-hand man, Stanley Tillman, to take Doug Asner's old job. All of the supervisors at the Main and at the Plant were going to receive sensitivity training.

Ron got Paul another beer, Shirley another Pepsi, refilled Angela's wine glass and went back in the kitchen, emerging with another scotch and soda. They started telling war stories, pretending it was just for Shirley's benefit.

Ron said, "Hey, remember the jump suit grievance?"

"Yeah, that was a fun one," Paul said.

"Two years ago, management put out a new instruction that jogging suits were not permitted at the Plant. It was stupid. The Plant is not open to the public and it really doesn't matter if people dressed informally. And if blue jeans and a flannel shirt are okay, what's wrong with a jogging suit? Anyway, one day Celia Derringer had been sent home with two hours left in her shift for violating this instruction. The thing is, she wasn't wearing a jogging suit. It was a *jump suit*.

93

"Red Collier didn't know much about fashion, and neither did I, for that matter. But I went to the mall and asked a salesclerk at a clothing store. A jogging suit is *two* pieces and a jump suit is a *one piece* outfit. I even got a written statement from the salesclerk. To thank the salesclerk, I bought a little something for my wife while I was there.

"Anyway, the grievance was denied at Step One, in spite of my evidence. All Red could say is it looked like a jogging suit to him. Before we reached Step Two, I got word that the policy on jogging suits was going to be rescinded. It was going to be posted in the Order Book soon. I told Celia, and the next day she wore the jump suit again. I was surprised, because I wasn't sure exactly when the new policy would be posted. Lucky for us, it was posted that day, although Collier hadn't seen it yet. He was ready to send Celia home again, but she smiled sweetly and said, 'haven't you read the Order Book today, Mr. Collier?'

"When I saw Celia at break, I just said 'that's a nice outfit you're wearing today.' Then we both laughed." Ron took a swig from his drink and added, "And by the way, she got paid at Step 2 for the two hours she missed."

Angela then told of a couple of grievances with Claudia Stinson, a relatively nice 204-B. "Once I lost track of the fourteen day time limit on a grievance about a Letter of Warning. Claudia didn't mind settling it anyway, but she was afraid her boss would be upset that she didn't stick it to me when she could. That Letter could've been on the record two years. But Claudia settled for six months, and to cover herself, we backdated the paperwork to make it look like we met on the fourteenth day. Claudia told her boss it had taken her a couple of days to get around to filing it away in the office. I really appreciated that. So, a few weeks later, I was filing a complicated overtime grievance. I was sure I could win, but Claudia had never read any of those Mittenthal arbitrations interpreting the overtime provisions. I offered to write up her position in denying the grievance on a Form 2608 for her. Then I wrote my Step Two, tearing her position apart. You know what? It was denied at Step Two. Labor Relations said Claudia did an excellent job explaining management's position. I couldn't believe it."

Everyone laughed at Angela's having done such a good job for the supervisor.

Paul chimed in with a tale about a Letter of Warning he handled with Harold Kline. "This was before he left the P.O. In fact, it was before I bid on eight-thirty to five. I hated that midnight shift, and on that particular night I was dead tired. For some reason, I had only gotten a couple of hours sleep the day before. So Harold was in the office, with me and Fred Kowalski. Well, you know how Harold always loved to talk. You could go to him with a simple question and end up talking for half-an-hour. And since he and Fred were friends, that's exactly what happened here. The Step One meeting started normally, I said a few things about how Fred's attendance record wasn't really all that bad, which it wasn't. Then Harold started talking and my drowsiness took over. At first my eyes closed but I was still listening. Fred responded and Harold started talking again. I think that's when I dozed off. I don't know how much of the conversation I missed, or even if anyone noticed, but when I woke up they were agreeing to take the Letter of Warning off Fred's record. I wrote up a settlement and they both thanked me. But I want to warn you Shirley, that's a technique that only works once in a while."

After the laughter subsided, Ron started to tell the story of his favorite edit grievance. "Rick Verkler used to supervise the Rochester LSM years ago, and there was a tall skinny black woman on the crew named Lashawn Daniels. Do you remember her Paul?"

Paul shrugged.

"Maybe that was before you hired in. Anyway, Lashawn had an edit with one error. There was nothing wrong with the letter, you could read the address clear as day. The machine was running at the right speed. I checked the random numbers table and it was her turn to be edited. I didn't see what I could do.

"Lashawn's real problem is her keying average was a hundred percent and she didn't want to ruin it. She wanted to stay perfect. I understood, but I didn't know what argument I could make to Verkler.

"Lashawn claimed while she was keying, with her long legs stretched out beyond the end of her console, the person sitting in front of her moved his chair back and hit her foot, distracting her momentarily. So that was my story at the Step One. Rick Verkler knew that even if that was true, there was no way to prove this distraction took place on the same letter she made an error on. I mean, from the time she sat down on her sweep to the time she got up after keying for forty-five minutes, she keyed a couple of thousand letters.

"I knew Rick was right. But I decided to try something creative. I asked Rick if he was a baseball fan. Turns out he was. So I said, you know what the official scorer does when the pitcher has a no hitter going and there's a sharply hit ball in the hole that goes off the infielder's glove? Ordinarily, it might be a base hit. But with the no hitter, the pitcher gets the benefit of the doubt and the official scorer calls it an error. So I said since Lashawn's got a no hitter going, let's give her the benefit of the doubt.

"Rick agreed to make it a zero-wrong edit, but he said next time, the error would count."

The other stewards broke out laughing.

Shirley got up and said she needed to leave – she had to take a nap before going back in to work. Before she gathered up her kids, Paul made one more comment. "Remember, everything we talked about here stays with us. Inside the steward's office, we talk among each other about people's attendance records and any situations we encounter. We need to share information like this, get advice, learn from each other. But if anyone out on the workroom floor asks us about Fred Kowalski's attendance, Celia Derringer's jump suit, or Lashawn Daniels' edit, it's not our place to tell them. People won't trust us with their grievances if they think their business will be spread all over the place. It sounds simple when I'm telling you now, but believe me, people are going to be asking you about everyone else's grievances. Sometimes it's tempting to say a few words – but it's a bad idea."

As Shirley left and Angela went to use the bathroom, Ron asked Paul how things were going with Emma.

"We broke up," he said.

"What? I thought you two were doing so well."

"I don't know what it is," Paul said. "When we break up, after a few months, I really miss her. Then we get back together, and it's really good at first, but then it seems like I'm disappointed somehow."

"I'll tell you what I think," Ron said. "Emma's going to lose patience with you and find someone else who isn't afraid of commitment. And you're going to lose a really good woman. You don't have to take my advice, of course, but just think about it. Want another beer?"

Ron headed back to the kitchen without waiting for an answer, and came back with a beer and his third (or was it his fourth?) scotch and soda. Angela rejoined them and declined an offer for more wine. Ron's wife Pam joined them just as they turned on the basketball game. It was the Bulls and Lakers, the network's national game of the week. As diehard Piston fans, Ron and Paul were in the habit of rooting against the Bulls no matter who they played, but Angela was a Michael Jordan fan. As Michael hit a jump shot that gave him ten points in the first quarter, they started talking about Shirley.

"It's good to have someone there on the weekend who can cover us," Paul said. "And she seems eager to learn. Do you think she'll stick it out?"

Angela looked at him and said, "You want to know my gut feeling? The answer is no. She just doesn't get what we're doing this for. I wouldn't be surprised if she goes into management eventually. I know she needs the money. And I just can't get a handle on what it is she believes. I can't tell you why exactly, but that's my take on her."

"From what Ron tells me," Pam said, "management isn't so bad there anymore. If Shirley goes that route, I couldn't blame her entirely. I'll bet the changes in management are making it easier on all of you."

"It's too early to tell," Angela responded. "It's calm now. It could be back to the way it used to be next month. They got rid of Herman and Borelli, but Newton's still there. It remains to be seen if sensitivity training will change him. And if it doesn't, are Potter and Tillman strong enough to keep him in line?"

"I doubt it," Paul said.

"One thing hasn't changed," Angela replied. "Married or not, Newton still goes after the nice looking women. There's a PTF, just got her ninety days in, who told me Newton was putting the moves on her. I'm not saying her name, this is girl talk I'm repeating here. Anyway, she strung him along 'till she got past probation, then told him to get lost. But that's just like him, using his power over people to try to get what he wants."

"Newton will never change," Paul said. "He's being careful right now, 'cause he knows which way the wind is blowing. But he just has a rotten character. You can't change that with workshops and training sessions. He reminds me of the bully who taught me to play fifty-one pick-up."

"What's fifty-one pick-up?," Pam asked.

"I must've been about ten at the time. This kid from the next block was over my house, and we were in the basement. He asked if I had a deck of cards, he was going to show me a new card game. I fell for it. I gave him the deck, and he fanned out the cards and asked me to pick one. I thought he was going to guess which card I picked after I put it back. Instead, he took the rest of the deck and threw the cards across the room. They scattered all over the place. He told me this game is called fifty-one pick-up, and he watched me pick them all up."

"That really is Newton's style," Angela said. "You know the stray letter belt at the end of the machine? All the letters that get lost in the LSM come onto this belt which empties onto this tray on the floor at the end of the machine. Anyway, I was passing by LSM Two one day and Newton asked me to get the letters from this tray. I wasn't even assigned to LSM Two, but I said okay and got down on the floor to gather up the letters. Newton said, 'I like to see a steward on her knees.' I'll never forget Newton saying that."

Paul said, "That's Newton's mentality exactly. He's like a young bully who never grew up, but now he runs Tour One. He enjoys sticking the knife in and turning it a little bit. He isn't just nasty, he's nasty with a flourish. He likes to taunt you. He likes to rub your nose in it. He's being quiet now, but he's never going to change. When all of this nice-nice stuff dies down, we'll see the old Newton again."

Eleven: APRIL FOOLS DAY

April 1st, 1994

Prosecutor: How did the defendant react when he was accused of harassing Melissa Robinson?
Witness: He was angry for the moment but we soon came up with a plan to deal with it.

"A steward was attending a national union convention in Las Vegas. From ten in the morning until the sessions adjourned at four, he was all business. He paid attention to the proceedings, took notes, even went to the microphone and asked a question. But after four, it was party time in Vegas. He went to a show Monday night, and Tuesday night he won a couple of hundred bucks playing blackjack."

Ron Davidson was telling the story in the Union Office at the Plant. Angela had a feeling she wasn't going to like where this story was going. Paul just hoped it had a good punch line. Ron continued.

"On Wednesday night the steward decided to spend some of his hard-earned money on a prostitute. Evidently, Las Vegas has quite a selection. But this steward had some principles. He would not do business with a non-union brothel.

"So he goes into one of the party city's finest houses of prostitution and looks around. He sees about a dozen absolutely gorgeous women there. He approaches the Madame and asks, 'Is this brothel unionized?' She says no. He asks, 'If I pay one-hundred dollars to spend the night with one of these fine young ladies, how much does she get, and how much goes to management?' The Madame answered 'The girl gets twenty, we keep the rest. What does it matter to you?' The steward said he didn't think that was fair, and walked out.

"At the next brothel, he asked the same questions and got pretty

101

much the same answers. Then he asked, 'Aren't there any unionized brothels in this town?' The Madame gave him an address and said. 'Are you sure that's where you want to go? We've got some lovely girls here.' The steward was tempted, but said 'I've got my principles.' The Madame just rolled her eyes and said, 'suit yourself.'

"The steward went to the address he was given and looked around. There was a lovely redhead named Rebecca, a truly sensuous black woman named Celeste, a number of women who looked to be in their mid-thirties, and a not very attractive woman named Edna who looked to be over sixty years old. It seemed odd, but as long as there was one woman he liked, that's all that mattered.

"He asked the Madame, 'Is this a unionized brothel?' She answered yes.

"He asked 'If I pay one-hundred dollars to spend the night, how much does the employee get, and how much goes to management?' The Madame answered, 'We just keep twenty-percent for overhead and expenses, and she keeps the rest.'

"The steward was happy now. He was practically drooling at the prospect of spending the night with the young redhead, who was smiling at him. And he could maintain his principles at the same time.

"He took a hundred dollar bill out of his wallet and said, 'I'd like to spend the night with Rebecca.'

" 'I'm sure you would,' said the Madame. 'But I have to explain something to you. This is a union brothel, and Edna has seniority.' "

Paul broke out laughing but cut it short when he saw the look on Angela's face. She looked hurt and upset. She didn't say a word; she just bolted from the room.

Paul and Ron analyzed the joke and determined that not only was it sexist, but its message was anti-union as well. "I still think it's damn funny," Ron said. Paul smiled.

A little while later Angela came back in the office. Ron was meeting with a supervisor in the manager's office, so she and Paul were alone.

"I guess that joke hit a raw nerve," she said. "A few days ago, I talked to Lisa Walton. Do you know her? She's a pretty young white girl, with blond hair, over on the OCR."

Paul nodded.

"Anyway, it seems Lawrence Harris was pressuring her to go to bed with him. She hasn't got ninety days in yet, so she was really afraid. Lawrence was promising she could have weekends off if she went along with him, and he hinted she might lose her job if she said no."

"What a pig," Paul said.

"You know, ever since they promoted Lawrence to full supervisor, he's been a real terror. It used to be all of the worst managers were white – Newton, Collier, and of course Borelli and Herman. Now you've got Harris and the new 204-B, Shirley Jones. I guess they're trying to be Equal Opportunity Terrorists."

"You sure called that one right about Shirley," Paul said. "I thought she was going to be a good steward."

"That woman's motto is Look out for Number One. I could see that from jump."

"So anyway, what happened with Lisa?"

"I talked to her, and we agreed we were going to file charges the next day. But she didn't come to work, and I haven't seen her since. I found out today that she went to the Main and handed in her resignation form, citing 'personal reasons.' "

"That's terrible," said Paul.

"I feel so bad. Lisa's a good kid. You know, she felt she had to explain to me that her not wanting to sleep with Lawrence had nothing to do with his being black. She said it's just that she has a boyfriend she's loyal to. She was almost apologetic. I told her she has nothing to apologize for. Lawrence is the asshole here. It makes me so mad. That's why Ron's joke hit me so hard. I'm just tired of men who think of women as nothing more than a hole where they can insert their johnson."

"Well, it seems like Lawrence, Newton, and the rest of them

have free reign again. All that sensitivity after the shooting didn't last long."

"You can say *that* again."

"But at least we had it better for a year or two. They say nothing's changed in Dearborn since last year's shooting. They're having a picket out there next month on the one year anniversary. They're demanding they get rid of the Postmaster and some of his cronies. And all the unions will join in – the Letter Carriers, the Mail Handlers, and APWU."

"I'll be there," Angela said. "From what I see around here, the postal culture is as bad as it ever was. I don't think Ron sees it though. He keeps talking like everything's been so mellow since management learned its lesson after the shooting at the Main. I guess he doesn't see the same crap we do every day. I wonder if he'll show up at the Dearborn picket."

Before Paul could reply, Aretha Simmons came through the door. Aretha and Angela were pretty close; they often took lunch together.

"There's some graffiti in a bathroom stall," Aretha said to Angela. "It says you're a dyke."

Angela was stunned. From the concerned look on Aretha's face, she could tell this was no April Fools joke.

"And now people are talking about you on the floor. You don't seem to have a boyfriend or anything, and they're saying you must be a lesbian. I said I don't think so. And in case people were wondering about me, I pulled out a photo of me and my boyfriend at a party last month. Then I felt stupid for feeling I had to prove to them that I'm not, well, you know…"

Aretha left and Angela just said, "This has not been a good day so far. And it isn't even half over."

They sat there in silence, Angela staring at the wall, Paul looking down, not knowing what to say. Then Angela told Paul where the rumor must have started. About six months ago, there was a lesbian in her work area. When coworkers picked on this woman Angela defended her. "You know, I have a cousin who's gay, and I know what he went through, and still goes through. He's a tremendous person, but he's having a hard time of it. So I defended my lesbian coworker. She bid on afternoon shift and I don't see her any more. I thought it was all forgotten, but I guess somebody remembers."

"Those rumors are so destructive," said Paul. "So cruel."

"Just so you know, I'm not gay, Paul. If anyone wonders why I don't have a man, I guess I'm one of those people who has trouble opening up to somebody else. I don't go out with men much. Once I had a very bad experience with a man I thought I loved. I was hurt badly. Don't ask about the details. Let's just say since then, I've been very cautious with my emotions."

"Hey, my love life isn't so great either," Paul said. "The last date I had was about a month ago. Arnold Foster set me up with his cousin. A lovely girl. We went to the movies, some sappy romance, but I thought she'd like it. I was about to lean over and give her a kiss when I noticed she had fallen asleep. I guess I have that effect on women."

Angela started thinking about the graffiti and rumors about her. "I'm going to feel weird when I go back on the floor. Whoever I talk to, I'll wonder what they think of me."

"If I heard that rumor about you, I wouldn't care. I was around when the gay movement hit college campuses in the early seventies. Some people I knew pretty well started coming out. I was shocked to see how many of my friends turned out to be gay. But then I realized these people still had all the good qualities I had liked about them before I knew they were gay. I stayed friends with them, and probably learned a lot of the same things you heard from your cousin.

"In any case, no rumor like that would change my opinion of you. You happen to be just about the best person I know. I really treasure your friendship. I never had a reason to tell you out loud, but I guess it seems appropriate now."

Paul paused for a moment and heard the clicking sound of a

retractable pen being pushed in and out. The pen was in his right hand. He laid it on the desk.

"This next thing is going to sound ridiculous. The only reason I never asked you out is I like you too much. I know the way most of my relationships end up, and I don't want our friendship to get all messed up that way. I guess I don't want to risk changing anything.

"But whatever rumors might get started, know that I totally respect you, and a lot of people on the floor think you're the best. You're intelligent, you're caring, you're resourceful, you're very good at what you do. The only people who usually speak up are the complainers, but if people start spreading rumors, trying to tear you down, your supporters will have something to say. You have more of them than you know – and it's because you're a good steward, and a great person."

Now they sat in an awkward, embarrassed silence. The phone rang, and Angela picked it up.

"I wish this was another April Fools joke," she said after hanging up. "Lawrence Harris and Jim Newton want to see you in the Manager's Office in fifteen minutes. They say you are harassing Melissa Robinson."

"I know what that's about," Paul said. "They've been making some of the new mail processors go seven hours before taking a lunch. I heard about it and asked Melissa to write a statement to document it for a grievance. She said she was scared, but she'd think about it. The next day I approached her while she was feeding mail onto the machine. I didn't notice Lawrence nearby. He chased me away and he and Melissa talked for awhile. They'll say I tried to pressure Melissa into filing a grievance. I think I better take my steward along to represent me at this meeting."

Paul felt a churning in his stomach and a tightening in his chest. It was a familiar feeling. He could go for months without an unpleasant encounter with Newton. Then his sixth sense would tell him he was dealing with Mr. Evil. Like a dog senses danger before the people around him do, Paul could tell when he had to be on full alert. He would watch every word he said, knowing they would be twisted around and used against him. Nothing Newton would say would be honest, nothing could be taken at face value in these situations. It had been awhile since he had dueled with Newton this way, but the tension, the attitude, the heightened alertness, were so familiar it seemed like yesterday. Newton would lie, Paul would know he was lying, and Newton would know Paul knew. Newton would anticipate Paul's next move and Paul would anticipate Newton's. It was like a tangled dance of conflict and ego. Paul felt fortunate that he wouldn't be caught by surprise this time, and that he'd have a friend with him.

As they walked towards the Manager's office, Angela said with a trace of bitterness, "They're accusing you of harassing Melissa, and we know that's not true. But Lawrence got away with harassing Lisa Walton out of a job. And the one craft employee who's harassing coworkers is Danny Vellarmo, and they're pretty much leaving him alone. I don't know if people are afraid to report him, or management is afraid to touch him."

"Angela, most people who have a run-in with him bid off the crew. Those who stay pretty much give him whatever he wants. And it's more than two years since that suspension he got, so his record is clean."

When they entered the Manager's Office, Newton was surprised to see Angela with Paul. So he shifted gears. "This is nothing but a Documented Discussion. It is not discipline, it is not grievable, and you do not need a steward. Angela, your presence is not required."

"Then what is Lawrence doing here?" said Paul. "You don't need two supervisors to give me a discussion."

Newton proceeded to meet with Paul privately. "You've been harassing Melissa Robinson. As you know, ever since the shooting a few years back, we've got to keep an eye on any situation that may cause tension in the workplace. Accordingly, you are not to go near Melissa, you are not to talk to her in her work area, you are not to talk to her on break, you are not to have anything to do with her. This is your only warning. Heed the warning or face the consequences."

Paul saw no point in disputing the facts in a one-on-one conversation with Newton. Both men knew what really happened, and one of them didn't care about the truth. But it was hard to remain silent. It took all the self-control Paul could muster to keep from yelling at Newton (which, of course, is what Newton wanted him to do). He did slam the door on the way out. Newton smiled.

Back in the Union Office, Paul and Angela discussed their options. Up until the recent management reorganization, he would have gone to Stanley Tillman. But now Tillman was at the Main, his mentor Potter was head of the District, and neither of them had any authority over the Plant. Newton's boss was the Plant Manager Norm Bradford, who seemed pretty weak. Bradford let the managers under him do pretty much what they wanted as long as the productivity numbers looked good. In fact, it wasn't clear to Paul exactly what it was that Bradford did to earn his considerable salary, but he knew he didn't interfere much with Newton.

The avenue of trying to get the Local Union President to intervene was fraught with danger too. Paul had vocally opposed an Amendment to the Local Union Constitution to raise the President's salary, and supported Humphrey's opponent in the last election. Humphrey was reelected, and he had been cool to Paul ever since, almost to the point of being uncooperative. If Paul went to Humphrey with this new problem, he wondered if Humphrey would stoop so low as to encourage Newton to keep on giving him a hard time. He would never be sure, because nobody would admit if anything like this was going on.

Finally, Angela came up with a plan.

"I'll talk to Claudia Stinson. Management expects me to talk to Melissa, they're keeping an eye on her. But Claudia also works in that area, and I always got along well with her. I don't know why the good people always get out of the 204-B program and the rotten ones get promoted. Anyway, I'll get Claudia to talk to Melissa, then she can write me a statement from what Melissa tells her. That should give you some protection."

Angela left the office to look for an opportunity to talk to Claudia discretely. Paul was still upset. He didn't know it, but Angela's plan was going to work to perfection. Within a couple of weeks, not only would all mention of harassment charges be dropped, but the PTF mail processors would be getting their lunches at a reasonable time. And Paul and Melissa Robinson would eventually become friends.

But he didn't know any of that just yet. All he knew is this was one April Fools Day that neither he nor Angela would ever forget.

Twelve: GOING BEFORE THE JUDGE

Summer, 1995

Prosecutor: Did the defendant accuse Mr. Newton of being a racist?
Witness: Yes.
Prosecutor: In your opinion was he a racist?
Witness: No.

Rudy Baylor boarded a Greyhound bus going from Memphis, Tennessee to Cleveland, Ohio. It was a 15 hour bus trip, but he couldn't afford to fly. Baylor was a struggling new lawyer who had just recently passed the bar exam. He was taking on the Great Benefit insurance company, whose headquarters was in Cleveland, and the purpose of the trip was to take depositions from some company officials. The Memphis law firm representing Great Benefit had the resources and experience to totally demolish him. They were not riding the Greyhound to Cleveland; they were flying first class and would be staying at a nice hotel. The five lawyers on the other side had a combined total of 58 years of legal experience. Baylor had never gone to trial in front of a jury.

Rudy Baylor had only one thing going for him. He was right. The insurance company had denied benefits to Donny Ray Black when he was dying of leukemia, and his life could have been saved with a bone marrow transplant. Baylor had spent some time with Donny Ray before he died, and now he was determined to bring Great Benefit to justice.

Paul Farley was reading "The Rainmaker" by John Grisham. He was identifying completely with the main character, Rudy Baylor. He, too, was about to go before a Judge for the first time. He was representing a young black woman named Earnestine Hall in an EEO (Equal Employment Opportunity) complaint. Earnestine had been fired by the Post Office, and all attempts at a compromise settlement had fallen through. Like Rudy Baylor, Paul believed in the justice of his case. Earnestine did not deserve to be fired any more than Donny Ray Black deserved to die. And like Rudy, he was going up against a much more experienced advocate. Nathan Zimmer used to be an EEO Counselor before he joined the Employee & Labor Relations Department at the Post Office. Nathan knew all the procedures, all the tricks, and all the people. He was on a first name basis with Administrative Law Judge Harry Worthington.

It was August 27th, and the hearing was a week-and-a-half away. In spite of the odds against him, Paul felt he had a chance to win. Reading the Grisham novel buoyed his spirits. He was two-thirds of the way through the book, and he was confident that Baylor would triumph. It gave him hope that he could obtain justice for Earnestine Hall.

Earnestine had been employed as a Transitional Employee (TE) for two years. She was fired for "Irregular Attendance" in July, 1994, after missing seven days in a ten month period. This was not a good record, but it was not that bad either, especially since the prior four months had been perfect. The real reason Earnestine had been fired was that the last day she missed was July 4th. Jim Newton got angry that a TE would dare to call in on a holiday, and instructed Red Collier to terminate her. The Letter of Removal stated Ms. Hall's attendance had been unsatisfactory from September, 1993 through July, 1994.

If Earnestine had been a career employee, she would not have been scheduled to work July 4th. And if she were a career employee, seven absences in ten months would not even have been cause for a slap on the wrist. In the days before the shooting, this attendance record probably would have given a career employee a Letter of Warning, but management had become pretty lax in the last few years. Paul knew of career employees with far worse records who had not even been talked to about their attendance, and he knew of TEs with worse records as well.

The category of Transitional Employee was introduced into the Postal Service with the 1990 contract. Management convinced an arbitrator they needed a new kind of long term, temporary employee who would be subject to layoff over the coming years. The arbitrator left it to the union and management to negotiate the details.

The terms of this agreement infuriated Paul. While the TE wage scale was not too bad, there were no health benefits. And worst of all, management could fire a TE without having to prove they had a good reason. Since the "just cause" provision of the contract did not apply to TEs, these removals could not be grieved unless the union could prove some other provision of the contract had been violated.

Paul felt this agreement was a betrayal of a basic union principle. How can we collect dues from someone who we won't protect if management fires them unfairly? As a human being, how can we stand back and do nothing while people are being treated this way? Paul sharply criticized the national leadership in an article the Local union newspaper (he was surprised his viewpoint was printed).

He also became a TE advocate on the workroom floor. He had a little bit of success. There was one young woman whose mother had died of heart problems and whose husband had died of cancer within a six month period. She had four or five lengthy absences, for which she was fired. But the reason for every one of those absences was well documented. She had been at the hospital with one of her dying loved ones. The supervisor who fired her would not look at the documents – the attendance is bad, the removal is not grievable, so don't bother me with any documentation. However, Paul set up an appointment to meet with Plant Manager Bradford, explained the circumstances and showed the documentation, and the young lady was permitted to return to work.

Paul had also succeeded in overturning the actions of an

overzealous 204-B who had fired three TEs in one day. This occurred on a Saturday night when the MDOs were not present, and neither of them had authorized the terminations.

But in most cases, Paul's efforts to resolve TE firings were futile. He would try to grieve them, but the Local Union would not appeal them beyond Step 2. This was a sore point between Paul and Local President Donald Humphrey, as if their relationship needed another conflict.

All but a handful of the TEs at the Plant were black, and every fired TE was black, while the majority of the career workforce was white. Paul thought he had a good grievance under Article 2 (Discrimination). Since Humphrey refused to appeal these cases, Paul went the EEO route. He represented about a dozen fired TEs, eventually lumping their cases all together into a class action complaint. Earnestine Hall had separated herself from the class action, and her individual case was to be heard before Judge Worthington. This was a conscious strategy. Earnestine had the best attendance of any of the fired TEs. Her case offered the best chance of a favorable ruling. Paul was convinced that if the Judge ruled in her favor, a settlement could be reached to put all of the others back to work without having to go through any more hearings.

On August 30th, Paul went over his preparations for the hearing with Angela and Ron, both of whom were scheduled to appear as witnesses. They were also offering much needed moral support. At times Paul was extremely nervous. But he kept reminding himself that the worst that could happen was an unfavorable ruling, in which case Earnestine would be no worse off than if he had done nothing.

The hearing would be held in an informal setting, a room in the basement at the Main. But the formal procedures of a court would apply. There would be opening statements, direct and cross examination of witnesses, and closing arguments, all taken down by a court reporter. He had to know what kind of questioning was permitted on direct and cross, and what kind of objections he could make when Zimmer was speaking. In short, he had to act like a lawyer.

Right now he was going over the theory of the case with Ron and Angela. He had to not only prove that Earnestine's firing was unjustified, but that there was racial discrimination.

Angela raised a good question. "I'm not sure we can prove Newton's a racist. I think he's got a bit of an attitude towards black people, but he's pretty much a jerk towards employees whether they're black or white. I mean, look at the way he treats you."

Ron added, "I know Earnestine didn't deserve to be fired. And that's probably true for some of the other TEs. But do you really think racism is involved? Isn't it just that management likes to abuse their authority, and with TEs they can get away with it?"

"The Post Office reflects the society we live in. Look at who has the lowest wages and fewest rights. The casuals and TEs, and most of them are black."

"So you believe it's intentional," said Ron.

"There aren't any explicit racist policies here," Paul said. "In fact there are programs against discrimination. But the racism is still a fact. There's an attitude among management towards the TEs as a whole. 'They don't have any rights, we can do what we want with them.' It's justified by the contract. But everyone knows most of the TEs are black. In your mind, when you say the word TE, you think of a young black person. Management thinks of an irresponsible young black person – that's their stereotype of a TE."

"Yeah, that is the prevalent attitude," Ron said.

"The way I look at it, the racism is masked by the different contractual provisions for TEs. When I wrote that article about TEs in the union paper, Larry Pendleton came up to me and called me a 'TE-lover.' I've known Larry to be hostile to black people before. I could tell this was a racist remark by the way he phrased it. When he said 'TE-lover,' what do you think he was really thinking?"

"Nigger lover," Ron replied, without hesitation. Angela winced.

"Exactly," Paul said. "And there are managers who think the same way, but I can't really prove that. What I can do is bring out the numbers. At the time Earnestine was fired, there had been 65 black TEs, and 26 of them had been fired or let go. That's 40 percent. Those numbers include a few who were fired and brought back, but it was management's *intent* to fire them."

Angela swore softly beneath her breath.

"Think about it," said Paul. "Out of any random group of employees, how likely is it that close to half of them are rotten? There's something else going on here."

"What about the white TEs?" Ron asked.

"They only have six, and none of them have been fired."

"Looks like you've got a case," Angela said.

"The only tricky part is, management will say you can only prove discrimination if a white TE with a worse record was working for the same supervisor. I can find two white TEs with worse attendance than Earnestine, but they didn't work for Collier. That's why I named Bradford and all of the MDOs on Tour One and Tour Three in the complaint. I'm saying you have to look building-wide. Collier didn't have any white TEs in his Pay Location. Does that mean he could fire the black TEs for no reason and get away with it?

Having explained the legal theory, Paul asked Angela to talk about Earnestine.

"First off, she was an excellent worker. All of her coworkers liked her. Butch Hobson praised her attendance and work habits when we were talking about her the first year she was here."

"Of course, Angela, Zimmer will object that what you just told me is hearsay. I want you to say it anyway. When they object, we can pull out the Letter of Recommendation Hobson wrote for her when she was applying for an office job at GM Headquarters. Zimmer probably doesn't know the letter exists."

"Paul, I can also talk about the absences. One was when her car was stolen. The police report is already part of the case file. The amazing thing to me is she only missed one day of work. Another absence was when her two-year-old was in the hospital. She's a single mother. What was she supposed to do? I also remember seeing her looking like hell, in here working, just before the Fourth of July holiday. I don't believe she took off because of the holiday. She didn't belong here on the third, but she tried her best."

Ron asked, "Aren't you going to have Earnestine testify about these absences herself?"

"Of course I will. But Angela will be kind of an expert witness, saying how this kind of record would ordinarily be evaluated. And you, Ron, are going to be an expert witness comparing her record to that of other employees who were *not* disciplined. You're going to conclude there's no way in hell a good employee like this should've been fired, so something funny must have been going on."

After going over the records, Paul talked about how this case had almost been settled six months ago. He had gone to Bradford with a proposal to resolve the entire class action. Of the fired TEs, there were eight, including Earnestine, who had lost an opportunity to obtain a career position due to their removal. Paul proposed to give all of them a new 359 day appointment as TEs. If they were evaluated satisfactory, they would then be converted to career. Bradford seemed receptive. But apparently after talking to the MDOs, he changed his mind.

"There's one other person Bradford may have talked to. Our fearless leader, Donald Humphrey. I don't know for sure what went on, but Humphrey made a sarcastic comment about my tentative TE settlement. I think he may have gone to Bradford and sabotaged it."

"Does our President hate you that much?"

"I don't know, Angela, but I wouldn't put it past him."

The hearing began September 6th at 9:00 AM. The participants were arranged around a U-shaped table that was really three long tables placed together. The Judge and court reporter sat at the center, and the respective parties each had their own side.

This case generated a mountain of paperwork; the stack was 18 inches high. Each advocate was allowed one technical assistant, someone to keep track of documents and exhibits and perhaps whisper words of advice when appropriate. Nathan Zimmer had Nancy Barber with him; they had handled many hearings together. Paul had Ron Davidson, who, like Paul, had never done this before. All of the witnesses (except Earnestine) were to be sequestered. Ron had to testify first if he was to be the technical assistant for the remainder of the hearing.

Earnestine dressed impeccably. She wore a long blue dress, not flashy, but attractive and dignified. Paul thought back to the time he had shown up at a house party given by another TE. Earnestine had been the first to greet him with a big hug. She wasn't flirting with him, just making him feel welcome, as his was the only white face in the house. He ended up dancing with Earnestine's sister much of that night.

Paul also thought of the times he had seen Earnestine at the Plant sneezing, coughing, looking like she belonged home in bed. He remembered seeing her dead tired, taking a 25 minute nap during lunch, then somehow going back to work energetically. He thought of the numerous attendance records he had seen, far worse than hers, of people still working at the Plant. And he thought of quite a few people who were not close to Earnestine in terms of character. Not only was she a good worker, Earnestine was "just good people."

He thought again about the Grisham novel he was reading. He had read most of it and then stopped. If there was a surprise ending, he didn't want to know it yet. Somehow, believing that Rudy Baylor had beaten Great Benefit in the book gave him confidence that he could do the same to the Postal Service. And he also felt it appropriate to save the ending of the book as a reward for himself after the hearing.

One advantage Rudy Baylor had in his trial was he knew the case file inside and out. He had been able to surprise Great Benefit's lawyers with embarrassing documents they didn't know existed. And if they lied on the stand, he would know exactly which document would prove them wrong.

Farley had some similar advantages in this case. He knew the details of almost every TE who had lost their job, because he had been there trying to help them. This was not just a bunch of documents he had to memorize; this was a history he had lived through. He knew the documents supplied by management were flawed, and he had a few surprises in store for them.

The opening statements went smoothly. Paul talked about Earnestine and her record, and he stressed that there was a pattern of discrimination against black TEs throughout the facility. It was important to plant this seed early in terms of the legal framework within which he wanted the Judge to view this case.

Ron Davidson was the first witness. He presented one of management's exhibits, a chart which purported to show the basic information about all of the TEs: race, job history, whether they had been fired, whether they had subsequently obtained career employment. Next to the name of Cynthia Stallworth, the chart said "Not Terminated." Paul then pulled out a removal notice with Cynthia Stallworth's name on it and entered into evidence. He had known management's documents had been slanted from the time he received them during discovery. He had relished the thought of embarrassing management at the hearing, and he thought the judge would be upset with management.

This tactic backfired. Judge Worthington asked if Paul had known about this all along. The Judge then stated that any problem in discovery information should have been addressed prior to the hearing. He implied Paul was being sneaky by not trying to get any discrepancies in the information straightened out before the hearing. In effect, Paul ended up being scolded for management's dishonesty.

Paul wanted Ron to compare Earnestine's record with some white career employees who work for Red Collier. Zimmer objected, and these records were kept out of evidence. The Judge said comparing career employees with TEs was like comparing apples and oranges. Paul argued that while the punishment for bad attendance might differ for career employees, the standard for what constitutes bad attendance was the same for everyone. He was overruled. It was a shame. There was a white girl with 17 absences in 9 months who had not even gotten a Letter of Warning from Collier. It was obvious that Earnestine had been treated unfairly, but Paul was having a tough time proving it.

Paul then introduced the attendance record of two white TEs. Zimmer objected, because they did not work for Collier. The objection was overruled, and Paul smiled. He finally got a ruling his way. When Paul asked Ron to draw some conclusions by comparing these TEs' records to Earnestine's, Zimmer objected again. He stated: "The records speak for themselves." The objection was sustained, and Ron could not talk about these records. Paul was told he could draw any conclusions he liked in his summary.

Paul had expected a pattern to emerge during Ron's testimony. It would be clear that black TEs were being judged more severely than white employees (career or Transitional). But with all the objections, the flow of the presentation had been disrupted and much of the information had been suppressed. Paul knew that in the Judge's mind, no such pattern had been established.

Earnestine's testimony was better. She discussed her career as a TE from the beginning. Paul introduced her attendance record from early 1993, which looked pretty good. Zimmer's objection that it was "out of the time frame" was overruled. Earnestine explained the reasons for each of her seven absences. When she was through, Paul was confident she had made a good impression.

This was important. In fact, Paul thought it was critical that the Judge like Earnestine. If he wants to put her back to work, the Judge will find a legal justification for that decision. But if Earnestine had come across badly, the case was probably lost.

Angela's testimony went off just like it was planned. The high point was the little ambush they had planned for Zimmer. He objected when Angela started talking about the fact that a supervisor named Butch Hobson thought very highly of Earnestine. The Judge ruled hearsay evidence was not permitted. Then Paul introduced Hobson's Letter of Recommendation, and you could see Zimmer's expression of shock. Zimmer was a pro, he knew he was not supposed to show that he had been zapped by this evidence, and he covered it up quickly. But Paul knew he had scored a point there.

The following day, Zimmer presented his witnesses. Collier was first. He stated that he was more lenient with Earnestine than with anyone in his Pay Location, TE or career. This was a lie, and everyone in the room except the Judge and court reporter knew it. On cross, Paul again tried to enter into evidence the attendance records of white career employees who worked for Collier. Zimmer objected and was sustained. Paul again argued with the Judge. Mr. Collier had opened up the area of white career employees with his testimony. If it wasn't relevant before, it was certainly relevant now, in order to cross examine him on what he said in his direct testimony.

The frustration in Paul's voice was evident. The Judge was not accustomed to having his rulings challenged by advocates, especially by an upstart like Farley, and especially in that tone of voice. "I have made my ruling," the Judge said. "Let's move on!"

Newton was the next witness. His testimony was boring. They went over the attendance records of the TEs one by one. He did slip up once. When looking at the record of a black TE that had been fired, he stated, "I'm sure that absence for his father's funeral wasn't counted against him. We generally don't consider absences for bereavement in discipline. It was all these other absences that precipitated the removal notice."

On cross examination, Paul pulled out the actual removal notice and showed this funeral date had been cited. He also pulled out the removal for another TE and showed a funeral had been counted against her. He then asked: "Are you saying that a death in the family is counted against a black TE and nobody else?"

It was a high point on an otherwise dreary day. For the most part, management's testimony was boring to the point of being deadening. The final witness was from the Personnel Department. He disputed Paul's claim that a termination as a TE would automatically deprive someone of a chance for a career position. On cross, Paul pulled out a letter addressed to Cynthia Stallworth which said precisely that. "Since you have been terminated for irregular attendance as a TE, we are not going to consider you qualified for a career position." This evidence would be crucial in terms of the remedy if the Judge ruled in Earnestine's favor. Paul was claiming the removal was the factor that prevented her from becoming a career employee, since she had been passed over on the hiring register. Paul was asking that Earnestine be reinstated as a career employee with full seniority and back pay from the time she was passed over (and back pay as a TE before that). The manager from Personnel insisted Paul was mistaken. In the hiring process, each case was evaluated individually. We have three applicants for each job and pick the most qualified of the three. There is no guarantee Earnestine would have been hired as a career employee even without the termination on her record.

Paul knew that even though management could pull out some regulations that appeared to back up this testimony, what happens in the real world is quite different. Unless there is some sort of problem, management generally hires the next person in line. But someone in Personnel had told him, "If they don't want them as a TE at the Plant, we're not sending them back to the Plant as a career employee. End of story."

The fact is, if not for the unfair firing, Earnestine would now have a secure career position. Again, everyone in the room except the Judge and court reporter knew it. But management's testimony made the issue seem muddy and unclear.

It was 3:00 PM when management's testimony ended. Paul hoped the Judge would schedule a third day for closing arguments. So many of his questions for witnesses had been cut off and he had been told to hold it for the summary. He needed an extensive summary to pull together the fragments of evidence into a clear pattern of discrimination.

Judge Worthington, however, wanted the case wrapped up quickly so he could have a long weekend. He allowed 15 minutes to each side for summaries. Paul tried his best, but couldn't find a rhythm. He made some points about Earnestine's record compared to the white TEs. He started to explain his theory that you had to go beyond the one Pay Location and look at the pattern within the installation as a whole. But the Judge said "time's up" and Paul half threw, half dropped his spiral notebook on the table. The Judge raised his eyebrows, but made no comment.

Management's summary started with the point that there was no similarly situated white TE so there could not be discrimination. The rest of management's summary sounded like a disorganized jumble of meaningless statistics gleaned from their defective chart.

Paul was drained. He was exhausted, discouraged and frustrated. And just a little bit angry. Earnestine gave him a pat on the back. "Win or lose, I really appreciate what you did for me. You put in a tremendous amount of work. It's good to know there are people like you in the world."

They would both have to wait another week to learn the outcome. Judge Worthington scheduled a session for September 14th to read his decision.

On September 12th, Paul ran into James Newton and Lawrence

Harris outside the MDO's office. Newton said, "You know, Lawrence, Paul thinks I'm a racist. What do you think about that?"

Lawrence responded, "You've got to be kidding me!"

Paul ignored these remarks.

On September 13th, Paul was denied any union time for the entire day. That had not happened for years. Even during the busy December "Christmas rush," he had always been allowed some union time. This day he was told he was needed in flats because the mail was heavy, and anyone who needed a steward could see Ron or Angela. His coworkers were surprised, since the mail seemed no worse than normal.

September 14th was the moment of truth. It was embarrassing. A typical EEO decision has three parts. First, the Judge says the claimant has proved a "prima facie" case. This means, on the surface, there is an appearance of discrimination. Secondly, the Judge says the Post Office presented business reasons for what they did. In the third part, the Judge weighs both sides' arguments, and makes a decision.

In this case, the Judge simply ruled there was no prima facie case for discrimination. Since there was no white TE working for the same supervisor, there was, by definition, no discrimination. All of the comparison employees Paul had pointed to were not "similarly situated." The case was dismissed.

Paul was stunned. He knew he might lose, but hearing the Judge say he didn't even have a prima facie case was quite a blow. After all that work, the Judge was basically saying the case wasn't even worth considering.

When he received the decision in writing, Paul appealed it to EEOC in Washington DC. There was one positive thing about Judge Worthington's decision. Since he dismissed it without saying anything about Earnestine's record, he really didn't say anything bad about her. Paul didn't think a Judge's evaluation of the merits of a person's record would likely be overturned on appeal, but an appeal on the theory of the case might work.

Judge Worthington had cited two prior EEO decisions as legal precedents. Paul called the Judge and asked for copies of these cases. At least, in this, he cooperated. He could have told Paul to go to the library and look for them. Instead, he mailed them to Paul's address, and wished him good luck on the appeal.

Paul put a lot of work into the appeal. He analyzed the cases cited as precedents and showed how they were different from Earnestine's situation. In the precedent cases, there had been employees of different races working for the same supervisor, but the complainant was unable to prove discrimination by that supervisor, and had looked to other work areas to find a comparison employee. In this case, since there were no comparison employees working for Mr. Collier, you had to take a wider view to determine if there was discrimination. Especially when 40% of the black TEs had been let go while employees with much worse records were not even disciplined. Paul included as documentation the attendance records of white employees who worked for Collier and did not receive discipline (the records that had been ruled inadmissible at the hearing). He even got the sick leave percentage for the Plant as a whole, and showed that over the course of her career as a TE, Earnestine's sick leave percentage had been better than average. Paul thought it was an impressive 20 page document.

Three months passed. Six months passed. Finally he called a number in Washington and was connected to a Mrs. Keller. It was not clear what her position was, but she was very friendly. "Yes, your appeal has been seen by one set of lawyers, and it was passed on to another set of lawyers for review. It raises some interesting issues. It will still be awhile before a decision is reached."

It turned out to be two whole years, and then Paul received a very brief denial letter. The EEOC agreed with Judge Worthington's decision. The letter did not address any of the issues raised in the appeal. It was quite a letdown, because Paul really had expected something more substantial. He'd gotten his hopes up, but now they were crushed.

At least Earnestine landed on her feet. She got a job at a bank and worked her way into a management position. She might not be good enough to work at the Post Office, but now she was making pretty good money and she didn't have to work those crazy hours in the middle of the night. It was the Post Office's loss.

The class action for the rest of the TEs was never certified. Three years after the Earnestine Hall hearing, all of the other TEs were sent letters giving them the option of reinstating their individual complaints. Most of them had moved and did not even receive these letters. Paul was able to negotiate an arrangement where two of the people had a special opportunity to take the career entrance exam, and if they passed with a high enough score, they would be hired (provided they met all qualifications, passed a medical exam and drug test, came up clear on a criminal check, etc.)

Of the two, only one, Samantha Chambers (Tawanna's sister) became a career employee in 1998.

So Paul's efforts on behalf of the TEs were not completely wasted. But he learned that these legal channels are hardly an effective way to fight for justice.

Thirteen: CANDACE, CLARENCE, AND CLARA

February, 1996

Defense Lawyer: Did Mr. Newton dislike you?
Witness: He hated me, and the feeling was mutual.

The three stewards were telling Supervisor Jokes. Some of these were recycled Dumb Blonde Jokes or Polish Jokes, and some were original.

Ron went first. "A supervisor took the orange juice out of the refrigerator, and then stood staring at it. How come?" The other stewards gave up. Ron said, "Because it said 'concentrate'."

Paul said, "A supervisor saw one of those yellow envelopes they mail x-rays in lying on the floor, but he didn't reach over to pick it up, he just left it lying there. How come?" The answer was, "because the envelope said 'Do Not Bend'."

Angela's joke was, "How many supervisors does it take to change a light bulb?" Her answer was: "Three – one to turn the bulb, one to give him a direct order, and one to harass him while he does it."

Angela's joke led into a discussion of how little decision making power any of the supervisors had. They can't even make a simple decision, the equivalent of changing a light bulb, without consulting Newton.

"I met with Stacey Kline on a Letter of Warning that should've never been issued," Angela said." Kline had recently been promoted to supervisor from 204-B. "Candace Brown was a few minutes late from break. Coming back from the swing room, she ran into a friend who'd been off sick, asked how she was doing, and talked for a few minutes. Stacey even admitted Candace is usually on time. So what's the big deal? I asked her to reduce it to a verbal discussion. That should've been a no-brainer. Stacey said: 'I have five days to get back to you.' Sure, the contract says they can take five days, but what is there to think about? I guess she means she'll

127

see if Newton will let her settle."

Ron said, "I think if I told a supervisor to go to hell, the response would be 'I have five days to get back to you on that.' Then they'd go to Newton and ask if they should accommodate my request."

"There sure is a lot of tension here nowadays," Paul said. "They're nit picking over every little thing, and issuing discipline like *crazy*."

"They say they have a business to run," Ron added. "They can't let anything slide. But it's a green light for supervisors who like to push people around. And those who treat people like human beings are under pressure to crack down. If they don't issue enough discipline, Newton thinks they're soft."

"Emma thinks there's going to be another shooting," Paul said. "I don't blame her, although you really can't predict that sort of thing."

It was February, 1996, a little more than four years after the shooting at the Main. Management was behaving as if they hadn't learned a thing.

Paul started thinking wistfully about Emma. If he asked her out again, would she give him another chance? His thoughts were interrupted when Clarence Day came into the union office. A thirty-five year old with a muscular build who always wore a black beret, he had a reputation as a militant black man. And he had a temper to match the image. But he was also an intellectual. He could talk to you about the Black Panthers, whom he admired but also criticized for their mistakes which left them vulnerable to attack. He could talk for hours about Malcolm X, particularly about the flexibility in the man's thinking. Malcolm had changed his views a number of times within just a few years, but always within the framework of an uncompromising desire for freedom for African-American people. Clarence hated to hear people oversimplify what Malcolm stood for.

While nobody would be surprised to hear Clarence talk about Malcolm or the Panthers, those who didn't know much about him would be shocked to hear him talk knowledgeably about the ancient Greek philosophers, the Renaissance, the history of genocide against the American Indians, or any number of historical subjects.

Paul respected the intellectual, thoughtful side of Clarence, and occasionally ran his own political views by him for feedback. Angela also had a healthy respect for Clarence, but she was not particularly close to him. Unlike Clarence, Angela did not project a strong consciousness of race. But it was there, right beneath the surface. To the degree she was proud of her accomplishments at Wayne State and her competence as a steward, she took pride as a black woman. And her insecurities about her personal life were the insecurities of a black woman.

From early childhood, Angela had been very much aware of how racism affected her life. She didn't feel she had to talk about it very often, it was just there. She had no trouble forming a strong friendship with Paul or forming close bonds with some of the employees she represented, regardless of race. She respected anyone who treated her with respect. If you didn't know Angela well, you might think racism wasn't an important issue to her. You would be wrong.

Paul liked both Clarence and Angela, but it was a different kind of friendship. Paul was always aware that Clarence was a black friend of his. Even if they were discussing nothing more important than last night's Pistons game, he was conscious that he was talking basketball with a black person. There was nothing negative about this attitude; Paul and Clarence liked and respected each other. It was just a lot different than his friendship with the steward he worked with, whom he thought of simply as that wonderful person, Angela.

Clarence and Angela had discussed their attitudes about race consciousness several times in the past. But that's not why Clarence entered the union office on this February day. He had received a Letter of Warning for a trivial offense. When he went out to lunch, he put his time card in his pocket instead of leaving it in the rack. When he came back to punch in, Jim Newton saw him take his card out of his pocket. Twenty minutes later, Day was paged to the office and given his discipline.

The three stewards were shocked. Clarence hadn't even been late from his lunch. The offense he committed was commonplace. In fact, some people carried their cards with them to stretch their lunch by punching in and out next to the swing room, but Clarence hadn't even done that. He punched out at the clock in his work area, and punched in at the same time clock exactly 50 digits (thirty minutes) later.

Clarence explained he thought Newton was particularly out to get him. A few days earlier, Clarence had been casing mail in 044. Among the letters on his ledge was an envelope with no mailing address and no return address. The words "Rent Money" were handwritten on the envelope, which was rather thick, apparently containing a stack of ten or twenty dollar bills. Clarence figured it was a set-up to see if he would steal it. He simply placed the envelope on the supervisor's desk. "I'm not losing my job by falling for a trick like that," he said.

Clarence had a good work record, with no discipline except for poor attendance. "You know, when I worked at Chrysler I could get myself sent home any time I wanted, and they wouldn't hold it against me. See, they had a nurse right there at the plant, and when you weren't feeling well, you could ask to see her. Right outside the nurse's station they had a vending machine. You could drink a hot cup of black coffee before you went in. Then the nurse would stick the thermometer under your tongue and your temperature reading would be way up there. She'd send you right home. Everybody did it, it's amazing they never caught on. But they don't have a set up like that here, so I've run into trouble with unscheduled absences. But when I *am* here, I do my job. I give them a fair day's work for a fair day's pay. I don't appreciate being disciplined when I've done nothing wrong. It's garbage."

Angela decided she'd try to talk to Newton alone before holding a formal Step One Meeting. Maybe she could talk some sense into him. Clarence went back to his work area.

Meanwhile, Clara Parsons came in to see Paul about a Letter of Warning for attendance. Clara was relatively new at the Plant, and she explained that she was still having trouble adjusting to the midnight shift.

"In fact," Clara said, "I was almost AWOL one day a few months ago. My off days are Tuesday-Wednesday, which is Monday and Tuesday night. So when I went home from work Monday morning, I forced myself to stay up all day even though I was tired, and I collapsed into bed Monday night. When I awoke, it was sunny, and my clock said 9:00. I did a few things around the house and started making plans for my night off. Then my mother called and we talked about a bunch of different things. When we were about to hang up she said, 'Have a good time at work tonight.' I said it was my night off, and she said, 'don't you work Wednesday night?' I was shocked. I had slept more than thirty hours straight. If my mother hadn't called, I would've been AWOL, and they never would have believed my story.

That was interesting, but it shed very little light on her Letter of Warning. However, looking at the attendance chart (Form 3972), Clara's record didn't seem too bad. She had missed five days in eight months and had been perfect for three months before that – a fact they never seem to mention in a Letter of Warning. It wasn't a great record, but Paul thought he might be able to get it reduced to a documented discussion.

They met with Lawrence Harris shortly before Paul's tour ended at 0500. Lawrence's main argument was Clara set a pattern because all of her absences were on Friday, Saturday, or Sunday. "Those are desirable weekend days," Lawrence said. "If it wasn't for the pattern, I might let it slide."

Paul responded that the pattern management usually looks for is when employees hook up their absences with their off days. "If Clara had always called in on Mondays or Thursdays, you'd say she was setting a pattern by extending her weekend. By this logic, whatever day she happens to get sick is automatically suspicious. That's ridiculous."

Paul also pointed out that on Tour One, Friday is not a desirable weekend day. "On Tour Three, that would be Friday night, when people like to go out, but on Tour One, that's Thursday night, which is just an ordinary week night. In fact, one of the days she missed was a pay day. Nobody calls in on pay day unless they're really sick."

Lawrence was convinced and told Paul to come in tomorrow and write up a settlement reducing it to a documented discussion. Paul thanked him, Clara thanked Paul and Lawrence, and then Paul punched out and went home.

The next day the three stewards were back in the union office. Ron had some inside information on Danny Vellarmo. "You know he landed a job with the Troy Police Department? It's a lucky thing for him they let him clear his record before he left."

"He still blames Newton," Paul said. "And he blames me. Everyone but himself. He threw a punch at Reggie Green, in full view of Gwendolyn Rogers and three craft employees. They were going to remove him. Newton read him the riot act, and actually had him scared shitless. Then he offered to let him resign. I just said 'Do it, please.' And Vellarmo thinks we both were out to get him. If he had that removal on his record, the police might have turned him down."

"They say there's a few rotten apples in every police force," Angela added. "We know Troy's got one."

Then Ron took a phone call and found he was needed at the BOBB to handle two Letters of Warning and a Suspension. A few minutes later, Stacey Kline called Angela and said she had decided to deny the grievance concerning Candace Brown's long break.

"What a waste of time," Angela said. "I have to write up a Step Two over a break that was a few minutes too long. Have they ever thought about how much time is going to be spent on something like this? My time, Candace's time, Stacey Kline's time, Nancy Barber's time – all over a matter of *three minutes*?"

"Well, good luck on your Step One with Clarence Day," Paul said. "Remember to have Clarence tell Newton how remorseful he is, and that he will never again commit the heinous crime of…" Paul paused as he dramatically pulled his time card out of his pocket… "carrying his time card in his pocket."

Chuckling at Paul's rule breaking behavior, Angela left to hold her Step One with Clarence and Newton, while Paul wrote up his settlement from the day before and went to find Harris and get his signature on it.

"I've talked it over with Newton," Lawrence said, "and we have to take all attendance infractions seriously. I'm willing to offer you six months on the Letter of Warning, but I can't let Clara go with just a discussion."

"But we agreed on a settlement yesterday! You gave your word. You're not allowed to renege. That's bargaining in bad faith!"

"We didn't sign anything yesterday," Lawrence said. "Six months on record, take it or leave it."

Paul ended up writing up a Step Two on Clara Parsons' Letter of Warning. He also took the time to get a witness statement from Clara that Lawrence had agreed to a Documented Discussion at the Step One Meeting. A second grievance was going to be filed. Paul would be the grievant and Ron would represent him. The issue was bad faith bargaining.

When Angela came back from her Step One with Newton she was steaming.

"That man is so arrogant. He made it sound like Clarence committed the crime of the century by carrying around his time card. He said there would be total chaos here if employees could break the rules whenever they pleased. He offered us a year on the record!"

"*What*?" said Paul incredulously.

"*And* he was trying to get Clarence upset throughout the

meeting. He kept taking little digs at him, trying to get him to lose his temper."

"How did Clarence react?"

"He was cool as a cucumber. He saw right through Newton. He was even expecting it more than I was. But he had to be seething inside. Newton's trying to railroad him, and over what? Something we shouldn't even be talking about. Oh, maybe they should ask him not to do it anymore, but I don't even think it should be an official discussion. Just ask him to leave his card in the rack from now on. It's so petty."

"Well, I'm glad your grievant was calm in there," said Paul. "I don't know if I would've been, in his place."

When Clarence got home he phoned his wife Lakeisha. They were separated, and Lakeisha had custody of their nine year old son Bobby. They lived in a downriver community. Bobby was having trouble with one of the teachers at school. In fact, Bobby was one of four black children in the school, and they all had trouble with the same teacher. Bobby's grades had always been B or higher, but he was failing in Mrs. Stith's Social Studies class. She claimed he hadn't turned in numerous homework assignments. The first time this happened, Lakeisha Day started keeping track; Bobby showed her the completed assignment before turning it in. Then Mrs. Stith still turned around and said she didn't receive a dozen of them. Lakeisha was not surprised to encounter some prejudice at a mostly white school, but she never expected to find a teacher deliberately sabotaging a student. It turned out that the other three black students also failed Mrs. Stith's class, and two of them were straight A students otherwise (the third had a C average).

Talking to the Principal had done absolutely no good. The four sets of parents asked the NAACP to intervene, but all they could do was recommend a lawyer. The parents had to come up with the lawyer's fee, and they all chipped in, including Clarence. The suit had been filed four months ago, and had encountered one continuance after another. It was finally slated to go to trial next week, if no informal settlement could be negotiated.

Lakeisha informed Clarence that there was no news. The school was not willing to change any of the children's grades, and there would have to be a trial. Clarence was upset. He and his wife had an amicable separation. In fact, Clarence realized that in some respects he was a hard person to live with. He had a girlfriend now, and they'd been going together for quite some time, but he still cared about his wife and loved his son. It took all of his self-control not to drive down to the school and commit some sort of act of violence. Maybe it's a good thing he lived about an hour's drive from the school.

There was one thing Clarence had neglected to mention to Angela when she handled his Letter of Warning. Perhaps it was none of her business. Clarence didn't know very much about Mrs. Lisa Stith, but he did know her maiden name was Lisa Newton. The teacher that Clarence's wife filed suit against was Jim Newton's sister.

Fourteen: SUMMER HEAT

Summer, 1996

Prosecutor: What was the defendant's reaction when management threatened to call the police on him?
Witness: He described Mr. Newton as a "monster."

Saturday, August 18th was hot and muggy. Paul stayed inside with the central air running all afternoon, except for walking two blocks to the 7-11. When he returned with a six pack of Budweiser to take to Aretha Simmons' birthday party that night, he was soaking wet.

He started getting ready about ten. He showered and shaved, put on some Dockers, comfortable dress shoes, and a bright red dress shirt. For Paul, this was dressing up. His normal summer outfit consisted of dungarees, gym shoes, and a T-shirt or tank top. There would be some people at the party dressed informally, but Paul knew he would probably be the only white person at this party, and he did not want to be perceived as showing any disrespect. Besides, he kind of liked dressing this way once in a while.

The party was at Aretha Simmons' house, and he had precise directions. From his home on the east side, he took Eight Mile Road west more than ten miles. He thought of Eight Mile as a symbolic divide between white and black, even if he lived on the incorrect side. Of course, some white folks lived in Detroit, south of Eight Mile, and quite a few black people had moved into Oak Park and Southfield to the north. But tonight, the symbolism seemed real. When he reached Greenfield, he went south a little more than a mile, turned left, then right, and looked for the house number.

It was 11:30 when he arrived, said hello to Aretha (who was still rushing back and forth to the kitchen where her sisters were helping her cook quite a feast), and sat in one of the thirty metal

137

chairs that had been rented for the occasion. It was an outdoor party in the back yard. A DJ had his equipment in the garage, and at the moment a song by TLC was booming out. Paul was sure it could be heard for several blocks. Paul put five cans of Bud in the cooler and slowly drank the sixth, waiting for the party to begin. There was a couple he didn't know; a woman in a backless summer dress and a young man in a suit jacket and tie, although he had taken off the jacket and hung it carefully on one of the metal chairs. The couple seemed very much wrapped up in each other, and Paul was pretty much alone.

Paul had been to a few parties thrown by black coworkers in the past. He knew that even though the handwritten invitation said "From 9:00 until...", the real party didn't start until much later. But he always underestimated just how much later that would be.

Paul spent the next 45 minutes alone with his thoughts. He didn't remember the first time he had gone to a party like this, but once he had gone he had been invited to more. There was always some nervousness in him, even though he knew he usually ended up having a good time. The nervousness gave him pause to think about questions of race, both in society in general and in terms of his own attitude.

Paul wished there were social events where black and white people partied together, but that was not usually the case. Paul found he could usually party with a group of white coworkers and friends, perhaps with a single black person in attendance, or else he could be the only white guy at a black party. He did both. Even at work among the card players, the whites mostly played euchre and the blacks played bid.

So here he was awkwardly sitting in a black person's back yard, in a black neighborhood. Why was he nervous? He certainly didn't consider himself a racist, and he got along just fine with people of all races at work. There was no rational reason to be nervous; nothing bad was going to happen to him here. He knew from experience what would happen. He would drink quite a bit. He would dance with a few different women, or maybe he would attach himself to one in particular. He remembered one time he had left with the phone number of a young lady he met at a backyard party. He had called, and she never did go out with him, but he did have a good time with her at the party.

He always started out nervous. His parents were liberals who had taught him not to be prejudiced (although they never were too thrilled when he expressed interest in a black woman). And he could go for weeks at work without being explicitly conscious of race, just treating people as people in the course of his daily life. And then, all of a sudden, he was acutely aware of race.

Of course, the nervousness wasn't entirely due to the racial aspect. There was always some nervousness at the prospect of some new encounter with someone of the opposite sex. He felt it on a first date with almost anyone – even someone he knew as a friend. Did other men feel the same way? None of his friends talked about it, they pretended to be super-confident, but Paul suspected his nervousness wasn't unique.

He would feel more comfortable when Angela arrived. At least he thought she was coming, since Aretha was a close friend of hers. It would give him someone to talk to in between occasional forays onto the dance floor. Once he found someone he knew to sit with his nervousness would subside, and Angela would be just perfect in that regard.

Little did he know that Angela had given Aretha some excuse for missing the party. She was actually watching a couple of old Hitchcock movies rented from Blockbusters. Angela usually avoided this type of party. She would tell people she didn't like rap music and the party scene, but the truth is she was insecure about men. She lacked confidence in that type of setting, so she tried to avoid it.

In a way, it was ironic. Angela was intelligent, competent, kind, compassionate, and not bad looking. She got along well with most people. In many ways, she would make an ideal mate for any number of men. Yet, like so many intelligent and basically good people, she had trouble getting any kind of personal life together. As she watched Cary Grant and Eva Marie Saint hanging on to Mount Rushmore for their lives, she tried not to think about Aretha, Paul, and everyone else at the party.

Paul hadn't come to the party just to talk to Angela. He could do that any time. The fact is, Paul was attracted to black women. It's not that he didn't like white women, but there was something different about his attraction to black women. He could try to analyze it backwards and forwards. Did this prove he wasn't racist or did this, in some way, indicate he really had some kind of a hang-up about race? He'd debated this in his mind long ago and decided not to worry about it. If he enjoyed the company of black women, then he should do just that – enjoy it – and stop trying to analyze it.

It was now after midnight and a few more people had arrived, but nobody he knew. The heat had subsided and there was a slight breeze. It would be a nice night for dancing when Paul finally was ready for it. Right now he was still lost in his thoughts.

Someone Paul knew finally walked into the back yard, but it was not who he was expecting. Supervisor Reggie Green and his wife made an appearance, and Paul shook their hands and returned to his seat. Paul immediately thought of a situation he and Reggie had just resolved. Arnold Foster, a clerk on the 110 Belt, had made a mistake in filling out the vacation chart at the beginning of the year. There was a week on the chart marked "25 - Dec. - 1," which Arnold thought was the week between Christmas and New Years. It was actually November 25th through December 1st. By the time the mistake was discovered, the week Arnold wanted had been filled. Green had agreed with Paul to let Arnold take Christmas week off, and Paul agreed that if anyone else in the section runs out of annual leave and has to cancel that week, it would not be reposted. It is really fairly common for people to use up their annual leave during the year, so in all likelihood the settlement would not leave management short staffed.

Reggie told Paul he had been chewed out by Newton for making the settlement. "But that doesn't bother me," he said, "I let it go in one ear and out the other. I hadn't been chewed out since last month."

It was a little after one in the morning when Tawanna Chambers and her sister Samantha showed up, together with a young man who turned out to be Samantha's boyfriend. Paul didn't ask where Tawanna's husband was. He just couldn't take his eyes off her. She was wearing a pair of tight shorts and a tank top that rode pretty low on her breasts. Every time she caught him looking at her, she smiled that warm, beautiful smile of hers.

He went out on the dance floor with her for a hard driving fast number by a singer he didn't recognize. The dance floor was just the back lawn and there were some bumpy spots so you had to be careful. Paul was not the most graceful dancer in any event, but he moved around and enjoyed himself. Paul was aware his black coworkers would mainly notice whether he was enjoying himself. To them, if he had a good time that meant he was comfortable with black people in a social setting. Nobody would verbalize it that way. But he remembered on more than one occasion when he got back to work after one of these parties and a coworker said, "Paul was really tearing up the dance floor the other night." It was not so much a comment on his dancing ability as a sign of acceptance.

Right now Paul didn't have to pretend to be enjoying himself. He liked Tawanna a lot, and he watched her graceful movements while his own arms, legs, and hips moved more or less in time to the beat. When the song stopped he put his arm around Tawanna, thanked her for the dance, and said we'll do it again later on. She smiled and went inside the house.

Paul danced with Samantha once and with a couple of women he didn't know. The one dance with Tawanna had made him feel totally at ease, and even a little adventurous. It didn't even matter that Angela had not shown up. He was having a good time.

Before the party ended he danced to a couple of slow tunes with Tawanna. Now there is slow dancing and then there is *slow* dancing. There is a polite kind of slow dancing where you kind of hold each other at arm's length and move in time to the music but never get too close. That was sometimes the way Paul danced with someone he hardly knew. But not with Tawanna. She pressed her body right into his. He could feel her ample breasts against his chest, and his right hand moved all over her back and down below, while she gave his rear end a friendly squeeze. It was sensual, it was exciting, and for Paul it was bliss. When it was over he kissed Tawanna on the lips.

Tawanna and her sister left shortly after that, and Paul found little reason to stay much longer. He kissed Aretha to say happy birthday and left. He went to bed thinking about Tawanna, and she was on his mind all day Sunday. His logical mind told him that Tawanna was married and the fact that she danced with him meant nothing more than that they'd had an enjoyable time at a party. But he fantasized about being her lover. His logical mind told him that even if he was successful in pursuing her, in the end someone would be badly hurt, and it probably would be him. The conflict between his fantasy and his better judgment would have to be resolved when he saw her again at work.

When Paul began his tour at 8:30 Monday night, the temperature outside was 95 degrees. The air conditioning in the building was totally ineffective. Laura Kress, a Tour 3 steward, told Paul she had complained to a Maintenance Supervisor, who told her the air conditioning was on full blast and there's nothing wrong with the system. It's just not strong enough to deal with the intense heat, especially with so much machinery running.

As the day went on, Paul kept looking for a chance to talk to

Tawanna alone. He saw her when he passed by her work area but knew he couldn't have the conversation he wanted there. She looked great, even in dungarees and a T-shirt. For Paul, the anticipation was building.

His thoughts were broken when he heard his name being paged over the loudspeaker. "Paul Farley, come to the supervisor's desk in automation." The voice was that of Lawrence Harris.

When Paul arrived there Lawrence said, "I'm sending Aretha Simmons home. Her shorts are in violation of the dress code. I just thought you should see them first, since you'll be representing her. You are familiar with the dress code, aren't you?"

"I think I've got a copy of it in the union office, but I don't have it memorized. Can I take Aretha back there so we can look it over together before you do anything else?"

Lawrence agreed but added, "When you're done, she has to go home and change. That's off the clock, of course."

Paul knew the dress code well enough to see that Aretha's shorts were in violation. The length was supposed to be no higher than half way between the knee and the top of the leg. Aretha's shorts were a good deal higher. But Paul had seen lots of shorts or skirts that were similarly in violation throughout the summer. If management wasn't enforcing this provision, it would not be fair to send Aretha home.

Paul and Aretha discussed their strategy inside the union office. Paul said he was going to go back out and try to convince Lawrence to let Aretha finish out the day if she agrees not to wear the same pair of shorts to work again.

Aretha also told Paul that when she asked for a steward, Lawrence had said Angela wasn't available, and she'd have to see one of the others. "I figure he knew Angela's my best friend and he just wanted me to see someone else. Little did he know you were over at my house this weekend. Thanks for coming, by the way. I hope you had a good time."

"I certainly did," Paul responded. "Thanks for inviting me."

On his way back to automation, Paul ran into Tawanna. He said, "Tawanna, you know of any parties next weekend?" She replied, "My husband's taking me to Toronto this weekend. We haven't been spending enough time together. It will be a nice getaway for the two of us."

Paul smiled gamely. He told himself it was for the best. It had been foolish to let his fantasies run wild. He could tell himself that again and again, but in fact, Paul felt deflated.

He continued on towards automation, hoping he would be up to the task of arguing with Lawrence. As it turned out, that battle was already won.

Clara Parsons was feeding the machine that Aretha had been taken off. Clara was new, and she worked the weekends. In fact, today was her normal off day, but she had switched with another new employee so she could hear a John Mellencamp concert at Pine Knob Wednesday night. On the night of Aretha's party, Clara had come to work wearing shorts very similar to Aretha's.

When Clara heard what was happening to Aretha, her mood changed. She kept feeding the machine whatever mail was in front of her, but her expression was grim. Soon the sweeper on the machine noticed all the mail was winding up in the reject bin. Lawrence Harris was notified. It turned out Clara had started running a different kind of mail without changing the sort plan on the computer. Technically, it was the supervisor's job to pay attention to the sort plan, but mail processors routinely took care of it. Clara simply said, "Sorry, I must've been distracted thinking about what you're doing to Aretha."

Two machines down, Ellen Rudny's machine kept jamming. She was running mail through it with addresses that were automation readable, but the mail pieces were very flimsy. The whole container of mail should have been sent to letter hand cases. But Ellen, too, was distracted.

By the time Paul arrived with his suggestion that Aretha be allowed to stay but warned not to wear the same shorts again,

Lawrence was willing to accept it. It offered him a face-saving way out. He gave Aretha a stern warning, Xeroxed a copy of the dress code and handed it to her, and told her to get back to work. When her coworkers saw Aretha feeding the machine again, everything went smoothly in the area. Charlie Valmont whistled at her and yelled out "nice shorts!" Aretha smiled.

Aretha was well liked by most people in the area, and that's one reason they stood behind her. Another reason was their dislike of Lawrence Harris. Add to that the unfairness of his picking on her, and the summer heat, and you had the ingredients for a job action by Aretha's coworkers. It worked better than the grievance procedure usually does.

Later that day, Paul was called to the Building on Big Beaver (BOBB). Randy Sochalski wanted to file a harassment grievance against Shirley Jones. It gave Paul an eerie feeling. The details were similar to an episode Shirley once handled as a steward.

There was an added complication. Randy said, "I think Shirley believes I'm still on my ninety day probation. I hired in four months ago in CFS. Technically that's connected to the District, not the Plant. After a month and a half, I managed to get transferred here to the Small Parcel & Bundle Sorter without a break in service. I've got more than ninety days total, but less than three months here on the SPBS. She can't fire me, can she?"

Paul looked it up in the Employee & Labor Relations Manual and found the regulations were clear. Randy had completed his probation and could not be terminated without just cause and due process. They decided before doing anything else, they should make sure that point got cleared up with Shirley.

It was 3:30 AM (0350) and time for lunch on the SPBS machine. Paul couldn't catch Shirley before lunch and decided he would talk to her the next day.

Back at the Plant, Clarence Day was seeing Ron Davidson about a suspension for attendance. It was his third suspension. Inexplicably, he hadn't filed grievances on the first two.

"I deserved those two," he said. "But this one is unfair. If they don't expunge it, I'm calling in for a few days before Labor Day, which will give me a nice long holiday weekend just before serving my suspension. You guys can get me back pay later. Fuck those assholes."

Ron was not pleased. "What you're saying reminds me of a silly rhyme my father used to sing. It went,

> Si and I went to the circus,
> Si got hit with a rolling pin.
> Si got even with the darn old circus.
> He bought two tickets and didn't go in.

"Do you get the point? Si didn't hurt the circus, he only hurt himself. That's what you'll be doing if you call in sick again. I might not be able to get this suspension off your record completely. I'll feel good if I can undo some of the damage you did to yourself by not grieving those other two. If I can reduce the days on this one and get all your discipline to come off your record one year from now, that'll give you a chance to dig yourself out of the hole you're in. 'Cause if you get in trouble again, it won't be a suspension, it'll be a removal. They usually settle the first attendance removal for a long suspension, but if you mess up again you're a goner. So get rid of the attitude, come to work for a year, and earn yourself a new start. You're a smart guy Clarence. Don't act dumb when it comes to saving your job."

Clarence left the room without saying another word.

At three in the afternoon Paul went outside to mow his lawn. He had put it off long enough, waiting for a cooler day. It was still above 90, and hot weather was forecast for the rest of the week. By four, his grass was short, he had filled five large garbage bags with grass clippings and was soaking wet. He took a shower and went to make a phone call when he noticed his answering machine was blinking.

The message was from the Union Office in Ferndale. Randy Sochalski had been fired at 7:30 that morning. Randy had not been allowed to see a steward. Shirley Jones told him he was on probation and could not grieve it. The Local Vice President had called Nancy Barber in Labor Relations. The situation was worked out. Randy would be able to report back in at 11:00 PM tonight. Paul should go over to the BOBB at that time to make sure everything went smoothly. Jim Newton had been called at home and a message had been left on his answering machine. He was to inform Shirley Jones to let Randy work.

It sounded like a nice plan. At 2300 Paul and Randy reported to the BOBB and went to the time clock by the SPBS. Randy's time card was not in the rack. Paul asked Shirley, "Are you going to give Randy his timecard?"

Pretending Randy was not standing right there, Shirley told Paul, "I'm busy, I don't have time to talk to you right now. If you have any grievances to discuss with me, catch me later in the day." Then she turned her back on both of them and walked in the direction of the SPBS.

Paul and Randy went to the union office at the other end of the building. Paul said, "I want you to write a statement about what just happened, while it's fresh in your mind. Get the conversation word-for-word, if possible. I'll do the same. Then go on home, and we'll get you paid for it."

Paul had a feeling Shirley might want to barge in, so he locked the door to the office, something he seldom did when he was inside. Sure enough, a few minutes later, there was Shirley at the door, peering in through the glass window.

"Randy has to leave the premises," she shouted.

"He'll leave when he's through writing his statement."

Shirley then tried the door and was shocked to find it was locked. She tried it again. Then she tried a third time while banging her shoulder against it, as if she could force it open that way.

"You can't do this!" she shouted. "If you don't open up, I'm calling the police!"

"You better check with Jim Newton first," Paul responded.

Shirley left her position by the doorway and Randy and Paul finished their statements, adding in a description of Shirley's behavior at the locked door. Then Randy went home and Paul went back to the Plant.

At midnight, he was in Newton's office.

"Didn't Labor Relations contact you about putting Sochalski back to work?"

"Oh yes. I just got in myself. I was just about to call Shirley Jones and let her know."

"You idiot! His starting time is 2300. She sent him home an hour ago, and threatened to call the police on us!"

Newton just smirked. Paul was sure he had intentionally caused the turmoil. Sochalski would surely end up being paid for the day, but that didn't seem to bother Newton. He enjoyed Sochalski's suffering and Paul's frustration.

Later that day the three stewards talked over this latest incident.

"Must be the summer heat," said Ron. Lots of people have been acting crazy lately."

"So how do you explain it when they pull stunts like this in the winter?"

"I still can't get over Shirley Jones," said Angela. "Threatening to call the police. I almost wish she had, it sure would've made her look stupid. There's nothing worse than an ex-steward turned manager."

"Yeah there is," Paul responded. "That monster we have in the MDO's office is a lot worse."

Fifteen: ELECTION TIME

November, 1996

Prosecutor: What type of gun did you sell the defendant?
Witness: It was a .22 caliber pistol.

"I don't understand it." Ron said. "When Jesus rose up from the dead, they called it a miracle. But when thousands of dead people in Chicago rise up and vote on Election Day, they call it fraud."

"I'm more concerned with *our* elections." Paul said. "We've got to get Humphrey out of there, and I think Joanna Carver would really do a good job."

It was the day after Bill Clinton had been reelected President, defeating Bob Dole. Local union elections were just a couple of weeks away.

"I'm sure glad Clinton won," Ron said. "He may not be perfect, but he did sign Hatch Act Reform and FMLA."

"I don't like Clinton," said Paul. "I didn't so much vote for him as against the Republicans. But he's almost a Republican, with his support for trade deals like NAFTA and so-called welfare reform – throwing all those poor people out on the street, while corporate welfare is more generous than ever."

Ron was about to respond but the phone rang. "Bad news," he said when he hung up. "Clarence Day just got a removal."

A few minutes later Clarence came into the Union Office, and Ron was upset with him.

"You were in here a few months ago with a suspension. Don't you take this seriously? You have to come to work! I don't want to sound like management, but I guess I've got to lecture you for your own good. Even if I get this knocked down to a suspension, I wonder if it'll do any good. If you don't get your act together, you're going to lose your job for sure Clarence. It might even be too late now."

"Don't talk to me like I'm a child," Clarence responded, trembling with anger. "My mother's been in the hospital, on and off, for the past two months. I've been taking care of her at home, too. That's what all of my absences are for, except one. This job ain't more important than my mother. If you can't understand that, you've got a real problem, Mr. Davidson!"

"Don't you know about FMLA?," Ron asked.

"What's that?"

"The Family & Medical Leave Act, that was signed into law by Bill Clinton. Paul and I were just talking about it. All union members were sent an FMLA booklet in the mail. I don't understand, Clarence, how you can be so smart about some things and so ignorant when it comes to your own job. FMLA protects you from discipline for absences due to the serious health condition of a parent, spouse, or child. But you have to document it. Did you turn in any paperwork at the time of the absences for your mother's hospitalization?"

"No way. I never missed more than three days at a time. Didn't you tell me you only have to bring in documentation if the absence is more than three days?"

"Yeah, but that's different. If you miss more than three days, you need documentation to avoid being AWOL. But with FMLA, for any absence covered with documentation that meets the criteria of the law, it doesn't count against you at all."

They looked over the 3972 (attendance chart) together, and Clarence pointed out the absences that were due to his mother's hospitalization. Ron decided it might not be too late to try to win this case outright, instead of compromising.

"Look," said Ron. "I'm sorry about what I said to you before. Maybe we can fight this thing. Hobson will probably want to reduce this to a last chance suspension. Then you'd be on the brink of losing your job if your attendance gets shaky again. But I want to do better than that. Try to get some documentation from your mother's doctor. Cover the dates she was in the hospital and whenever she needed special care at home. Try to get your absences covered. I'll argue the discipline should be expunged completely. Even though it's not a violation of the law to use these absences against you, there is no just cause for the discipline. That'll be our starting point, and if we have to, we'll compromise on a suspension."

The following Sunday afternoon, Paul was at Ron's house. The Lions' home game was not televised because it was not a sellout, and the Packers - Bears game on the tube wasn't even close. Brett Favre threw three TD passes in the first half, and Chicago's offense could do nothing right. They left the game on but paid no attention.

Ron got out the gun he had been planning to sell to Paul. "It's a .22 caliber pistol, easy to handle for a beginner. I first got it for Pam, before we moved out to Sterling Heights. She doesn't feel so much like she needs it here, and she never practices with it anymore."

Paul had already obtained a permit to purchase a firearm. He didn't know much about guns, but thought it might be a good time to learn. A couple of his neighbors had been broken into recently.

"We can go down tomorrow and make the sale official, get it registered in your name," Ron said. "Then we can go down to this gun range I like, over on Gratiot in Roseville. It's not all that far from your place, either. I'll show you how to use it and you can practice until you get the hang of it."

"Do the targets look like Jim Newton?" Paul said.

"No, you'll just have to use your imagination."

Their discussion turned to Clarence Day's removal. They agreed that Butch Hobson might buy Ron's argument and expunge it, if left alone to make the decision. But if Newton took an interest in the case, Hobson might not have a choice.

Paul mentioned he was taking a day of annual leave towards the end of the week to campaign for Joanna Carver.

"You know, I heard some people saying she was a Communist," Ron said. "But you know her better than I do. What do you think about that?"

"I think Humphrey's desperate, and a little bit vicious. He's got a whispering campaign going against her, spreading all kinds of rumors. That's just another reason not to vote for him. He's got no union principles."

Paul got himself and Ron a fresh drink and settled into an old stuffed chair.

"I spent a lot of time talking to Joanna at the Union Picnic last summer," Paul said. "She was a bit of a radical in college, like a lot of people. All I can say is her heart is in the union. She believes in organizing the members, and she sets the example where she works. The Sterling Heights office is tight. Management is afraid to mess with people, not just because Joanna will file a grievance but because the employees out on the floor will make it rough on the supervisor. I haven't talked to anyone from Sterling Heights who isn't impressed with her. But she'll need to carry the Plant to win. That's why I'm handing out her fliers."

"What about her lack of experience? She's Chief Steward at her office, but she's never been a Vice President or even Local Craft Director."

"Don't worry, she's very smart. And she's got the right attitude. Humphrey's got experience, but it's the wrong kind of experience. He knows how to cave in to management and to control opposition within the Local. That kind of experience we don't need."

"Well, old buddy," said Ron, raising his glass. "I hope what you're doing doesn't come back to bite you in the ass."

A week and a half later, Angela and Paul were sitting in the union office while Ron and Clarence were holding a Step One with Butch

Hobson in the Manager's Office. There was a new poster on the wall that said: "The Labor Movement, "The Folks Who Brought You the Weekend." Angela and Paul both knew that how much Clarence Day appreciated the labor movement would depend on the outcome of his Step One Meeting.

Ron had waited until the 14th day, the last day a grievance would be timely. It had taken Clarence a while, but he was able to document and prove that almost all of his absences were related to his mother.

Meanwhile Martha Huntington came into the Union Office with a question. "I would like a Leave of Absence for six months. Do you think management will allow it?"

Angela asked what her reasons were and she said they were personal. Angela said she could talk to Newton about it, but unfortunately, he would probably say no, they weren't very generous with this type of request.

"I have an idea," Paul said. "Didn't you hurt your arm recently and go on light duty?"

"Yes."

"If you can get your doctor to write a note that you can't lift more than ten pounds, they won't let you work. Apply for light duty in the letter hand cases. They'll say you have to be able to lift fifteen pounds, otherwise they have no work for you. It's a stupid policy, and the union objects to it, but this time we can use it to our advantage."

"Let me get this straight. If I tell them I want a Leave of Absence they'll make me work. But if I tell them I want to work on light duty, they'll tell me not to work?"

"That's right, *if* you can only lift ten pounds. Every thirty days bring back a new light duty form requesting work with ten pounds lifting. They'll send you home, and they can't use the absence against you in discipline. You wanted to work, and they told you no."

"Are you sure this will work?"

"Positive. They consistently deny light duty requests for ten pounds."

"This place is weird," said Martha. "They prevent you from working for all the wrong reasons. They do everything backwards."

Paul and Angela both caught the reference to the incident five years earlier when Martha had been put off work when her boyfriend attacked her. At least this time her absence would not be a traumatic experience.

"Oh well, I'm off to see the doctor," she said on her way out of the office.

Ron came back in as Martha was leaving, dropped Clarence Day's grievance file on the table, and said nothing. It looked like Ron was holding back tears.

"It can't be that bad," Angela said. What happened, is it going to Step Two?"

"It's settled," Ron responded. "Clarence thinks I sold him out. I used my best judgment; I was afraid Labor Relations would be even tougher. And yet, it really isn't fair to suspend Clarence for taking care of his mother. So I'm caught in the middle."

"What did they offer?" Paul asked.

"Fourteen day suspension, one year on record. Hobson said he couldn't expunge it. Even though he understood the circumstances, the absences weren't covered by FMLA so they still counted. He only cut us one break, and I'm not sure Clarence understands it. He didn't include any language about this being a 'last chance.' That means if he's disciplined again, of course it will be issued as a removal, and management will probably try to make it stick, but there might be some wiggle room, depending on the circumstances. I was afraid Labor Relations would insist on 'last chance' language, and maybe keep it on his record for eighteen months. They often do that with first removals, and I haven't noticed much compassion from the E&LR Department lately. So I told Clarence it was up to him. Go a year with good attendance and he'll be in the clear."

"What did Clarence say?" Paul asked.

"He wants you or Angela to handle any grievances he has in the future."

"I don't get it," said Angela. "Why wouldn't Hobson expunge it?"

"It was Newton," Paul said. "Had to be. He told Hobson to really stick it to Clarence."

I think that's exactly what happened," said Ron. "Hobson gave the most lenient terms he could get away with."

On Friday evening, Paul was an observer for Joanna Carver as the ballots were counted by the union's Election Committee. It was a mail ballot, and the Election Committee went as a group to the Post Office to pick up the ballots. Then, each group of ballots was tallied by more than one pair of Election Committee members. It seemed that cheating was not possible, and the main role of the observers was to notify the candidates of the final results. The counting was done in the basement of the Union Office in Ferndale. The Election Committee members sat around the conference table, while observers sat in chairs against the back wall. President Humphrey was upstairs in his office. Joanna was home, sitting by the phone.

The Election Committee tallied the other races first. Many of the positions were uncontested, but there were Chief Steward races in Mount Clemens, Dearborn, and Sterling Heights, and there was a contested race for Clerk Craft Director.

It was about 9:00 PM when they started counting the ballots for President. Paul got up from his seat and stood directly behind Committee member Laura Kress. It's not that he suspected foul play, he just wanted to look over her shoulder and observe voting patterns as they developed. It was nip and tuck for a while, then Humphrey seemed to take a slight lead with a little more than half of the ballots counted. But a different trend emerged from that point on. It wasn't exactly a landslide, but in the end it was a fairly comfortable margin of victory.

Paul dialed Joanna's number before anyone went upstairs to talk to Humphrey.

"Hello," Joanna answered nervously.

"Madame President. Congratulations."

Sixteen: INSANITY REIGNS

January, 1997

Prosecutor: I'd like to introduce as evidence an article written by the defendant called "Insanity Reigns."
Defense Lawyer: Objection!

"It looks like we've got another removal case to handle," Ron said. "Wayne Fontes just got canned. I don't want to handle this one, though."

Angela looked puzzled.

"The Detroit Lions just fired their coach, Wayne Fontes," Paul explained. "I could defend him, though. He usually gets them into the playoffs. They just don't have the defensive talent to go all the way. Barry Sanders and an exciting offense can only get you so far. That's not Wayne's fault."

"No way," Ron retorted. "Fontes just doesn't instill the toughness needed to get to the Super Bowl. We need a new man at the top."

"I'll handle the grievance," Paul quipped. "If I can't settle at Step One, I can probably get a 'last chance' settlement from Labor Relations. This is a first removal, isn't it?"

The phone rang and Angela picked it up. It was Red Collier calling from the Stephenson Highway Operation (SHO), the third building that comprised the Plant complex. This building had nothing but the most modern DBCSs. They sorted each carrier's mail to the order in which the carriers walked their route (Delivery Point Sequence or DPS).

There were no regular eight hour positions at the SHO. That left PTFs who had an awful schedule – six days, approximately six hours per day, in the middle of the night. Six days on midnights meant you spent your one off day trying to recover and sleep at night like a normal person. But there was no overtime pay, as you were not even working 40 hours a week.

One of the mechanics had nicknamed the building the Stephenson Highway Institute of Technology, ostensibly because of the modern machinery there. But the acronym seemed to fit the working conditions there, especially since Red Collier had become boss. Most employees and even some supervisors picked it up.

"I'm going to the SHIT," Angela said as she put down the phone. Red Collier just fired a PTF on her first ninety days. She asked for a steward. He said he doesn't even have to let me see her. He just wants me to explain to her how probation works. I'm not looking forward to it."

It was Tuesday morning, January 6th, and Angela had to drive through a heavy snowstorm. It took her 15 minutes for what normally was a five minute trip. When she arrived, she heard a story that broke her heart.

Teresa Matson was a short woman with a milk chocolate complexion and a little bit of baby fat sill hanging on. She had a soft-spoken manner of speaking, and as Angela perceived it, a sincere face. Angela had seen Teresa at the Plant occasionally, as some of the PTFs from the SHO volunteered to throw letters there after the DPS mail was done on days when mail was heavy. But this was the first time they had spoken.

When Angela read the Notice of Removal she couldn't believe her eyes. It seems Teresa had felt a little twinge in her back on January 2nd, but thought the pain would go away and didn't report it. She just kept on working. On January 3rd it was still bothering her. When she came to the Plant to finish her tour throwing letters, the 204-B there noticed she was walking stiffly and asked her what had happened. Teresa explained, not at all thinking she had done anything wrong. The 204-B sent Teresa to the clinic, where she was given some pain pills and told she could return to work on her next scheduled day, after her off day on Sunday, January 4th.

Red Collier had been on vacation from Christmas Day through the weekend after New Years. When he received a note from the 204-B, he typed up a Notice of Removal for "Failure to Follow

Instructions." It seems Collier had given a Service Talk telling everyone to report all injuries immediately. Teresa Matson had not done so, therefore she had not followed instructions and was to be terminated.

Angela knocked on Collier's door and opened it. Collier was on the phone and held up a finger in a "wait a minute" gesture.

"Red, I know about the rule to report injuries right away," Angela said. "But working through pain is usually the sign of a conscientious worker. She thought the pain would go away. It's really a judgment call and she used good judgment. The clinic sent her back to work."

"Angela, I don't even have to talk to you about this. She's on probation. She's fired. End of discussion"

Angela went back to the little room in which she had talked to Teresa (there wasn't a union office in this building). Her message was the opposite of what Collier wanted her to tell Teresa about probation.

"I'm going to find a way to file a grievance on this. The contract doesn't allow for grieving removals for probationary employees, so I won't use Article sixteen. I'll file under Article two for discrimination. They're discriminating against you because you're handicapped, even if the handicap is temporary. If Collier won't hold a Step One with me, I'll note that and appeal to Step Two. They would be within their rights to deny it under the contract, but I hope someone in Labor Relations has some common sense. Probation is for weeding out the *bad* employees, not the good ones."

Teresa looked puzzled. "What's going to happen?" she asked.

"I'm going to see what I can do. No guarantees. I've never grieved a probationary before. It's an uphill fight. We're on shaky ground, technically speaking. But we're on solid ground morally. And its just common sense, you're a good worker, they should keep you. I'll fight for you, that's all I can say."

"How long will it take?"

"Probably a couple of weeks, give or take."

"I guess all I can do is pray."

"By the way, do you have the thirty day and sixty day evaluations they gave you?"

"I've got them at home. I was satisfactory or outstanding in every category."

"I'll need to get copies from you"

Teresa slowly made her way out of the building, looking dazed and miserable.

Meanwhile, Angela talked to a few of the PTFs who already had their 90 days in. She agreed to treat them to breakfast at Denny's, provided they would write a truthful statement about what kind of worker Teresa Matson was. She knew her case was contractually weak, but she thought she could show Labor Relations it was in management's interest to put Teresa back to work.

<><><><><>

Paul was alone in the Union Office when the phone rang. It was Emma. She had been off work most of December with pneumonia. Now her doctor said she could return to work, but management wouldn't let her.

"When you've been off work more than 21 days," Paul explained, "you have to get clearance through the medical unit at the Main. Your doctor can fax the medical info to the nurse at the Main, and she can fax a note saying you've been cleared to the Plant."

"I know that," Emma said. "The nurse said she faxed the clearance over on Friday. But Friday night for Saturday I came in and they sent me home. They said they never received any clearance. I looked for you but you weren't there."

"Sorry. I called in."

"Anyway, I called the Plant this evening. I was sure they would have gotten it straightened out during the day Monday. But they said no. So now I'm calling you."

"I'll tell you what, Emma. How about meeting me for lunch in Royal Oak tomorrow. We can go to the Big Boy on Woodward. Then we'll go to the Main together, and get a copy of the nurse's note clearing you. I'll personally hand it to your supervisor when I get in at eight-thirty, and you can bring a copy in too. Then we'll grieve for back pay."

"Is this how you normally handle these cases?"

"No, but I'd like to see you again."

"That's okay, Paul, but you should understand I'm seeing someone else now. If we have lunch at Big Boy, we're just meeting as friends."

"Okay," Paul said, trying to conceal his disappointment.

His mood picked up when Tawanna came in to the office. "I need to file a grievance. My doctor said I was unable to work, and they tried to force me to work."

Paul broke out laughing.

"What's so funny?"

"I was just on the phone with someone else. Her doctor said she *was* able to work, and they wouldn't let *her* work. Is this place crazy or what?"

"We've known that all along, Paul."

"Let me guess, Tawanna. You were hurt on the job. They would've had to pay you anyway, so they gave you a job offer they said was within your restrictions."

"That's right. I strained a muscle and went to their clinic at about seven in the morning last Thursday. The doctor wrote 'No lifting for three days' on my paperwork. I turned the papers in to Newton and he made me wait while he called the clinic back. He said 'can't she even lift a few pounds?' I didn't hear the other end of the conversation, but he added the words 'more than 2 pounds' after 'no lifting.' He wrote it right on the paperwork signed by the doctor. Then he typed up a job offer for me, saying I could throw letters, lifting up to two pounds at a time. I thought you had to lift 15 pounds to throw letters."

"That's only if your injury occurred off the job. If they have to pay you anyway, they think you can be productive lifting only two pounds."

"Anyway, Paul, I went to my doctor the same day – that was January second. He put me off work entirely until today. I want to make sure I get paid for that day and Newton gets what's coming to him for trying to pressure me back to work."

"I'll be happy to handle it, T. You should be paid COP for the day. That stands for Continuation Of Pay. It means you get paid for eight hours and they don't use your annual or sick leave. It should be no problem getting that straightened out. The grievance against Newton will be a hot one. He altered medical documentation – that's a serious offense. I want to take care of the COP first, before we start causing controversy with Newton. I'm going over to the Main tomorrow. If you sign a release, I can talk to someone in the Injury Comp department for you."

"You'd do that on your own time? For me?"

"Certainly, dear."

Tawanna blew him a kiss as she left the room. Paul enjoyed Tawanna's visit and was happy to help her. But he couldn't help feeling a bit frustrated over his luck with women. A part of him still longed for Tawanna, but he knew that was impossible. Her flirtation was just a form of friendliness – she had made the limits clear on more than one occasion. It looked like he had blown it with Emma.

Maybe it was time he took a good look inside himself. He must be doing something wrong. Was he too self-centered to have a meaningful relationship with a woman? That couldn't be. His work as a steward proved he cared deeply about other people. He often put his own self-interest last, and gave freely of his time to help others.

But why did he always seem to be chasing after a woman that, deep down, he knew he'd never get, while ignoring women like Emma? Perhaps somewhere inside his psyche there lurked a

Groucho Marx complex with regard to women (Groucho once said he'd never join a club whose standards were so low that they'd accept *him* as a member).

His thoughts were interrupted by the phone. It was Lashawn Wyatt, a casual employee. Casuals were a category of temporary employee who were not even permitted union representation. They were hired for 89 days at a time, often working several 89 day terms in a row. They had fewer rights than TEs. Their wage scale was arbitrarily set by local management (it was $7 per hour at the Plant) and they had no benefits at all. The TEs at least earned annual leave as they worked, and they had gained some protection against unjust removals in the most recent contract. The casuals had no such protection. As with the TEs, most of the casuals at the Plant were black, including Lashawn Wyatt.

"I don't know if you know me," said Lashawn. "I'm a Tour Three casual – at least I was a Tour Three casual. I was fired by Tour One management, so I want to talk to a Tour One steward."

"This is Paul Farley. I know who you are Lashawn. I come in at eight-thirty, and I've seen you taking a bascart to automation to bring mail back to the letter hand cases. They usually assign you to gather mail for the hand cases, don't they?"

"That's right. I didn't think you'd remember who I was, Paul."

"So what happened?"

"On New Year's Eve, we were scheduled to work until eleven pm. Then at the last minute, they decided that Tour One needed us for two more hours.

"A 204-B gave us some friendly advice. She said if we write notes saying we were ill, they would have to let us go. Some of the girls and one guy wrote notes like that, and I'm sure they went out to party. But I couldn't lie. I needed to go home to watch my two year old boy. My mother promised to watch him until I got home at eleven fifteen, but she was attending a church service at midnight. She's very religious. So I wrote 'baby sitter leaving' on my note, and was denied. They told me I had to stay, but I left along with the others. Friday night, Jim Newton came in early just to fire me before I punched out at eleven. I guess I expected someone to give me a hard time, but I never expected this. They must know all the others left to drink and dance and party."

Paul marched right in to the manager's office. Newton was on the phone. "No Allison, I don't have time to talk to you now." There was a pause, during which Paul retreated to a respectful distance. "Please don't call me at work again. We can talk when I get home!" Newton's voice was too loud for Paul to ignore. After another pause, Newton said, "I love you too!" and slammed the receiver down.

Paul wondered if Newton treated his wife the same way he treated employees. But that was not his concern.

"I want to talk to you about Lashawn Wyatt," he said.

"She's a casual, Farley. You can't represent her."

"But she had a very good reason for leaving."

"Farley, I'm not paying you to be on union time to represent a casual."

"Okay, I'll talk to you on my own time, after I punch out at five. I know she's a casual, but her situation is extraordinary. You can at least take the time to listen."

"No dice, Farley. Everyone who gets fired has a hard luck story. Bottom line, she didn't want to work when we needed her. We'll replace her with someone who will."

"But she's a Tour Three employee. Don't you think you ought to ask them what kind of worker she is?"

"That's enough Farley. I've already made up my mind. Come back when you want to talk to me about someone you can legally represent."

Paul stormed out of the office, angry but determined to see justice served.

Lunch with Emma at Big Boy was nice, but a little strange. Emma had the soup and salad bar, and picked away at her salad, leaving over half of what was on her plate. Paul had a burger and fries. The conversation was friendly, but muted. At times Paul got the feeling Emma wished in her heart things had worked out with him. Perhaps part of her still wanted him and she was making a conscious effort to suppress any such feelings. Then again, maybe Paul was imagining these things.

In any event, the trip to the Main was fruitful. They got copies of Emma's clearance from the medical unit. Then Paul went on to the Injury Comp department and talked to a gentleman who filled out a 3971 authorizing COP for Tawanna and signed it right then and there.

When Paul got in to work at 8:30 he approached the afternoon shift supervisor in the letter hand cases. Sharon Demarco said she hated to lose Lashawn Wyatt; she was a conscientious worker with good attendance. But she declined to put her opinion in writing. "I know how much clout Newton has around here. If I write the statement you want, Lashawn will still be fired and I'll just get heat for supporting her. There's really nothing I can do, and nothing you can do either. Maybe after some time passes, Lashawn can ask that her record be cleared and she can get another eighty-nine day appointment down the road. Tell her I wish her good luck."

Paul wasn't done. He wrote a three page typewritten letter to Plant Manager Norm Bradford on Lashawn's behalf. He included all of the circumstances. He contrasted her reason for leaving with those who claimed they were sick. This part was carefully worded to avoid implicating any individual. He wrote "Maybe one or two were sick, but don't you think Lashawn had a better reason for leaving, and was more honest, than some of those who left?" He asked Bradford to talk to Sharon Demarco. "She would not go out of her way to upset the apple cart by putting anything in writing, but if you approach her personally, I think you'll find you're losing a valuable employee in Lashawn Wyatt."

This is the kind of situation Paul lived for. He was fighting injustice. The odds might be long; some might even say he was tilting at windmills. But he knew he was right. Even if his personal life was disappointing, he truly felt alive when he was fighting for someone like Lashawn. There was a spring in his step as he walked to the office to place the letter in Bradford's in box.

A few days later, Paul was holding a Step One with Newton about his altering of Tawanna's medical documentation. Newton denied the grievance, saying he was only writing down what the doctor dictated over the phone. "And by the way," Newton added, "Norm Bradford sent me the letter you wrote him about Lashawn Wyatt. He said it was up to me to handle, and I've already made that decision. She's fired, and she stays fired. But I have a bone to pick with you. You didn't write that letter to Bradford on the clock, did you? Were we paying you to represent a casual?"

"No sir," Paul lied.

"Good. You know we would have to take some kind of action against you if you abused your union time and handled that on the clock."

Paul left the room shaking his head. The good feeling that came from fighting the good fight was replaced by frustration and despair. Lashawn was a good worker, and a good person. Paul had anticipated a better outcome, since it was in management's interest to retain a good employee. But it was not to be. His rotten mood was a jumble of his anger at Newton, compassion for Lashawn, and the blow to his ego that came with failure. It was hardly the first time Paul had experienced this combination of emotions.

The Friday before the Super Bowl, Angela and Paul both had

their Step Two Meetings at the Main. Paul revised his work schedule to start at midnight and work until 8:30 am, so he would be on the clock for his 8:00 meeting with Nancy Barber. Angela was to meet with Nathan Zimmer. Afterwards they were going to meet for breakfast at Big Boy.

Paul argued his heart out for Tawanna. Newton had no business trying to pressure her back to work. A weaker person than Tawanna might have caved in, and possibly injured herself further. And it was unethical to pressure the doctor into changing his work restrictions.

Nancy Barber held to the position that all Newton had done was "obtain clarification" from the doctor. That was perfectly okay in her opinion. And, in any case, Tawanna wasn't forced in as it turned out, so no harm was done.

Paul felt there was a time when Nancy Barber would have been appalled by Newton's behavior, and would have met with Newton's boss to talk about it. The political climate within management was different now. That was why the grievance was denied.

Nathan Zimmer denied Angela's grievance about Teresa Matson's termination for working through pain without reporting it. "Once we start overturning the firing of probationaries, we open up a whole can of worms. Everyone else who doesn't make probation will file grievances, EEOs, whatever. We'll never see the end of it. We have to be consistent. When you're fired on probation, you're fired. She may have been a good kid, like you say. But I'm denying your grievance."

When Paul finished his pancakes, and while Angela was still working on her ham and cheese omelet, Paul said, "I've got the title of my next article for the Commentator. It's called 'Insanity Reigns.' And I have the opening lines: 'Let's get rid of some good employees. If the doctor says you can work, we won't let you work. If you doctor says you can't work, we'll pressure you to work. Yes brothers and sisters, insanity reigns at the North Suburban P&DC nowadays. And the most insane person of all is an MDO on Tour One who shall remain nameless…' "

Seventeen: THE SUPERVISOR SHUFFLE

July, 1997

Defense Lawyer: What kind of discipline did you get over Celia Derringer's pay issue?
Witness: I got a 14-day suspension.
Defense Lawyer: Was there anything unusual about the manner in which the discipline was issued?
Witness: Mr. Newton went out of his way to humiliate me.

It was a hot sticky day, and the building did not cool off much at night. Clouds had moved in overhead, sealing in the day's heat. The humidity was rising and rain was threatening. The Plant's air conditioning system didn't seem to be having much affect, and the fans were just blowing the hot air around.

Rachel Parker was in the Union Office complaining about the heat. Ron Davidson tried a little humor to cheer her up.

"This is all the result of a union grievance, you know. Back in January we had that big snow followed by days of sub-zero temperatures. People complained to us, so we filed a grievance about the weather. It was denied at Steps One and Two and went up to Step Three in Chicago. They settled the case in March and it started warming up. But just like with everything else they do, management went overboard. Now we've got this extreme heat and humidity. I'll file a grievance for you, but I can't guarantee they won't go too far in the other direction by the time December gets here."

"You're crazy," Rachel said, shaking her head as she left the room. But she was smiling a little, in spite of herself.

Paul entered the room a few minutes later.

"I just came from the SHIT. I've got a class action grievance that will get the PTFs some money. Collier hasn't been giving them Level Five for doing breakdown. When they feed and sweep

169

the DBCSs, we know that's Level Four. But when the trucks are unloaded, they have to determine which mail goes to which DBCS, and that requires more knowledge of the mail.

"I had Collier call Lawrence Harris and Shirley Jones and they confirmed it. So now he's paying them an hour of Level Five per day."

"That's not a lot of money, is it Paul? Something like seventy-five cents per day?"

"The point is, when people are treated like those PTFs at the SHIT, it's an insult to short them even a few pennies. It may not be much, but the union is doing something for them."

"So it's a victory of principle, eh?" said Ron.

"That's right. And then there's the issue of back pay. Some of these PTFs have been working eight to ten months. Seventy-five cents a day going back that far adds up to something. I held a Step One with Collier and he said it was untimely, that I could only go back fourteen days asking for back pay. I can't accept that. I'm going up to Step Two, but first I'm going to talk to Newton."

Angela walked in the room and Ron said, "Hey Angela, you wanna hear something funny?"

"No," she said."

"I'm telling you anyway. Paul thinks he can convince Newton to give the SHIT mail processors ten months of Level Five back pay."

"What kind of drugs are you on this week?" she asked Paul.

"Hey, you can't assume the worst before you start. You've got to present each case as if you are dealing with a reasonable manager who might settle with you. I learned that in steward training years ago. You never know, depending on the phases of the moon or something, Newton might decide to do the right thing."

"And if not," Ron said, "you can imagine his face in the middle of the target next time you go to the gun range."

"I do that anyway."

The talk then turned to the shuffling of supervisors that had started when Collier went to the SHIT, which set off a chain reaction. The latest move was that Reggie Green asked for the position in Flats to get weekend off and got it. Then they gave Stacey Kline the 110 Belt job Reggie vacated. Once Stacey got the position, they turned around and changed the off days so she had weekends off, too.

"Reggie's really pissed," Ron said. "He never would've left the belt if he knew he could get weekends off there."

"Can he appeal through NAPS?" Angela asked. "Isn't that what they call the supervisors' union?"

"I don't understand exactly how their appeal process works," Ron said, "But I know one thing. Their union rep is none other than James Newton. It'll never get anywhere if Reggie tries to appeal."

Paul and Angela couldn't believe it, so Ron explained.

"I heard the NAPS members at the Plant were afraid not to vote for Newton. So now they get no representation against their own boss, and Newton gets a few more perks, like an occasional trip to Washington for a little lobbying and some sightseeing."

"What do you think's going on with Newton and Stacey?" Paul asked. "I've heard some rumors."

"I don't know for sure," Ron said, "but I think those rumors are true. They've been pretty discrete about it so far, but this latest supervisor shuffle is going to fuel the fire."

The next topic of discussion was whether Stacey was a natural blond. Paul and Ron said she was, but Angela thought she used hair color.

"I've been coloring my hair," Paul said, "but I do it selectively. Every month I color a few more hairs gray. Have you noticed it?"

"It's very becoming," Angela said.

Paul then noticed the new poster on the wall. "Who put that one up?" he asked.

The poster read, "I can only please one person per day. Today is not your day. Tomorrow doesn't look good either."

The other stewards didn't know where it came from either.

Angela didn't like the new addition to the room's decor.

"I can understand that whatever steward put that up gets frustrated sometimes. We all do. But it sends the wrong message to the people we represent."

Just then Celia Derringer came to the office without knocking. Since Angela had a Step One to handle at the BOBB and Paul wanted to talk to Newton about back pay at the SHIT, Ron talked to Celia. She looked like she had been crying.

"I've just got a letter from Finance. They want to take seven hundred thirteen dollars away from me. I had a week of jury duty in March, and I took court leave. They say they sent me a letter in April and another in May asking me to turn in the fifteen dollars a day I was paid by the court. I never got the letter in April. I did get the one in May and wrote them a check for seventy-five dollars. I guess they never received it, but I don't know 'cause I haven't tried to balance my check book since then. I've got a big credit card balance to pay off and I really can't afford this right now. Why can't I just pay the seventy-five dollars now? Why do I have to pay back the court leave they gave me?"

"You work in Flats now, right? I'll talk to Reggie and see what I can do."

It was just before five when the three stewards got back together. Angela had gotten Shirley Jones to drop a Letter of Warning down to a documented discussion. "I surprised myself with that one," she said.

"No, you're just good," Paul said. "You don't realize how good you are."

Ron had talked to Reggie Green about Celia's court leave. Reggie was sympathetic but said he couldn't resolve it without an okay from Finance. He volunteered to call them when their department opened at 0800 and plead Celia's case. Reggie was hopeful it could be resolved without a grievance.

But the best news came from Paul's meeting with Newton.

"At first he was giving me all this crap about timeliness. He said 'You're an experienced steward, Farley. You know you've got fourteen days to file a grievance.' But it turned out that wasn't the real problem. Newton said the pay adjustments would be an administrative nightmare. For each PTF, a separate pay adjustment would be needed for each week of each Pay Period. Some of the PTFs would need as many as forty different pay adjustments. With something like sixty people involved, it would take forever. He said the man-hours required to process the pay adjustments are worth more than the few pennies the PTFs would get.

"But I found a way to solve the problem. I said let's not do separate pay adjustments for each week. Let's issue each PTF one lump sum check that estimates the amount of money they lost. We'll use a formula of seven-fifty per Pay Period. Some will get a check for ninety dollars, some seventy-five, whatever. It won't be exactly what they're owed, but it'll be close. I'll do the calculations and you or Collier can double check them. The amount of money won't be huge, but neither will the paperwork. And it'll improve morale at the SHO – I almost blew it by saying SHIT."

"And Newton *went* for it?" Angela asked, wide-eyed.

"Newton went for it."

"Will wonders never cease."

A week later Ron Davidson talked to a frustrated Reggie Green. "I can't get anywhere with Finance," Reggie said. "It's like talking to a brick wall. They're going to take the money out of the next two checks. But don't bother filing a grievance. I've got a way to even things out. I'll fill out a 1260 crediting her with working twelve hours OT in each of the next two Pay Periods. Timekeeping will process it as if she had worked those hours. That'll be twenty-four hours at time-and-a-half or the equivalent of thirty-six hours straight time. That plus the seventy-five dollars on the check they never cashed should just about make her even."

Ron was stunned. It was a rare supervisor who would stick his neck out like this to correct an injustice done to one of his employees. All he could say was, "You're a good man, Reggie."

But three weeks later, Reggie was in hot water. Someone in timekeeping had gotten suspicious about Celia's authorization for twelve hours overtime the second Pay Period in a row. It had come to the attention of Jim Newton, who had reamed Reggie Green out.

"Don't you know this is falsification," he screamed. "You could get fired for this, and that's just what I should do!"

In the end, Green was given a suspension. There was something unusual about it though. Normally, disciplines given to supervisors were either Letters of Warning or "paper suspensions," in which the discipline was entered into the supervisor's file but they never missed any time from work. That way the supervisor wasn't publicly embarrassed. Management liked to discipline their own quietly, so as not to undermine the supervisor's respect in the eyes of those he supervised. But this one was different. Newton gave Green a 14 day suspension, and actually had him off work without pay for two weeks. And he made sure word leaked out to the workroom floor that there was an issue of falsification involved.

"Isn't there anything Reggie can do about that?" Angela asked, as the three stewards talked about it on a hot August night.

"Sure there is," said Ron. "He can talk to his union rep – Jim Newton."

Eighteen: THE REMOVAL

September, 1997

Prosecutor: How would you characterize the series of events leading up to Clarence Day's removal grievance being ruled untimely?
Witness: That was dirty, even for Newton.
Prosecutor: What was the defendant's reaction?
Witness: He was steaming.

It hurt him just as much as if a girlfriend he really cared about had dumped him for another guy. There was an awful feeling in the pit of his stomach. It wasn't logical. There was no way to explain why it bothered him so much. But Paul couldn't accept the fact that his number one grievant, Tawanna Chambers, had gone into management.

"I need the money, Paul," she explained. "We bought a new house in Southfield and we've got steep mortgage payments and higher utility bills. I understand how bad management is here, but I'm going to be different. I won't mess with people. I'll be like Reggie."

"Yeah, and look what they're doing to Reggie."

"Well I'll be careful, Paul. I won't falsify anyone's pay, but I'll try to work with people. You'll see, it'll be okay. And we'll still be friends, of course."

Paul thought Tawanna understood there was a sharp line between labor and management, a line she should never cross. He had seen other people go into management saying they would be people-friendly bosses, only to change completely under pressure from Newton.

Another part of his reaction was, he had to admit, kind of messed up. He made it a point never to have a manager or 204-B as a girlfriend; that would compromise his role as a steward. But

175

he still had a lot of desire for Tawanna, even if it wasn't realistic to act on it. By crossing. that line, Tawanna punctured his fantasy.

Angela understood the first part of his reaction, and intuitively sensed more than he realized about the second. She tried to cheer him up.

"I know you'll miss your number one coming back here, Paul. But you'll still get to see her. She'll probably be a little soft when you handle attendance discipline with her. And once you find a new number one you'll be ahead – you'll have a favorite supervisor *and* a favorite grievant."

Just then the door opened and Clarence Day burst in.With his beret, his military fatigues, and the angry glare on his face, he looked intimidating. Even though his anger was directed elsewhere, Paul's heart skipped a beat.

"Do something about this bullshit," he demanded, throwing a couple of sheets of paper on the table. "And don't let Davidson get his hands on it, either!"

As Paul feared, it was a Notice of Removal. Fifteen minutes later, Paul was back in the room with Clarence's 3972 (attendance chart), which he had obtained from Butch Hobson. For 1997 there were four instances of sick leave totaling 40 hours, two latenesses, and two instances of emergency annual. Seven of the eight instances had occurred before May 31st. The only recent absence was an emergency of some sort.

"You know what my last absence was? My uncle's funeral! Back around Memorial Day I knew my attendance was getting close to the edge, so I did what I had to do. I started being 'regular in attendance.' I hadn't missed in three months. But I had to go to that funeral. My mother isn't as strong as she used to be, physically or emotionally, and her brother's death really tore her up. I had to be there to support her. And I only took one day. She needed me around for a *week*."

"I'm going to do a lot of work on this, Clarence. I'm going to send to Finance for your clock rings going back to when you returned from suspension in early December. I'm sure you've worked a lot of hours since then. I'll calculate your sick leave percentage, and I'll bet it's no worse than the Plant average, which is close to five percent. I'll argue that it's not proper to punish you for the funeral. I remember Newton giving testimony at an EEO hearing to that effect. I still have the transcript. Your record isn't that bad this year. I think we can win this case."

"That sounds good," said Clarence. "When will we meet with Hobson?"

"I'm going to take my time. I want to get the clock rings, get all my information, get all my arguments prepared. Today is September second. We have until the sixteenth – that's a Tuesday. I'll try to be ready by the end of next week. I want to do it right."

Paul had another conversation with Butch Hobson the following day. Hobson was a little defensive about citing the funeral, but pointed out that it wasn't immediate family, like a parent or child.

That got Paul upset, but he exhibited a controlled anger that was quite effective. He asked how can you judge how close a particular family member is. Some people are almost as close to their aunts and uncles as to their parents, while others hardly ever see these relatives. Besides, his mother was falling apart and needed support.

That put Hobson back on the defensive and he said he'd give it some thought. But he pointed out that Clarence had been absent quite a bit before June, and he could've been removed then. "It's kind of hard to let that slide, Paul," he said. "Mr. Newton wouldn't be happy if we did that."

Paul figured out what was going on. If Clarence went until November without getting further discipline, he would have all prior discipline removed from his record. Management didn't want him to go scot-free. But since June 1st, Clarence had made a determined effort to avoid absences. Knowing this, management must have already decided that the next time he missed they would fire him. When he missed work for the funeral, they knew it wasn't the ideal absence to nail him for, but they were afraid they might not get another chance.

Paul felt he could move Hobson to save Clarence's job, depending on whether Newton allowed him to settle. He planned to argue hard to expunge the removal, based on all the arguments he had prepared. He would have a full discussion, maybe arguing this position for about half-an-hour. If he couldn't convince Hobson to expunge it, he had a fall-back position. He would propose an unusual kind of settlement. Management would rescind the removal if the union agreed to alter the settlement of the prior discipline which would clear Clarence's record in November. He would propose adding six months to it, and he would even be flexible about that time frame. That would alleviate what Paul perceived to be management's legitimate concern – that after having years of poor attendance, and after having shaky attendance up until the end of May, Clarence could go a few more months without missing work and wipe out all of his previous suspensions. With this proposal, Clarence would have to go a long time with good attendance. He would have to prove himself to get his record cleared.

By the end of the week Paul received the clock rings he requested. It would take some time to do the mathematical calculations, but at first glance it looked pretty good. He mentioned to Hobson that he might have something interesting to tell him about Clarence Day's sick leave percentage when they held their Step One. Hobson said okay, but he neglected to mention he was going on Annual Leave the following week.

On September 13th Paul Farley and Clarence Day met again to go over their strategy one final time. They would have to hold the Step One on September 16th, Hobson's first day back. Clarence fully understood and agreed with Paul's strategy. He also explained in detail everything he remembered about his absences. One of his latenesses was back in February when his furnace blew up and he stayed home until the new one was installed. He had the receipts. The other lateness was when he was pulled over by the Troy police on his way to work.

"Did they give you a ticket," Paul asked.

"No, my only offense was Driving While Black. They were hassling me for no reason, Paul. When they let me go, I didn't even have a piece of paper to show why I was late."

There was one other point Paul wanted to raise, but he wasn't sure how. It wasn't really relevant, but it could affect the case. Ron Davidson had told Paul and Angela that he heard that Clarence had asked Stacey Kline out. Given the relationship between Stacey and Newton, that could give Newton a strong attitude. Angela expressed disbelief, as Clarence didn't seem like the type who would chase white women. Paul wasn't sure, but wouldn't rule it out.

"You know, Angela, I would never ask out any supervisor, but I could almost make an exception for Stacey. She just has an appeal that transcends those barriers."

Whether it was true or not, Paul worried that if Newton had heard the rumor, he would tell Hobson to really put the screws to Clarence. And Ron's information usually came from an inside source, which meant if Ron heard this rumor, it was likely that Newton had heard it too.

Now, in the union office with Clarence, Paul broached the subject carefully, without revealing where he heard the rumor. Clarence denied it completely.

"Since I separated from my wife, I've only had one girlfriend. She's all I need, believe me. And in any case, I'm not stupid enough to make a play for Newton's bitch."

"When Paul came in at 8:30 PM on Monday night for Tuesday

September 16th, everything seemed normal. His supervisor, Reggie Green, wasn't due in until midnight. The Pay Location had Flat Sorting Machine operators who started at midnight and a few manual throwers like Paul who worked 8:30 to 5:00. The supervisor reported with the majority of the crew. At 8:30 Paul reported to the afternoon shift supervisor and went on union business. Hobson and Clarence Day weren't due in until after midnight, so Paul took care of some other cases and once again reviewed every document and all of his notes in the Clarence Day file.

There were two surprises after midnight. The first was that Reggie Green had annual leave for the day and Lawrence Harris was running flats. Lawrence told Paul he could stay on union business for now, and Lawrence would call him back if mail got heavy.

The other surprise was that Hobson was nowhere to be found. This was the 14th day; if a grievance wasn't filed today it would be untimely. Paul went into the manager's office and found Newton sitting at his desk.

"I need an extension on the time limits for Clarence Day's grievance. Hobson wasn't here all of last week and he isn't in today, which is the 14th day. I can meet with him when he comes back."

"Don't worry Paul. I just talked to Hobson on the phone. He had a little emergency but he expects to be in by two, three o' clock at the latest. You don't need an extension."

At two-thirty Paul was paged back to the work area by Lawrence Harris, who explained flats were heavy and he was needed to throw mail. "In fact, mail is heavy throughout the building tonight."

Paul explained that he needed to meet with Butch Hobson on a grievance that would be untimely if no meeting were held today. He asked Lawrence to inform him when Hobson came in. Any time Lawrence could release him for the Step One meeting would be fine. And if Lawrence couldn't release him long enough to have the meeting, Paul requested five minutes once Hobson got in so he could get a written extension. Paul was willing to cooperate with Lawrence as long as it didn't jeopardize his grievance. Lawrence said he understood.

At three o' clock there was an announcement over the PA system that all clerks on the 8:30 - 5:00 shift would be scheduled for overtime – four hours for people on the Desired Overtime List and two hours for non-list employees. Paul was non-list, so he was scheduled to work until 0700.

At 3:30, Paul heard Jim Newton's voice paging Butch Hobson to the Manager's Office. Since Hobson was obviously in, Paul approached Lawrence Harris and asked about the Step One Meeting.

"This is what I'm going to do," Lawrence said. "I'll keep you here in flats until we get our 5:00 dispatch out. After that you'll be on overtime, but we'll mostly be catching up on our third class mail. I can let you do your Step One then."

That sounded like a workable plan to Paul.

At five minutes to five, Elliott Drummond made another announcement on the PA system. "There's a change in the overtime call for the eight-thirty to five shift. There is no overtime for non-list employees. Employees on the Desired Overtime List will stay for two hours. Thank you."

Paul bolted from his work area without asking permission. He went to the supervisor's desk in Butch Hobson's area, but Hobson was nowhere to be found. The employees were busily rolling mail out to the dock. In fact, the whole building was frantically pushing mail from various areas towards the dock, trying to get the dispatch done in something close to a timely fashion.

Paul ran to the Manager's Office. Newton wasn't there, but Drummond was.

"I need an extension on a grievance, Mr. Drummond. I was supposed to meet with Butch Hobson today but he was late coming in. I was called back to Flats. Lawrence said he'd release me on overtime, but now you've canceled it."

"I canceled the overtime because good employees like yourself worked hard and got a lot of mail out. We appreciate it."

"But I need an extension for just one day. I'll write it out, and I'd appreciate it if you would sign it."

"You really should approach the supervisor," Drummond said.

"But I just looked and couldn't find him. Can you get him in here for me?"

Drummond limped over to his desk and sat down. He'd been favoring his left leg a lot recently. Sometimes he tried to hide the problem with his leg, but he made no such effort now. He sat down facing Paul and spoke again.

"Now is not a good time to work this out, Farley. Some areas are still dispatching. Take it up with Hobson tomorrow, I'm sure he'll understand. If not, you can talk to Jim Newton to get it straightened out. He's more involved with this case than I am. But right now it's five o' clock and time for you to punch out. We're not paying you overtime to do something you could do at straight time tomorrow."

Paul went to his area and punched out but he did not leave the building. He looked all over for Hobson or Newton and couldn't find either one. He went to the Union Office, which was empty. Evidently Angela and Ron had been summoned to their work areas due to the mail volume. Paul paged Hobson over the PA system, asking him to call the Union Office. There was no response.

At five-thirty an extremely frustrated Paul Farley left the Plant. Something was extremely fishy. He was worried sick about Clarence Day's job. He went home to bed, but could not sleep.

Nineteen: THE FLY

*Prosecutor: How did the defendant react to the denial of
Clarence Day's grievance?*
Witness: The defendant threatened Mr. Newton's life.

The light on Maple Road turned yellow. Paul hit the accelerator
and made it through the intersection. He told himself he had
timed it just right, or close enough. Then he saw the flashing light
on top of the police car and pulled over.

"God damn it," he shouted. He was running late for work, and
now he would be late for sure. That was one reason he had tried
to beat the light. The other was that he had a bad habit of driving
aggressively when he was angry about something. It had gotten
him a few tickets in the past.

September 16th had not been a good day for Paul. He went to
bed about 6:30 AM after the fiasco with Clarence Day's grievance,
but was up at ten, having tossed and turned more than slept. Since
he couldn't sleep, he made a pot of coffee so at least he'd be alert.
But he was already a bundle of nerves – he was worried sick about
the removal grievance. The caffeine got him wired up even more.
He was certain the overtime call, Lawrence's decision to keep him
in Flats until 0500, and Hobson and Newton's disappearance had
been carefully planned. He paced back and forth in his living room.
As he paced, he started doing a monologue out loud, directed at
Jim Newton. "You asshole. You were out to get Clarence Day.
You don't care that he had to go to his uncle's funeral. You don't
care about any human being. You're the scum of the earth. The
scum of the earth!"

Anyone hearing his monologue would think he was crazy. Paul
didn't care. He also didn't care that he'd promised himself to stop
doing this when he was angry. It never made him feel any better.

He realized he needed to calm down. He also realized he shouldn't jump to the conclusion that he wouldn't be able to hold a timely Step One. Maybe it would all be straightened out tonight, as Elliott Drummond had indicated. He thought about times in the past he had worried for hours about something he feared would happen. Often it turned out he was worrying for no reason. But he had a bad feeling about this one. His sixth sense told him Newton was up to his dirty tricks. And this time, a man's job was at stake.

He really wanted to call Angela. Talking to her would make him feel better. But she probably was asleep by now. Why wake her, especially since there was nothing to be done until he went to work in the evening.

He couldn't concentrate on anything that required logical thought. He decided to occupy his time by doing some housework. He put Springsteen's "Tunnel of Love" CD on and scrubbed the bathroom sink and bathtub. He washed the mirror above the sink and then did the floor. He washed the kitchen floor for the first time in he didn't remember how long. Then he went to K-Mart and bought some white socks to wear with the gym shoes that were always on his feet. They came six pairs to a package. He needed new ones because some of his socks had holes in the toes (maybe he should cut his toenails more often).

These chores partly got his mind off the Clarence Day situation. He wasn't consciously thinking about it, but his mood was very much affected. It was like there was a cloud over him. He couldn't laugh or smile. He was sleepwalking through these simple chores.

He sat down at his computer to play solitaire. But the game did not take his mind off the situation at work. Whenever Paul played solitaire, he imagined he was playing against Jim Newton. In his mind, Jim had challenged him to try to win one game out of five (these rules gave him a reasonable chance). At stake was some grievance – whatever was on the table at the time – and pride. If Paul got nowhere in the first game, he imagined Newton smiling at his misfortune. If he came close in another game, only to get stuck because one key card was still covered, Newton would enjoy his frustration. If Paul belatedly noticed a mistake ("Damn, I should've put the seven of clubs on that red eight"), Newton would be laughing at him. But if after losing four games he pulled the fifth one out, Paul would smile broadly and Newton's big ego would be deflated. It was, truthfully speaking, kind of a sick game, but one that Paul played frequently. Today he was losing.

He went to a local diner for an early dinner. Years of living alone had taught him where all the good neighborhood diners were. Not the really nice restaurants where it would be awkward to go by yourself, but the decent ones. He sat at the counter and didn't say a word to the waitress after ordering his pork chops and apple sauce.

At five o' clock he realized he needed a little sleep or he surely wouldn't do Clarence any good. He went down to the bar in his basement, drank a shot of whiskey, and lay down again. He set the alarm for 7:30 but it didn't go off. He woke with a start at a few minutes before 8:00 – it turned out the alarm was set for 7:30 AM instead of PM. It seems when one thing goes wrong, everything does. He splashed some water on his face, put some deodorant on his underarms, and started out for work. If he hurried there was a chance he could make it without being late.

It was completely irrational. His attendance was good enough that he could afford to be late. He should have called in to work, told them he would be about half-an-hour late, and taken his time. He felt stupid when the cops pulled him over and gave him a ticket.

The Tour 3 supervisor in Flats had him fill out a 3971 for being late. Then Paul stayed in his work area and threw mail until lunch time.

Reggie Green released him for union business after lunch. He headed straight for Butch Hobson's area. Hobson didn't wait for Paul to speak; he knew what Paul wanted.

"It's untimely, Paul," he said. "If you want an extension, talk to Newton."

Ten minutes later Paul was sitting across from Newton. He

looked at the sign saying "The Buck Stops Here." He looked at the picture of Newton and his wife, and wondered about Stacey Kline. Then he saw the beginning of a smirk – just a slight upturn of the lips – on Newton's face. He had seen that look before. It was not a good sign.

"Mr. Newton, yesterday I requested an extension on Clarence Day's grievance. You said I could see Hobson before 0500, but Lawrence Harris didn't release me. I'm asking for a one day extension right now. A man's job is at stake."

"Fourteen days is fourteen days, Farley. The grievance is untimely. I can't start bending the rules, especially for someone who never came to work."

"But the only absence in the last few months was for his uncle's funeral. That's what triggered the discipline. That's really not fair. You even testified at Earnestine Hall's EEO hearing that *funerals* are *not* to be used in discipline."

"That was for immediate family, Farley. Mother or father, son or daughter, husband or wife. You know your FMLA, don't you?"

Paul realized it would be fruitless to point out that the Family & Medical Leave Act had nothing to do with funerals. He realized there was no point in appealing to Newton's sense of humanity. So he tried to address the procedural issue.

"Mr. Newton, the reason for the fourteen day time limit is so the union won't surprise management with a grievance that comes out of the blue. You know, an employee gets sore at a supervisor and digs up an incident from two months ago to file a grievance on. This isn't like that. I told Hobson week before last that I'd be analyzing Clarence's sick leave percentage before I held the Step One – and by the way, Clarence's sick leave percentage is lower than the Plant average. Anyway, Hobson never told me he was going on vacation. If I had known, I might have held the Step One before he left. And yesterday I approached you for an extension when the grievance was still timely. You assured me I didn't need one. Then Harris didn't release me. If ever there was a situation that justified an extension, it's this one."

"I don't see it that way Farley."

"A man's job is on the line, Mr. Newton. Please, just give him a chance to have the case heard on its merits. Even if it is denied at Step One, let Clarence have his day in court higher up."

"You know, you could have turned the case over to Ron Davidson yesterday. He could have met with Hobson after five."

"That's ridiculous. I did all the work on the case. And anyway, when I looked in the Union Office after five I couldn't find Davidson."

"That's a shame, Farley. A real shame."

"Please, just sign an extension."

"I won't sign an extension. For one thing, there were several days before Hobson went on vacation that you could have met with him. It's not my fault you put it off until the last minute. And if we grant him an extension, soon *everyone* will be asking for extensions. I'm going strictly by the procedures, Farley. There will be *no* extension."

Paul just stared at Newton. The corners of his mouth were turned up a little bit more. Paul couldn't stand the smugness with which Newton disposed of Clarence Day's career and all logical arguments.

"And by the way, Farley," Newton added, "if you don't want to end up like Day, make sure you get to work on time. I understand you were late today."

Paul just glared at the person across the desk. All he could think of was what a rotten excuse for a human being Newton was.

Paul knew that unionism was not about a contest of egos between supervisors and stewards. That there was no point in trying to out-macho management. That Newton was trying to get him to lose his temper and enjoyed watching him squirm.

Paul knew that the best thing he could do with this grievance was write it up to Step Two, explaining all the circumstances, and hope for the best. He knew real unionism involved coworkers helping each other and showing solidarity. It had very little to do with stewards having personal confrontations with managers behind closed doors.

Paul knew all of these things, but none of that mattered. Right now, all he could think of was how much he hated the man who was just sitting there with that smirk on his face. Paul just kept glaring at him.

Then a fly landed on the desk, closer to Paul than to Newton. Paul stared at the fly. Far better to take out his aggressions on this insect than on Newton. He extended his arms, palms inward, about a foot-and-a-half apart. They were six inches above the table. He did this gradually. He very slowly brought his palms closer together, about a foot apart, with the fly in the middle. Then suddenly and rapidly, he clapped his hands together once, with a good deal of force. Newton jumped from the noise. Paul turned up his palms. There was a dead fly in his left hand.

"It's a trick my father taught me," Paul explained. "Most people would slap their hand down on the table where the fly was resting. That doesn't work. It flies away before your hand hits the table. You miss the fly, and hurt your hand in the process. But if you clap your hands above the fly's head, the fly's instinct is to go straight up as soon as it senses danger. If you time it right, you'll catch the fly between your hands. It seems stupid – the fly would be safe staying where it is. But it works more often than not. The trick is not to scare it away when you're getting your hands in position."

"That's very interesting Farley."

Then Paul was moved by a crazy impulse. He stood and leaned across the desk, extending his arms in Newton's direction. As Newton watched, Paul slowly brought his hands closer together, then slammed them palm to palm, right over Newton's head. Newton flinched. For a moment Newton stared at Paul in disbelief. Then the confident half-grin returned. "Sit down for a moment," he said. He opened the door to Elliott Drummond's office and asked Drummond to get another male supervisor to come with

Drummond to Newton's office.

When Drummond and Lawrence Harris entered the office, Newton addressed Paul Farley.

"You showed me your technique for killing a fly. Then you tried the same technique on me. That constituted a threat on my life. You are being placed on emergency suspension, pending charges of removal. Mr. Drummond and Mr. Harris will escort you from the building. You are not to return unless notified. The Notice of Removal will be sent to you by certified mail."

Twenty: SOLIDARITY

Late September, 1997

Defense Lawyer: Did you blame the defendant for your grievance being untimely?
Witness: No I blamed Mr. Newton. He hated me and I hated him.

"I'm going to handle your grievance personally, Paul."

Joanna Carver was trying to reassure Paul Farley as they talked at the Union Office in Ferndale. She sat behind her cluttered desk in an expensive executive style chair that had been purchased during the Humphrey administration. The fancy chair made her uncomfortable; it clashed with her style of unionism. But here, on the afternoon of September 17th, there was a lot more to feel uncomfortable about. She wished she could just reach out across the desk and tell Paul she was absolutely certain everything was going to be all right. But Joanna was a straight shooter. The only assurance she could give was that she would put all her energy into helping him.

"I don't often handle a Step One grievance but I'll do this one and I'll write up the Step Two. This Local will do everything in our power to fight your emergency suspension and removal. It's not just an unfair discipline, it's an attack on the union." She leaned back in her chair. "But first let's talk about the case you're handling for Clarence Day."

"If the grievance is untimely," Paul said, "we might have to go through other channels. Do you think filing charges with the NLRB about the way the Step One was handled would help?"

"I don't know, Paul. The NLRB will ask whether we filed a separate Article Fifteen grievance. If we said no, they would tell us to file. The NLRB would then wait to see what happened to the grievance. If our Business Agent signed off on some language

191

about both parties cooperating in the scheduling of timely Step One Meetings in the future, then the NLRB would defer. That is, they'd say the dispute was voluntarily settled to both parties' satisfaction, so there's no reason for the NLRB to pursue it. Of course, I could call the Business Agent and ask him not to settle for anything less than that Clarence Day's grievance be considered timely. Management would deny it and it would be certified for arbitration. Then the NLRB would defer to whatever the arbitrator decided.

"So we could just file a separate Article Fifteen grievance without wasting our time with the NLRB. The problem is, this is a contractual grievance, so it will take years to be heard. The grievance you're filing on the removal will get to arbitration long before that. If we win that case, we don't need the contractual grievance. On the other hand, if an arbitrator upholds the removal, it'll be hard to get another arbitrator to reverse it on procedural grounds years later."

Paul was glum.

"There was a time I would have suggested Clarence go to EEO," he said, "but now I know better. You have to have another employee who is in the exact same position, or 'similarly situated' as they say. We'd have to go out and kill the uncle of one of the white guys in Hobson's Pay Location and see if the absence for the funeral is cited in discipline."

Joanna didn't smile.

"I know the best way to handle timeliness," she said. "On the Step Two Form in the space for 'date of the Step One Meeting,' write "Supervisor refused to hold Step One.' That's pretty much what happened. You've written that before, I know. Usually it's when a supervisor says, 'Go away Paul, don't bother me.' This is a little different. Write out a detailed statement about your efforts to hold a Step One or to get an extension. We'll include it in the grievance package. Maybe we can get Labor Relations to accept the grievance as timely at Step Two. In any event, I guess you'll have plenty of time to work on that case, until we get you back to work."

"Okay, how do you think we should handle that," Paul asked.

"First, I'll make some phone calls. Bradford, Drummond, Labor Relations. See if I can talk some sense into any of them."

"The way I see it, Joanna, they don't have any kind of a case. I didn't threaten him. It was a silly thing to do, I guess, but it wasn't a threat on his life. Can't they see that?"

"You know what the Zero Tolerance Policy is Paul?"

"Sure, that's the policy they adopted after the wave of postal shootings a few years back. Any threat of violence, even if it's made as a joke, will be taken seriously. Is that what they're using?"

"I'm sure it is, Paul. I've heard of people in other parts of the country being fired under Zero Tolerance for some flimsy reasons. Sometimes they get ridiculous with it. You know, an employee tells a supervisor 'you drive a silver Cadillac Seville, don't you?' Management construes it as a threat to follow the supervisor home or do some damage to the car. They fire the employee. A lot of these cases are denied all the way up to arbitration. We win the more ridiculous ones, most of the time. But not always. I agree you really didn't threaten Newton with violence. He was never in fear for his life. He just wants to get rid of you and now he thinks he has a good excuse. But I'm not sure if the case goes to an arbitrator, you'll automatically get back to work with all your back pay. You've got a good chance, but it's not a slam dunk. So let's not rely on the grievance procedure alone."

"What else do have in mind?"

"Like I said, I'll get on the phone tomorrow and see if I can work it out informally. While I'm at it, I'll try to get Clarence's grievance declared timely. That was bullshit, the way they handled that.

"If I don't get anywhere this week, we'll start organizing your coworkers. When I made that part of my election campaign, it wasn't just a slogan. I'll start working on a flier – you can come by Monday and look at the final draft. We'll explain how putting

193

you off work was an attack on the union and an attack on each and every employee.

"Tour One has the strongest union presence at the Plant, and I think you've got a lot of support. The other stewards will help. We'll ask everyone to wear something black on Friday night as a sign of solidarity. Maybe some of your coworkers will come up with additional ways to get the message across to management. I'll hint at that in the flier without getting too specific."

Joanna rose from her chair and walked around her desk. "I'll hand out the fliers personally, starting at 8:30 PM. We'll ask Ron and Angela to help, but the main thing they can do is organize support inside. If they don't settle this thing when I call them this week, we need to really send management a message next week."

She gave Paul a hug and walked with him to the door. As he left the building, Paul felt the anger and frustration start to melt away. He was still nervous and uncertain. But it felt good to have the full support of his union.

Two days later the news wasn't good. Joanna called Paul at home and told him about the phone calls she'd made. As far as Clarence Day's grievance was concerned, Nancy Barber wouldn't commit to considering it timely. She said she'd look at the facts when Paul presented the case at Step Two. "I know he's not allowed in the Plant anymore," she had said, "but he can come here for the Step Two. After all, it wasn't *my* life he threatened."

Joanna wasn't the least bit amused by Nancy's remark – not when Ms. Barber was being so unhelpful.

As for Paul's removal, Nancy just said she'd look at the case when it got to Step 2. Joanna's calls to Bradford and Drummond proved no more fruitful. They wouldn't interfere with Paul's removal; there was a grievance procedure to determine if the discipline was for just cause.

On Saturday Paul received the certified envelope containing the Notice of Removal. Some people would've refused to sign for it and pretended they never got it. But Paul wasn't playing that game. He knew management would see to it that he received a copy one way or another. And he didn't want to play games; he wanted to fight.

He waited until he thought Angela would be awake and gave her a call at home. He got her answering machine.

Angela was on a double date with Ed Crawford, who she'd met at a barbecue in Aretha Simmons' backyard. He was Aretha's neighbor. Aretha's boyfriend was Sean White, a former TE who was now a PTF mail processor.

The four of them went to Belle Isle, a large park on a beautiful island in the middle of the Detroit River. It was a sunny day in the 60s, quite nice for what was actually the last day of summer. They walked around the island admiring the view. They could see the Renaissance Center and the rest of the Detroit skyline. Ed brought a camera and they took turns taking pictures of each other with the river and skyline in the background. Then they walked some more, stopping by the river's edge to throw small rocks into the water and watch the expanding circles. Eventually they settled down for a picnic lunch. After that Ed lay down on his back with Angela beside him, resting her head on his chest as she looked up at the beautiful sky. Aretha and Sean went for another walk. It was a great way to enjoy a beautiful day. They probably wouldn't see weather this nice again until spring.

Sunday morning Angela returned Paul's message. She apologized for not answering sooner, and told him about her day. Paul momentarily forgot his situation. Angela was always so secretive about her personal life that he was intrigued. As far as he knew, she never went out with anyone.

"Actually, Paul, he's the third guy I've been out with this year. But he's the first I went out with more than once."

"What does he look like?"

"He's fairly tall, and dark-skinned. He's got a nice face and a wonderful smile. He's pretty muscular, but he doesn't try to show it off. I like that. And what I really like is, there's nothing phony about him. He doesn't use a lot of come-on lines or anything like that. He's just real easy to talk to and to spend time with."

"Well maybe you've really found someone. If so, I'm happy for you. You're a great person Angela, and you deserve something good to happen to you."

"Hey, not so fast, Paul. We've only been out a few times. As far as I'm concerned, we're still just friends. He seems eager to push the relationship to the next level, but I'm not in a hurry to do that. I would enjoy a lot more days just like yesterday."

"My only advice, Angela, is keep an open mind and an open heart. If he's the right guy for you, then open up your heart and let him in. If he's a nice guy, but not quite the right one, then act accordingly. Just do what your heart tells you."

"Okay, Paul, thanks for the encouragement. But you probably called to talk about your situation. I'll have you know I didn't forget about it at all. We talked about it quite a bit while we walked all over Belle Isle yesterday. Ed wasn't too interested, but Aretha and Sean are outraged. If Ed hadn't asked us to stop talking about the PO, we would've come up with twenty-five different ways to torture Jim Newton."

Paul went on to tell her about the plans for the coming week, and Angela was enthusiastic about helping.

Paul couldn't resist one last remark about Angela's new boyfriend. "It's great to hear you so upbeat, Angela. This guy sounds like he's been good for you."

"Well, Paul, even if he turns out to be no more than a friend, it's good to get out and enjoy myself." Paul couldn't tell whether these cautious words were meant to keep Paul from jumping to conclusions, or to keep Angela's own emotions and expectations in check.

Later that day, Paul called Clarence and brought him up to date. He also urged Clarence to apply for unemployment benefits. There was still over a week before his removal took effect, and Paul urged him to apply on the first day. "If you get turned down, appeal and ask for a hearing, I'll be glad to represent you. From what I understand, if the PO doesn't send a representative to the hearing, you'll probably win. And even if they do send someone, you stand a good chance. It's not a kangaroo court like the grievance procedure at the PO."

Paul also told him he thought there was a 50-50 chance he could settle the grievance at Step 2. He didn't want to get Clarence's hopes up any higher than that.

Clarence thanked him. It was good that he didn't blame Paul for how his case had been handled. He understood the dirty game management was playing. He put the blame on "Fig Newton and Bitch Hobson."

<><><><><><>

The following Wednesday morning at 8:00 AM, Joanna Carver met with Newton on a Step One for Paul's removal. The meeting was a farce. Newton pretended he had been afraid for his life. It was all a ridiculous game. Joanna made her position clear, took notes on whatever Newton said, and left with a denial. She didn't let Newton get her upset. She hadn't expected anything positive to come out of this meeting. She just needed to meet with Newton before writing the grievance up to Step Two.

That night Joanna and Angela leafleted Tour One. Ron Davidson begged off. He had taken his daughter to the doctor in the afternoon and needed to get some sleep before work.

On Wednesday and Thursday nights, Angela spent a lot of time in automation, in Lawrence Harris' area in particular. Lawrence suspected she was up to something that he wouldn't like, but he didn't know what. He thought it would be a good time to try to discredit her. He walked up to Sean White and said, "I see you've been talking to that dyke, Angela Roberts."

Sean just said, "You're a fool Lawrence. She's got a boyfriend who's out of your league."

On Friday night for Saturday, the response to the leaflet was impressive. About 75% of the employees wore black. In some work areas, the participation was nearly 100%. The Flats section was a sea of black as Reggie Green handed out the timecards at midnight. Lawrence Harris' area was the same way.

Elliott Drummond surveyed the building and was impressed. He asked Newton if perhaps they had gone too far with the Farley removal. Newton said, "What do you mean? The man threatened my life before, remember?"

Drummond was noncommittal. "I don't know, maybe I'm getting too old for this sort of thing,"

Lawrence Harris ran one of the three automation Pay Locations in the Plant. His area was a union stronghold, with people like Aretha, Sean, Charlie Valmont & Ellen Rudny and the former 204-B, Claudia Stinson. Randy Sochalski had bid to this area from the BOBB, and he remembered how the union had protected him when Shirley Jones wanted to get rid of him. In addition, since this area was short of people on Saturdays, they brought over a couple of clerks from other areas – Rachel Parker and Emma Friedman.

Strange things started happening to the mail in this area. Mail was run with the wrong computer program and ended up in the reject bin. Another machine kept jamming. Other people ran out of mail and were too confused to figure out where to get more – the people borrowed from other areas of the building were especially good for this.

When there was a machine breakdown that required a mechanic, the employees didn't go to the phone and page one as they normally did. They waited until Lawrence came over and noticed the machine wasn't running and only then did they tell him to page a mechanic. "It's your job to page the mechanic, isn't it?" they asked. Twice this happened while Lawrence had left the building to take a cigarette break.

Finally, after the mail was run, the sweepers were a little careless about which APC they put the full trays of mail in, and some mail was misdirected. In short, both the productivity and accuracy were a disaster.

In Flats, productivity was down, but not as dramatically. People wanted to help Paul, but they were not anxious to hurt Reggie too much.

At the end of the day, Drummond was convinced. "I think we should do something," he told Newton.

Newton was livid. "We can't let the employees bully us around. We should find out who's responsible and punish the ringleader."

Drummond just said let's think about it and talk again Tuesday (Monday night, their first day back after their off days).

Angela was ecstatic when she called Paul the next day to tell him what had transpired. She felt some employees went overboard by misdirecting mail, but she was proud that her coworkers had taken a strong stand. She made the call from Aretha's house, and put Aretha on the phone too. "I've never seen Lawrence lose his cool like that before. He didn't know what to do."

When Paul thanked her for the job action she had organized in automation, she declined to take the credit. "You deserve the credit, Paul. They did it for you. If they didn't respect you, it never would have happened."

Paul acknowledged Angela's point, but he still thought the organizing was mainly her doing. He didn't understand why she was being so modest. Either she lacked confidence in herself, or she just had a whole lot of class.

On Monday morning, Elliott Drummond called Plant Manager Norman Bradford. Drummond had no desire to see things get totally out of hand at the Plant. Bradford agreed. It wasn't often that Newton was overruled, but together the two of them did exactly that on this occasion.

So at 11:00 AM, Drummond called Joanna Carver and informed her of the decision.

"Paul's removal is being administratively reduced to a two week suspension. You can grieve that suspension through the usual channels. It's been almost two weeks that he's been off on emergency suspension. If it's all right with you we'll make the dates coincide and he can come back in a few days."

Joanna agreed. In spite of what appeared to be some technical violations in what they were doing, it was still a victory for the union.

"I assume this means all the furor at the Plant will die down now," Drummond added.

"What do you mean, is management so upset about people wearing the same color shirts?"

"A lot more was going on than people wearing black shirts. It was getting out of hand."

Joanna replied, "I wouldn't know about that, but I'm sure when people see Paul back at work they'll calm down." Actually, Joanna had gotten a full report from Angela over the weekend. She smiled in the knowledge that solidarity on the workroom floor had made management back down.

Then she said: "Are you going to do anything about Clarence Day?"

Drummond replied, "We can't overrule Newton on everything. You can take that up with Labor Relations."

A week later Paul Farley met with Nancy Barber on Clarence Day's removal. She wouldn't budge, claiming it was untimely. When he argued about the games Newton had played, she replied "I don't know why you and Newton can't get along. You guys should work that out over at the Plant."

Paul couldn't figure out why Barber was being so hard-nosed. Maybe she resented the job action a week-and-a-half ago. Maybe her philosophy was that management had made a big concession on one case so they should take a hard line on the next one. In any event he left the meeting sorely disappointed.

At least Clarence Day wasn't starving. As Paul had predicted, the Post Office didn't send a representative to Clarence's unemployment hearing. He collected unemployment while he waited for his grievance to be processed to Step Three and probably arbitration.

Twenty-One: THE RALLY

Spring, 1998

Prosecutor: What was your reaction when the union started publishing a bulletin called the "Activator?"
Witness: It was another avenue to attack Mr. Newton.

They met at a coffee house in late March. Carol was in her early 40s, but like Paul, she looked a good deal younger than her age. She had beautiful shoulder length red hair and freckles on her face. Paul didn't think it was a beautiful face, more a warm, friendly one, and he was comfortable talking to her.

Paul never would have set foot in this establishment if his old friend Frank Silver hadn't moved back to Detroit. Frank liked the relaxed, comfortable atmosphere of this coffee house on Woodward north of Nine Mile Road. The decor was informal. Posters on the wall advertised classic movies like Bogart's "Casablanca" and Hitchcock's "Psycho." There were posters with political messages like "Work for Peace."

At one table a couple of men were playing chess. At another, a group of young people were reading some magazines, occasionally making a remark. Many of the patrons looked to be between the ages of 18 and 21.

Paul and Frank sat at a table where some people of their own generation were discussing the efforts of the Christian right to ban the teaching of evolution in the schools. One of those who vehemently disagreed with these zealots was Carol.

"Instead of banning evolution in the schools, they should make it mandatory to watch 'Inherit the Wind' with Spencer Tracy."

"Yeah, that's a classic," said a bearded man, as he raised his coffee cup to take a sip.

"It's the Neanderthal right-wingers that haven't evolved," said Carol.

Nobody at the table was dressed up. Carol wore a pair of tan slacks and a green T-shirt that said "Commit Random Acts of Kindness and Senseless Beauty."

Before the evening was over, Paul learned that Carol had a part-time (30 hours a week) secretarial job. Actually, with her computer knowledge and considerable office skills, she was paid much better than a secretary. In her spare time she was a painter. She painted for her own satisfaction, never even trying to sell her work. She had many of them hanging in her house in Royal Oak, which was paid off by now. Her expenses were manageable and she could afford to live on a part-time income. Her one child, a daughter, was about to graduate from Wayne State University. Carol was divorced, and didn't want to talk about her ex.

A week later she invited Paul over to look at her art work. He was afraid it would be awkward if he didn't like the paintings, but that turned out not to be a problem. He didn't know much about art and he couldn't categorize her paintings, but the creativity was evident. The faces of people were alive, the landscapes were expressive – recognizable for sure, but not like photographs. Another painting was just a jumble of colors that didn't represent anything specific but was quite striking.

Over the next few weeks they spent a lot of time together. They went back to the coffee house, they went to the movies, they went to the Detroit Art Institute, they saw a concert at the State Theater featuring Collective Soul and the Cranberries. And sometimes he spent the night at her house.

In mid-May, Carol got involved in the union's preparations for a national day of protest against postal privatization. The Local had put Paul in charge of organizing it, and he formed a committee with Angela and a few volunteers from various Post Offices within the Local. The plan was for a couple of hours of picketing followed by a few speeches. Carol helped with the picket signs and some artwork for the fliers. She also made a couple of costumes, a huge mask that looked like Postmaster General Runyon, and a "Mr. Greed" costume representing the big business types who would profit from the job slashing, wage cutting, and poor mail service of privatization. She got the "Mr. Greed" idea from a song by John Fogarty. Paul really appreciated Carol's contribution. He believed protesting should be fun, and she definitely added to the atmosphere.

On Wednesday, May 27, the day of the protest, Stacey Kline met Jim Newton for breakfast at the Chef's Hat for the second straight week. She had been a bit nervous the week before but was more relaxed this time. Newton talked about the need to make sure they find out who attends the protest. "If anyone who called in sick today shows up at the picket we should nail them. I've got someone there taking down names."

Stacey had something of a more personal nature to share.

"I'm pregnant Jim. I'm not sure whose it is. I haven't even told Harold yet."

Newton looked up at the ceiling. Then he looked back at Stacey and asked, "Do you think it's mine?"

Actually, since Stacey and Harold now slept in separate bedrooms, she knew it was Jim's. But what she was about to say would go over better if Jim didn't know that.

"I can't be sure, but it doesn't matter. I'm not going to have the baby, Jim. I'm getting an abortion."

There was very little emotion in her voice, which was a good trick under the circumstances.

Newton had always voted for political candidates who opposed abortion. But this wasn't a political issue; this affected him personally. He actually felt relieved that he wouldn't have to take any responsibility for the child, if it *was* his. An image formed in his mind of Stacey gaining weight with the pregnancy until she was huge. It wasn't pretty. He wanted everything to stay just the way it was. So he said, "Do whatever you think best, Stacey."

A few hours later the sidewalk in front of the Main Post Office was filled with 300 rowdy picketers, a much better turnout than at previous pickets. A few television news crews showed up, and they got good shots of the masks and costumes, as well as the picket signs. Paul's favorite was "Union Jobs, Quality Service – That's Our Priority," a takeoff of the USPS advertising campaign for Priority Mail, which was being contracted out to Emery Worldwide Airlines. A few suburban newspapers showed up, but the major daily papers had not been invited. There was a bitter labor dispute at these papers, and it would have been like scabbing to invite them or cooperate with them in any way. In fact, the striking newspaper workers provided the postal workers with the same sound system that they had used at countless rallies in front of the Detroit News building. And one of the invited guest speakers was Angela's old friend Louise Henderson, the Detroit Free Press reporter, who had been active in the strike from the beginning. After Louise expressed her support for the postal workers and urged them to continue boycotting the Free Press, Detroit News, and USA Today, Joanna Carver took the microphone:

"It's good to see so many different people out here today. I see Teamsters, newspaper workers, auto workers, and representatives from other unions here. I see our own members from the Plant and at least a dozen different Post Offices. I see people of all races, new hires and old timers. And I'm sure I see people who fall in the political spectrum from conservative, to liberal, to somewhat radical. But none of that really matters. Because as radio commentator Jim Hightower says, the real political spectrum in this country is not from left to right, it's from top to bottom. And the vast majority of us on the bottom realize we aren't even in shouting distance of the top any more.

"The people at the top in our society, the CEOs of the corporations and the multi-millionaires, are systematically stomping all over the rest of us. And it almost doesn't matter who you are in America today. You could be the owner of a small business and the big corporations are squeezing you out. You could be a family farmer and the agricultural conglomerates are taking over. You could be a worker in private industry and the corporation that owns your plant is threatening to move overseas and pay children fifty cents an hour to do your work. Or, like the newspaper workers, they could provoke a strike and then lock you out and hire scab labor. Or you could be a nurse at a profit-making hospital, and your staffing levels are being cut to the point that you are so overworked that your patients aren't getting quality care.

"It's happening all over. Corporate greed is ruining America. And now they want to take over the US Postal Service. They want to take it over piece by piece. And they don't care about the postal workers who'll be displaced if they are allowed to go ahead with their plans. They don't care about our families. They don't care about the thousands of people in every community in America who need good jobs and won't be able to get a job in the Postal Service if they are allowed to go ahead with their plans. They don't care that for the general public, mail service will be in chaos if the Postal Service is fragmented into ten or fifteen or twenty pieces. They only care about their own bottom line. And the bad news is that our opponents have a lot of money, they have a lot of influence, they have a lot of power, and they are very much accustomed to getting whatever it is they want. But the good news is there's a lot more of us than there are of them, and if we build a mass movement of all the people who would be harmed by privatization, brothers and sisters, we can win this fight!"

After the rally a bunch of people decided to go to Mr. B's for some burgers and a pitcher a beer. Angela was walking over there with Aretha and Sean, and they were consoling her about having to break up with Ed Crawford, who had gotten a job as a photographer with the Chicago Sun-Times.

"Don't feel bad for me," said Angela. "We had a lovely few months together. It was my first relationship in some time, and it felt good. But I'm not heartbroken, I never felt like he was 'the one.' We're still friends. I just got a letter from him. All in all it was good for me. I feel better about my personal life than I have in a long time."

Aretha didn't know if this was really how Angela felt or if she was just putting the best face on things. Even though they were close friends, Aretha found Angela's emotions almost impossible to decipher.

Once they got to Mr. B's there was a lot of enthusiastic talk about the rally. They talked about the turnout, Joanna's speech, the number of TV cameras they saw, the colorful picket signs and costumes, and some of their favorite chants. Aretha was proud that seven people from her Pay Location turned out. The enthusiasm was contagious, and they started discussing follow-up. One idea followed another, and soon they were talking about putting out a shop floor newsletter at the Plant.

Paul said: "We'll call it the 'Activator,' to go along with the Local's 'Commentator.' It can comment on what's happening at the Plant and even help organize job actions when appropriate. It can inform people specifically of their rights – like how to resist management pressure to force them to work when they're injured on the job, things like that. It can even talk about broader issues, like privatization, but more informally than the 'Commentator.'"

Aretha said, "Yeah, we can talk about these issues based on the mail we run every day. We run mail on the DBCS that has already been carrier sequenced by the mailer. They get something like a ten cents discount to do this, even though it doesn't do us any good to get one company's mail sequenced. It has to be mixed in with the other mail so it all can be sequenced together. That discount is just a gift to big business. Now, the stuff that's been carrier routed and bar coded does save us the trouble of running it on the OCR, and big business gets a discount for that, too. But the discount is a lot more than what it would cost to run it in-house. Somebody's making a profit hiring cheap labor to do our work. We can explain a lot of things, starting from the mail people see and work every day."

"Good," Paul said excitedly. They decided that Angela would write a report on the rally and Aretha would work on "Privatization – the Inside View." Paul would write about his favorite subject, the problems with Tour One management. Carol would draw a cartoon.

The day after the Activator came out, Ron Davidson was telling the other stewards about some interesting developments in management.

"NAPS had their elections recently, and Reggie Green ran against Newton. It was close, but Newton won."

"That's too bad," Angela said, but I guess it's nothing new."

"Reggie better be careful," Paul said. "Newton is a vindictive son of a bitch."

Twenty-two: A FATEFUL AUTUMN BEGINS
September, 1998

*Defense Lawyer: What happened after you challenged Mr.
Newton for a leadership position in the supervisors' union?
Witness: I started getting obscene phone calls at home.*

For Paul, the first working day of the fall was Monday night
for Tuesday, September 22nd. Celia Derringer came back to see
him about a Letter of Warning for irregular attendance, issued by
Reggie Green the previous week. Since Reggie's days off had been
changed to Tuesday and Wednesday, they would have to wait until
Thursday to grieve it.

Celia had missed work four times in seven months. Paul felt
Reggie had jumped the gun. It wasn't a great record, but Reggie
was usually more patient.

Celia explained that her most recent absence was to take her
sister to the hospital. Paul felt that might be all that was needed to
get Reggie to drop it. "FMLA doesn't cover sisters and brothers,
but Reggie has a little bit of humanity in him. Maybe we can
resolve this at Step One."

Two days later they met with Reggie Green. They explained
the circumstances of the most recent absence and Reggie seemed
to waver for a minute. Then he said he still wasn't sure he could
expunge the Letter of Warning.

Paul said, "How about if we word it like this: 'Letter of Warning
is expunged, however all absences cited in this Letter may be used
if discipline is issued in the future.' That way, Reggie, you know
she has to come to work every day, because she'll be on the brink
of being disciplined again."

Reggie signed the settlement. It was strange. The language
Paul offered to add meant Celia's circumstances were exactly what
they'd be if the Letter of Warning had never been issued. Reggie

211

and Paul both knew that. The wording Paul suggested gave the settlement a tone of compromise, as if each side had given up something. In reality, Celia got what she wanted.

Later on, Reggie confided to Paul that he was under a lot of pressure from Newton. That's why he issued the discipline in the first place. That's also why he liked the language that gave the appearance he wasn't just being soft. "I'll tell Newton I read Celia the riot act about her attendance when we inserted that language."

"Reggie, it sounds like that man dogs you as much as he dogs the employees."

Reggie didn't tell Paul he was getting obscene phone calls at home. His wife took the first one, and Reggie answered many others. The voice was disguised. All it said were words like "Motherfucker," "Bitch," or a variety of racial epithets. Caller ID didn't help him trace the calls; it simply identified the calls as "Out of Area." That was how calls from the Plant showed up on his caller ID, but that didn't prove anything, as many other phones would appear the same way. The calls were always on Tuesday or Wednesday morning (Reggie's off days), very early, when Newton would be at the Plant. They started back in May, when Reggie challenged Newton for the NAPS position. They had continued, sporadically, ever since.

Nor did Reggie tell Paul about the call he made to a friend in Area Headquarters in Illinois. If, for some reason, Newton loses his position, there's a good chance his friend could use his influence to get Reggie promoted – to a position he truly deserved in the first place. And the added income would come in handy, since Mrs. Green had drained their savings by overzealous use of her Visa card.

Reggie didn't want to discuss any of this with Paul, but did say, "I may have a surprise for Newton pretty soon."

On Saturday afternoon, Paul and Angela visited a mail processor named Ron Daltry at his home in Hazel Park. Ron was off work, his Workman's Comp claim had been denied, and the two stewards were helping him appeal the decision.

It was a complicated case. Ron's injury was not originally suffered at work. After two years in the Army, during which time he never left the country, he had been on the Troy police force for 13 years. That's when the injury occurred, but it was not in the line of duty. He and some fellow officers were playing basketball at a gym. One of the cops dove for a loose ball and crashed into Ron's left knee. It required reconstructive surgery, and even then it was never the same.

He left the police force and freelanced as a private eye for seven years. That was the most interesting and challenging work he had ever done, and not as physically demanding as being a cop on the beat. But eventually, he opted for the steady income of a postal job.

He hired in as a mail processor, but he had no idea what kind of physical demands that job would entail. He had pictured himself sitting at a letter case tossing letters into cubbyholes. But sweeping the mail on the DBCS machines, with the constant walking, bending, and stretching, wore out his leg. He was barely through his 90 day probation when his doctor put him off work and he filed the claim. He was in considerable pain and his doctor was afraid the reconstructed knee would disintegrate completely if he kept at it. Management, of course, controverted the claim.

Ron was a big man, a little over six feet, 195 pounds, with his hair cut short, almost in a crew cut. His nose looked a little crooked, which was hard not to notice on his narrow face. He had walked with a limp for years, and now the limp was more pronounced. On his left arm he had a tattoo, with a heart and the name Cheryl (a girl he no longer knew but had thought he was in love with when he was 18). He was not a handsome man, but he always had self-assurance and a look about him that said here was someone who knows what's going on. He had a street sense and a knack for reading people that many supervisors or union officials lacked.

Paul and Angela looked through the medical documentation, and Ron explained how each document fit in with his case. They discussed what additional paperwork would be helpful, and how the doctor should word it. They discussed the various avenues for appeal, and decided to ask for a hearing. Paul offered to represent him, saying it could probably be scheduled within the next six months.

"Thanks a lot Paul," Ron said. "I owe you one, for sure."

"You don't owe me anything. We haven't won anything yet, and you're still not earning any money."

"Well I guess I'll see if I can get any P.I. work. I can handle it physically, most of it's driving around, which only involves my right foot since my car doesn't have a stick, or talking on the phone, or using the Internet. I'll earn some money while I'm waiting for my hearing."

They had expected to be at Ron's house until late Saturday evening, but as it turned out they were finished a little before seven. Angela decided to go home and read. "I've just started a mystery called "The Perfect Witness," by Barry Siegel. In the first chapter, a Postmaster is murdered."

"That sounds like a terrific book, Angela."

"It's not what you're thinking, Paul. It seems the Postmaster was a nice old man that everyone liked. I don't think the book will even have much to do with horrible conditions at the Post Office, but I'll let you know."

Meanwhile, Paul decided to get a quick bite to eat at the Rialto on Woodward, and then drop in on Carol by surprise.

Carol's Honda Civic was in the drive along with a Ford Escort. Paul figured the Escort must be her daughter's car. He rang the bell and got no answer. He tried it again and waited a full minute, timing it on his watch. He rang again and pounded on the door. Finally, Carol appeared in her bathrobe. Sitting in the living room was a man he recognized from the coffee house. Paul knew the man's name was Seth, but he knew very little else about him, except that right now, his full beard and rather large stomach made him seem like one of the ugliest men on the earth. The fact that he was not wearing a shirt, shoes, or socks, and that his belt was unbuckled, made it obvious he'd just come from the bedroom with the woman Paul had started to really care about.

Carol said nothing. Paul had an impulse to scream at her and call her every nasty name he could think of, but he couldn't bring himself to do it. He turned around and left, slamming the door on the way out. He found a bar and drank gin and tonics until it closed at two.

When he woke up Sunday, there was a pain in his head, a hole in his heart, and a message on his answering machine from Carol. It had been left there Saturday night, shortly after he left Carol's house. He didn't return the call.

Paul was pouring cold water into his coffeemaker when the phone rang. It was Carol. She was really sorry. She really cares about Paul. Seth never meant that much to her and she's not sure how they ended up in bed. It certainly wasn't her plan for the night, it just happened. And it was really important for her to see him again.

Now, all the insulting words he had refrained from using the night before poured out. Maybe it was easier to do this over the phone, when he couldn't see her reaction. Perhaps she was sincere, and perhaps it was stupid to burn his bridges behind him and throw away a relationship that had been good for six months, but that's what he did. All of his anger came out, with intensity. Paul had, earlier in his life, been influenced by the feminist movement, and he probably would not be proud of some of the language he used while he yelled at Carol. But when he hung up, he didn't even remember exactly what he had said. He just knew he wasn't seeing Carol again. And that he felt worse than he had before the phone call.

He went through the same routine that he had tried when he was angry about Clarence Day's grievance. Just occupy the mind with simple things. Put on some music and do some housework. But be careful about the music; no love songs.

His funk lasted all through the weekend and he decided to call in sick Monday night. He drank beer and watched the Monday night game and then some late night comedy. He didn't laugh once.

Another person was in a funk that weekend, for reasons that were not all that different. Allison Newton, wife of Jim Newton, had been hurt badly. Every year, her parents had a party on the weekend closest to their anniversary. It was a two hour drive to their home just outside of Lansing. For the second year in a row, Allison had to make the drive alone. This time, her husband said he had to meet with Elliott Drummond about some business venture they were involved in together. She didn't understand why they had to meet on that particular Saturday night. Especially since she had reminded him about this party so many times. When he missed it last year he promised to make it up to her the next time.

Allison's life revolved around her husband. Her love for him was, in reality, a combination of admiration, fear, genuine affection, and a generous dose of self-deception. When he disappointed her in private, she could overlook it and convince herself she still had a good marriage. She certainly had security, a beautiful home in the suburbs, and they did have some nice moments together. But when he didn't come to his parents' anniversary party for the second year in a row, *that* was really embarrassing. She had wanted so much to show her parents how successful her marriage was, partly by showing them how successful *he* was. But he was off meeting with Drummond, whom he saw at work every day of the week.

Newton always said "I love you" to Allison, and she had always taken these words at face value. But the signs that this wasn't so were becoming too blatant to ignore. As Newton left for work Monday night, Allison poured herself a glass of Merlot and turned on the television. She sat there, in her nice suburban home, not laughing at the same Jay Leno jokes that Paul wasn't laughing at in Detroit.

By Tuesday night for Wednesday, Paul realized he had to get back to his normal routine and go back to work. He might even feel better that way. He ended up throwing mail for most of the day, going to the Union Office for about an hour after lunch, and then returning to Flats. Shortly before 0400, a clerk on the 110 Belt asked to see him about an overtime grievance. The 204-B in Flats asked Paul to help with the dispatch until 4:30, and see the employee just before he went home.

Paul quickly listened to the complaint. It looked like the employee was not entitled to any back pay, but should be given a make-up opportunity to work two hours overtime. He thought he might be able to get a quick verbal agreement from Stacey Kline before he went home. He got to the 110 Belt at about five minutes to five, but Stacey was nowhere to be found. He asked a casual named Toni who was pushing a hamper out to the dock if she knew where Stacey was.

"You know Paul, it seems like Stacey scoots out of here a little early every Wednesday."

Then Paul remembered that it had been almost a week since he had handed Jim Newton a request for some information on another class action grievance, and he hadn't gotten a response. Paul kicked himself for not remembering to ask Newton about it when he'd gone on union business earlier. He punched out at 0500 and decided he'd stop by the Manager's Office and remind Newton about it before he went home.

Elliott Drummond was in the office, but Newton was gone. When Paul asked if Drummond knew where Newton was, the reply was, "I'm not his keeper. I'm sure whatever you've got can wait until tomorrow. You're not on the fourteenth day, are you?"

"No, I've got time," said Paul. He headed back to the Union Office to gather all of his things, and from a distance, he saw Jim Newton leaving the building by the side door.

<><><><><><>

At the Chef's Hat Diner, Jim Newton asked Stacey about her husband.

"You know Jim, he isn't intimate with me very often, and I need a lot more. But in his own way, he still cares about me. And he trusts me. I'm sure he doesn't suspect a thing about us. And I'm sure he's not seeing anyone else either. Or if he is, he certainly isn't spending any money on her. We still have a joint checking account, and I see his credit card statements, too."

"Maybe the man's just too cheap to fool around."

"No, that's not it, it's the job. There's some funny business going on there."

"How bad is it?."

"I'm not sure. But Harold hired a private investigator to look into it - I saw the expense on his credit card. I asked why he needed to use his own money for that, and he said his boss is involved. If he catches the boss red-handed, he could end up getting his boss's job. I wish him luck, that job is so important to him."

"But he doesn't suspect about us?"

"No, Jim, I'm sure about that. He's never home when we meet

– it's always during the day. What about your wife?"

"She believes everything I tell her, bless her soul. She really does."

The following day Paul decided to see if he could find out what Reggie Green had meant when he said he had a surprise for Newton. Reggie was tightlipped, but Paul got the information from an unexpected source.

It was 4:30 AM, and Paul was alone in the Union Office when the phone rang. He picked it up and heard a familiar voice.

"Hi sugar, it's Tawanna. How ya doin'?"

It had been a year since Tawanna Chambers had gone into management, and six months since she had been detailed temporarily into a position as the Plant Manager's secretary. The woman who formally held this position had accumulated close to a year's worth of sick leave, and was using it up before retiring. She had a doctor's note covering her absence. So now Tawanna was on day shift with a plum job, for the time being.

Tawanna never saw Paul anymore since she was on day shift at the BOBB. She had just decided on the spur of the moment to call him as she was getting ready to go to work.

"I've got to be in at six this morning, instead of eight. They want me to present at some kind of meeting involving Bradford, Newton, and Drummond. So how's it going over there?"

"About the same, Tawanna. Newton hasn't changed any, I'm always fighting with him. In fact, I'm sure you hear management's version of some of those disputes in your position."

"Well, I hear a little bit, but I'm not going to talk about it. There is something going on with Green and Newton though. Green wrote to Bradford saying Newton is finagling the productivity numbers to make Green look bad, and cheating on the EXFC mail."

"I know their bonus is based on their EXFC scores. If they meet their goal of ninety-two percent overnight delivery of mail from those zip codes, they all stand to be richer. But what do you mean by cheating? I know they try to work the mail from those zip codes first, but I don't know if Bradford would consider that cheating. Do you think they're specifically identifying the test letters?"

"I don't know, Paul. Maybe I'll find out more at this meeting, but I don't think I should even tell you if I do. I'm just telling you this because you might see some fallout from the dispute at the Plant. I'll tell you, if Reggie thinks Bradford's going to come down hard on Newton, he's sadly mistaken."

"He *likes* Newton?"

"He's just not anxious to tangle with him. At least that's what I think. The whole thing will probably backfire on Reggie, and Newton will fuck with him some more. If you see Reggie acting strangely, don't be surprised."

"Well, it's almost five, I've gotta go Tawanna. It's real nice to hear your voice again."

"Bye, sugar."

Paul smiled when he hung up. A year ago he'd been hurt and upset when Tawanna went into management. His relationship with her would never be quite the same, but it still felt good to talk to her. He left work in much better spirits than he'd been in several days.

Twenty-three: THE ARBITRATION

Defense Lawyer: Did you distribute this limerick at the plant?
Witness: No.

Thursday, October 1st was the day Clarence Day had waited over a year for. His removal grievance was to be heard by an Arbitrator. His unemployment benefits had run out and he was badly in need of a source of income.

The hearing was at the Main, in the same room in the basement where Paul had presented Earnestine Hall's EEO case. Nancy Barber presented the case for management. She had Drummond and Newton present, along with the supervisor who issued the discipline, Butch Hobson. John Huxley, a Business Agent from Chicago, was the union advocate. In addition to Clarence and Paul Farley, Joanna Carver showed up for moral support.

Huxley explained that the case had almost been settled earlier in the week:

"I offered to pre-arb it for a last chance suspension for time served, on the record for two years, which would be until next September. Nancy was considering it and said she'd call me back. I think Newton nixed it."

As expected, management asked the Arbitrator not to rule on the merits of the case, but just to hear arguments on the timeliness of the grievance. Management wanted the case declared untimely, which would make it unarbitrable on the merits and would allow the removal to stand. Procedural wrangling over how to conduct the hearing with respect to this issue consumed almost half-an-hour. Eventually, the Arbitrator went with John Huxley's suggestion. First, he would hear arguments and testimony on the question of timeliness. Then he would hear arguments and testimony on the merits of the case. He would then take his time to consider all of what he heard, and would issue a written decision in a few weeks.

On the timeliness issue, Paul was the union's only witness. He was sequestered when Hobson, Drummond, and Newton testified. So he didn't hear Newton lie and say Paul had never asked him for an extension. Paul was brought back again to testify during the second part of the hearing, stating that based on his experience as a steward, Clarence Day's record didn't justify a removal, especially considering the circumstances of the last absence. At this point, John Huxley attempted to introduce into evidence the transcript of Jim Newton's testimony at the EEO hearing in 1995, when he said he doesn't count funerals in discipline. Management objected that the EEO forum is irrelevant to this proceeding. Paul was surprised when the Arbitrator kept it out of evidence.

Paul's testimony followed Clarence Day's, which he had been not permitted to hear. He also didn't hear Hobson's testimony that the decision to fire Clarence had been his and his alone. And Hobson deflected the argument about the funeral as skillfully as possible. He stated any employee, good or bad, will occasionally have an absence that is unavoidable. The point of being regular in attendance is to have such good attendance throughout the year that the occasional unavoidable absence wouldn't hurt your record. Hobson said the reason he wasn't taking into account the circumstances of the last absence was that Day's attendance had been horrible for years. All the prior disciplines and the other instances of sick leave, lateness, etc. that were cited in the current discipline added up to a record that called for removal. It wasn't the last absence, it was the overall picture of irregular attendance for as long as anyone could remember that guided his decision. Hobson's testimony was effective; he had been well coached.

On October 2nd, Shirley Jones picked up the phone at the BOBB and called Newton's office. Years ago, it had been Newton who talked Shirley into leaving the union and going into management. Now she had a favor to ask.

She had heard another management reshuffling was being contemplated. Green was going to lose his position in Flats and become a swing supervisor, covering the 110 Belt on Sunday and Monday, and the dock on Saturday. On Thursday and Friday he would go over to the BOBB and cover the Small Parcel & Bundle Sorter. His off days would still be Tuesday and Wednesday.

When she started talking about the management shuffle, Newton thought Shirley was going to ask for Green's old position. But she had her eye on a day shift vacancy. She wasn't sure whether she should ask Newton, whose official authority extended only over Tour One, or go to the Plant Manager.

Newton considered Shirley to be one of his loyal people, so she wasn't surprised that he offered to help. But the way he worded it was a bit of a shock. "Leave it to me. Bradford's a wimp, he'll do what I say."

Not sure what to make of the conversation, Shirley decided it wouldn't hurt to talk to Bradford on her own. But according to his secretary, Bradford was out of town. It might not have been a smart thing to do, but she relayed Newton's comment about Bradford to the secretary, a young woman named Tawanna Chambers, whom she knew from her days at the Plant.

On Saturday night, October 11th, a Troy policeman named Danny Vellarmo responded to a complaint of a drunk and disorderly patron at a sports bar on Livernois near Big Beaver Road. Vellarmo put the offender in the patrol car and roughed him up a bit while his partner drove to the station. They didn't book him, they just let him go. It was almost time for the bars to close and this person wouldn't cause any more trouble.

Three weeks later a police brutality complaint was filed by a

28-year-old man named Roger Newton, son of James Newton. An informal meeting to discuss the complaint was scheduled for some time in early December.

Meanwhile, Vellarmo began receiving obscene phone calls. They would wake him up at around five in the morning. He had the calls traced to a phone booth at a gas station on Big Beaver and John R – about a half a mile from the Plant.

On October 15th the Arbitrator's decision was faxed to the Union Office in Ferndale, and Joanna Carver and Paul Farley read the fate of Clarence Day in stunned silence. The Arbitrator decided it wasn't necessary to rule on the timeliness of the grievance because, in his opinion, the removal was justified. He ruled against the grievance on its merits. His brief explanation largely echoed the testimony of Supervisor Butch Hobson.

Joanna's take was that the Arbitrator had been influenced by the procedural issues, even though he didn't come out and say so. The timeliness issue was a messy one to rule on. The Arbitrator wasn't sure he could rule it timely, but he wasn't completely comfortable calling it untimely, given the management antics Paul had described in his testimony. The way to get around the procedural issue entirely was to deny the grievance on its merits, which made the procedural issue irrelevant. On one level of logic, it was a safe way to handle it. But it was neither fair nor logical as far as the facts of Clarence Day's case were concerned.

"In any event," Paul said, "Newton got exactly what he wanted. It only shows that being a heartless, lying, conniving bastard works. Now, we have to go tell Clarence." Paul reluctantly volunteered for the unpleasant task of breaking the news.

As word spread through the Plant about the decision, a few people started to fear another shooting. Clarence's militant image scared a few people, but Paul thought he knew Clarence better.

After a long talk with Clarence, Paul was convinced Clarence had taken this blow as well as could be expected.

It was quite a shock to Paul, and to everyone else, when about 50 copies of a limerick, typed on a computer, on 8½ x 11 sheets of paper, in 18 point bold type, were scattered around the Plant on October 20th. These fliers were mostly placed in the swing room and men and women's locker rooms. One was put in Jim Newton's mailbox in the Manager's Office. It read:

> **I'm sure that you have enjoyed bootin'**
> **Me out of the door, Jim Newton**
> **You've got all the clout**
> **But you better look out**
> **When I come back, I might be shootin'**

It was unsigned.

Although the Postal Inspectors investigated, they could not tie the threatening limerick to Clarence Day. He did not even have a computer in his home. Nobody had seen Clarence in the building since the Arbitration decision was announced. Fingerprint analysis was tried on a few of the fliers. There were dozens of fingerprints, as the sheets had been passed around and looked at, but none of the prints matched Day's. Despite an announcement of a thousand dollar reward for information, nobody came forward to say they had observed someone placing these fliers around the Plant.

A flier was lying on the table in the union room. "Do you think Clarence typed this up?" Ron asked.

"No way," said Paul. "It doesn't sound like Clarence. It sounds more like someone trying to sound like Clarence."

"I was talking to Sean White," said Angela. "His theory is Newton printed them up himself, trying to frame Clarence on criminal charges."

"That's a little far-fetched, don't you think?" said Ron.

"I agree," said Paul. "It's probably some twisted person's idea of a joke."

"Some joke," said Angela.

Paul didn't mince words in his article in the Activator called "Fig Newton Must Go." In a short piece, he talked about Newton's dishonesty, vindictiveness towards employees, and general lack of decency. There was a vague reference to Newton's mistreatment of good managers, and there was a brief summary of Clarence Day's case. It was a blistering piece, going beyond anything Paul had written before. In the past, Paul had used the Activator and Commentator to expose specific instances of wrongdoing or unfairness, but he had not publicly called for Newton's ouster.

Drummond and Newton sat reading the article in the Manager's Office.

"We have to remove him," Newton stated in a matter of fact tone of voice.

"We can't do that Jim. You know that."

"Do you think I could sue him for slander?"

"I don't know. You could talk to a lawyer, I suppose."

"Well, I'll tell you what, Elliott, that Farley's going to pay. He doesn't know who he's dealing with."

Twenty-four: NOVEMBER 17

November 17, 1998

Prosecutor: What did the defendant say about the targets on the gun range?
Witness: He said they were looking more and more like Mr. Newton.

Paul dragged himself into work on Monday night at 8:30 for Tuesday, November 17th. It was the start of another week. After two weeks of hell, Paul was beginning to dread his job.

It had started when Red Collier was moved from the SHIT over to the Flats section, replacing Reggie Green. Not surprisingly, Red was given Saturday and Sunday nights off.

Newton and Collier orchestrated the disruption of Paul's union business. Nobody bothered him before midnight; he could take 3½ hours of union time at the beginning of his tour if he needed it. So he couldn't file a grievance about not being released.

The first thing Paul noticed was they never let him in the office at the same time as Angela. He would be called back to Flats some time between midnight and 0100, just before Angela's supervisor released her. Then they'd let him go again around 0400, when the dispatch was starting. It was strange. In the past, Reggie and other supervisors in the area said 0400 was the time they needed him the most. But 0400 was when Angela was called back to her area, and that's when they let Paul go again.

Occasionally, if an employee asked to see Paul some time between 0100 and 0400, he would be released for 15 minutes and told he would be given time to finish up later. It was always timed to coincide with a Step One Meeting Angela was having elsewhere in the building, her scheduled break, or a time when she had gone to the SHIT or the BOBB.

Paul also started noticing other difficulties. Simple requests

227

for information he sent to supervisors were getting lost. He was having trouble scheduling Step One Meetings; supervisors would tell him they were "busy" until ten minutes to five, then make him rush through his presentation. Then the supervisor would say "it's five o' clock, you have to go, and I'm not convinced, let's send it to Step Two." Issues that should have been easily resolved, like an overtime make-up opportunity for someone who was passed over, were being denied and sent to Step Two.

He was angry and frustrated. He'd always been an efficient steward, settling the easy cases and thoroughly preparing for a fight on the hard ones. Now his effectiveness was being undermined. One obstacle after another was being thrown in his way to prevent him from resolving even the little issues, or even to effectively gather information and interview witnesses.

His phone conversation with Angela the day before indicated she was facing some harassment herself. The only steward they were leaving alone was Ron Davidson, who they pretty much let come and go as he pleased. It was the old game: divide and conquer.

At 0400, Paul was in the Union Office with Ron.

"I might call in tomorrow, it's really getting to me Ron. I've never felt so discouraged. Sometimes I have trouble holding my temper, but there's no point in yelling at the supervisors and 204-Bs who are doing what they're told, they're just puppets. But if I go to the man who's pulling the strings he'll deny everything, with a smirk on his ugly face. And I can't grieve it. It's not like they're denying me union time, they're just making it ineffective. And I miss seeing Angela back here more than you know."

"Don't let Newton get to you, Paul, that's what he wants."

"It *is* getting to me. That man has no principles. Not even management principles. He'll cause chaos on the workroom floor, harming productivity, just to flex his muscles. And his number one priority right now is fucking with me. He doesn't deserve to be in a position of power. Sometimes I think he doesn't deserve to exist.

"Meanwhile, I haven't really gotten over what happened with

Carol. I don't feel the same way about her I once did. I probably never will. But I still feel the pain, and the loneliness."

"You live alone, don't you Paul?"

"Yeah."

"You got a dog or a cat? Or any pets?"

A strange look came over Paul's face. "I had a little family of pet mice not too long ago. They were real cute. I used to feed them peanut butter. But they suffered tragic accidents when their feeding dishes snapped on their heads."

It was the kind of sarcastic, sick humor Paul thought Ron would appreciate. But Ron just looked at him with concern on his face.

"Hey Paul, I've got annual for tomorrow. I was planning to take my wife and kids to the Red Wings game. I've got four tickets. But if you're going to call in, maybe you'd like to come instead of Pam. I'm sure she wouldn't mind. They're playing the Avalanche, should be a good game."

"No thanks, Ron. With my luck, someone from work will see me there and I'll get nailed for falsification. No, I think I'll get some of my aggression out by going to the gun range. That target is looking more and more like Newton all the time. And I'm getting pretty good at it. Then maybe I'll catch the Wings on cable. Don't worry about me Ron. Go out with your family and enjoy yourself."

Twenty-five: COPS AT THE DOOR

November, 1998

The sun had not yet risen on the morning of November 18th, but it was gradually getting lighter. Danny Vellarmo usually looked forward to the sunrise because it meant the end of his shift was approaching. But on November 18th, the adrenaline was flowing, and the position of the sun was the farthest thing from his mind. Danny and his partner, Fred Antonelli, were about to question a murder suspect.

The patrol car was slowed by the early stages of rush hour traffic. There was no need to put on the siren and race to the scene. They figured the suspect had already returned home and would pretend to be asleep. Traffic on I-696 was a little heavy but not too bad. However, I-94 heading towards downtown slowed to a crawl at Vernier Road a couple of miles before the exit they were looking for.

"I knew this guy when I worked at the Post Office," Danny told his partner. "Even back then, everyone knew he hated Jim Newton. He's our man all right, he must've called in sick just so he could bump Newton off."

It was light enough to see Paul Farley's brick house clearly. There was no car in the driveway, but they couldn't see into the garage, so Farley might have been home.

Danny sent his partner around the back to be sure the suspect couldn't escape. Then he rang the bell, with one hand on his gun. There was no response. He rapped sharply on the front door. Still no answer. Danny rapped harder. "Police, Open up!" After waiting another minute he was about to go to a back window when he heard the sound of the chain sliding inside the door. It opened, and he saw Paul Farley in his pajamas. He called out for his partner to join him at the front door.

"Where have you been for the last few hours?"

231

"Asleep."

"You didn't answer your phone!"

"I was asleep."

"You didn't hear the phone?"

"No, I was asleep."

"Is there anyone here who can verify that?"

"No, I live alone."

"And you didn't hear the phone? Three different people called you."

"No, I didn't hear it. I had the ringer turned off." Paul switched on the porch light. "Now what's this all about Vellarmo?"

"Do you own a gun?"

"Why do you need to know that?"

"There was a murder committed this morning. If you own a gun, we need to check it out."

"You think I murdered someone?"

"We don't know who did it. We have to check out all possibilities."

"Who was killed?"

"Can't you tell us?"

"No, I...You damn well better tell me what the hell's going on!"

"Jim Newton. We know you hate his guts, and you have no alibi. We need to check out any guns you might own."

"I do own a gun. You can run whatever tests you want on it. It wasn't the murder weapon."

"We also want to bring you down to the station for questioning. And we'll want to run a GSR test on your hands."

"What's GSR?"

"Gunshot residue. There will be traces of nitrates and other substances on your hands if you've fired a gun recently. You didn't know that, did you?"

"Your test will be positive, because I did fire a gun a little more than 12 hours ago – at the shooting range. That's *legal*, isn't it?"

"No need to get sarcastic with us, Farley. We don't make the call on who gets charged here. We have orders to bring you in to the station. Are you going to cooperate?"

Two days later police were back with a search warrant. Paul watched with rising fury as they opened drawers, overturned furniture and turned his already messy house into a disaster area. All in the name of looking for evidence.

Homicide investigator Eddie Logan had talked to enough people at the Plant to convince him Farley was their man. The .22 caliber pistol Farley had freely submitted to be tested was similar to the murder weapon they were looking for. But it was not the same gun. If they were lucky, the search would turn up the murder weapon.

"No wonder he turned over that gun so easily," Logan told Vellarmo. "He thinks he can fool us. If we don't find an eyewitness and we can't find the weapon, the prosecutor will have to decide whether to go forward with a circumstantial case. But he's the killer, I feel it in my gut."

When no other gun was found, smoking or otherwise, Logan was convinced Farley had planned out the murder thoroughly. "He knew we'd run some tests. He purposely went to the gun range to cover for the GSRs. And he handed us another gun to try to clear himself. But he doesn't get off that easy."

After one more strategy session between police and prosecutors, a decision was reached. On the day before Thanksgiving, Danny Vellarmo and Fred Antonelli once again rapped on Paul Farley's door.

When Paul opened it, he saw Vellarmo take the handcuffs from his belt while Antonelli recited those familiar words from TV cop shows: "You are being placed under arrest. You have the right to remain silent. Anything you say can be used against you in a court of law..."

Twenty-six: ANGELA COMES TO VISIT

January, 1999

Angela's voice on the phone was a source of comfort. He could barely see her through the dirty glass. This was the only type of visit permitted for friends and family of prisoners in the Pontiac jail.

The last two months had been a nightmare. The arrest was followed by arraignment at Troy District Court, and then a preliminary exam was scheduled, where the prosecution presented a condensed version of their case. There were a couple of witnesses – the medical examiner, forensics experts, etc. There were a few exhibits – results of the GSR tests, and copies of the *Commentator* and *Activator* to show how much the defendant hated the victim. The prosecution didn't have to prove its case beyond a reasonable doubt at this stage of the game, so they saved their most damning and most surprising evidence for the trial. The judge ruled there was enough circumstantial evidence that Paul Farley had the motive and opportunity to commit the crime.

Paul's court-appointed lawyer had then argued for bail. If bail had been granted, he could've gotten some help in paying it. Frank Silver had offered a loan of $5,000. His union had secretively offered to dip into their treasury – knowing the money would be repaid at the time of the trial. It wasn't proper procedure, but Joanna Carver was willing to pull some strings at the national level to make it happen.

But there was no bail. The Judge said he never grants bail in a first degree murder case. The prosecution argued further that the defendant had no family ties in the Detroit metropolitan area so he was a flight risk. The character witnesses the defense presented could not sway the Judge from the decision he probably had reached before the proceedings started.

Paul couldn't afford a private lawyer. The union might cover court costs for a steward if the charges against him were related to union activities, but that wasn't the case here. If Paul was guilty, the union couldn't stand behind him. If he was innocent, he'd have to prove it without union funds, although Joanna and Angela were personally supportive.

His parents had lost a lot of money in the stock market and were unable to pay for an experienced defense attorney. The lawyer he had, Alan Lewiston, was younger than Paul. He was 35, with blond hair and a pretty-boy face. He had a speech impediment, making it hard for him to pronounce the letter "r" properly, making him sound like a child. But he seemed "pwetty" smart – Paul figured he could've done worse.

Lewiston had one strategic idea that Paul felt was either brilliant or naïve. If a trial isn't scheduled within six months, Lewiston would file a motion for Paul to be released on his own recognizance. "The law says they have to do it," he told Paul. "Usually the defense files a bunch of other motions, challenging forensic evidence and things like that, which end up delaying the trial. If the defense contributes to the delay – which most of the time we do – then they won't release you in six months. But we have no reason to file any of those motions. I want you out in six months. They'll never schedule a trial that fast. Oakland County is all backed up. Then you can help prepare your own defense – you'll think a lot more clearly when you're out of this dump."

Calling the Pontiac jail a "dump" was kind of like calling cancer a "minor ailment." Anyone who's never been in jail has no idea what it's like. The worst part wasn't the cold, or the unique rotten smell. It wasn't the food, even though it went down easier if you closed your eyes and held your nose. The worst part was the feeling of being trapped. Paul paced back and forth like a caged animal, which is exactly what he was. He had seen movies where inmates banged on the bars and screamed at the top of their lungs. Paul did the same thing. Often.

This was not a place where people were rehabilitated. Nothing in this experience prepared you for a return to a useful and productive life in society. They just stripped you of your humanity and, in some cases, brutalized you.

Paul had escaped the worst of it so far. He was fortunate that his cell mate, Big Jake, decided to protect him. Jake, who had two more years to serve on an armed robbery rap, was a huge black man, 6 feet, 6 inches tall and weighing 275 pounds. Nobody messed with him. Jake didn't fight much anymore, as he had found religion. But everyone knew he could take care of himself.

Maybe it was because Paul had black friends come to visit him (nothing was a secret in this place); maybe it was because Paul seemed like a sincere person; or maybe Jake would protect whoever his cell mate happened to be. In any case, Jake took Paul under his wing. Paul knew that without this protection, he would already have been gang raped while the guards looked the other way.

So Paul could truthfully tell Angela that jail wasn't as bad as he'd feared. Even though the real truth was the experience was messing up his head in a way that was unbearable. The only things that restored any semblance of sanity to his life were the regular visits of Angela and occasional visits by Joanna, Frank Silver, and coworkers like Emma, Tawanna, and Aretha. And, surprisingly, Reggie Green had come by once.

Angela told him about her latest conversation with the private investigator who was working for free – Ron Daltry. Since Angela had taken over for Paul on Daltry's OWCP appeal, Ron was using his spare time checking into the whereabouts of some other possible suspects on the night of the crime.

She also told him the latest ridiculous story from work. Rachel Parker had been off on maternity leave for five months. Management sent threatening letters that she would be AWOL if she didn't come back to work. She came back on a Friday night for Saturday – and they sent her home. Management said she needed clearance from the medical unit because she had been off for more than 21 days. She didn't even have a medical condition; she'd given birth four months ago and was just taking as much time off as possible to be with her little girl. Since the Monday following her attempted return was Martin Luther King's Birthday, it wasn't until Tuesday night that this mess was straightened out and Rachel came back to work. And Angela was filing a grievance for Rachel to get four days of back pay.

"Sometimes they mess with people intentionally," she told Paul, "and sometimes they do it because they're just so stupid that they trip over their own regulations."

"So killing Newton didn't do any good, whoever did it."

"Oh, it's getting better at the Plant. There's not as much outright nastiness. But there's still a long way to go."

"Boy, I miss the Plant. I miss you, Ron, a lot of the people. I even miss the annoying things – the PA system, the idiotic squabbles, the coworkers who want to file grievances over nothing. The supervisors who try to sound intelligent giving us Newton's ridiculous excuses for denying a grievance. I miss all of it. Even though we called it a prison in the paper, at least you could punch out and go home at the end of the day."

Hearing stories from the Plant took Paul's mind off his own situation. But the feeling turned into it's opposite as soon as Angela left. He was angry about being trapped in this cell. And he was worried sick about the outcome of his trial. There were times as a steward that he'd felt totally frustrated, but he'd gladly return to that type of frustration if he could.

The other thing he really missed in his life was women. It's not that he'd been having sex that regularly or that often. And unlike some of the prisoners, he didn't have a picture in his cell of a girlfriend or wife. There was no special someone in his life. But he missed seeing women on a daily basis. The smile of a pretty woman, a friendly word from a woman he liked; these things used to recharge his batteries. Now there was nothing but frustration.

He often thought about Carol. He went over it again and again in his mind – that scene in which he found her with another man and reacted so angrily. What he wouldn't do to see her again now! He should have forgiven her, even if not right away. His pride had gotten in the way. She had really liked him, and he had felt the same. It wasn't just the great sex. Her spirit, her personality, everything about her was right for him. Or so it seemed, looking back at it from his lonely cell.

He thought about every argument he'd ever had with Newton. From the time Newton tried to get rid of him as a new steward to the business with the fly, to the problems with union time at the end. Even though Newton was dead, he still tormented Paul with accusations from the grave. That's why he was in this cell.

The visit from Angela had helped, even though he had trouble hearing every word over all the static on that phone. Unlike some of the other inmates, he had a friend who cared about what happened to him. To someone in jail – rightly or wrongly – that is so very important.

Paul clung to the hope that Lewiston was right about the six month thing. He knew lawyers sometimes strung their clients along. But he had to believe. Now, was that six months from the day of the arrest or from the preliminary exam? He didn't remember. Paul took the worst case scenario and figured it was the end of June. It was now late January. He wondered what shape his mind and his spirit would be in after five more months as a caged animal.

He looked at his cell mate, hovering over his prayer book. He wanted to talk, but you don't disturb Jake when he's praying. Paul wasn't religious, and didn't believe in prayer. But he hoped Jake was saying a prayer for him.

Twenty-seven: THREE PHONE CALLS

February, 1999

"Forget everything you've seen on TV about private eyes. I can get you interesting information about almost anyone you name. But it doesn't mean I'm going to find your killer so Paul's lawyer can act like Perry Mason and get someone to confess on the witness stand. It doesn't work that way in real life."

Ron Daltry was on the phone with Angela. They were trying to develop a strategy for Paul, in the absence of any real direction from Lewiston.

"The thing that gets me," Angela said, "is anyone who hated Newton enough to even think about killing him is someone I like. I mean, I'd hate to find out the real killer was Clarence Day. Or even Reggie Green."

"You gotta let the chips fall where they may. Find out what the facts are and see where it leads. If those people are innocent, fine. If not, you don't want Paul to be convicted, so we gotta do what we gotta do."

Angela agreed, though with a heavy heart. Then she added, "Hey Ron, this is kind of a long shot, but why don't you check into that cop Vellarmo? He left the Post Office with hard feelings towards Newton, and towards Paul. If Newton gets killed and Paul does time for it, that's perfect for Vellarmo."

"When did Vellarmo get fired?"

"I think it was a few years ago. I can't see someone waiting that long to get revenge. On the other hand, people do strange things, especially killers. Maybe it wasn't a coincidence Danny was the first cop on the scene."

"No problem checking on him, Angela. I've still got friends on the force."

"Also, do you think you could dig into Newton's private life and see what you find? Maybe his wife knew about Stacey. We keep

241

thinking it was a postal worker who got mad at him, but it could be something else entirely."

"I've got time on my hands. I'll see what I can do."

After hanging up, Angela called to cancel her dinner date with Tyrone Wheeler. He was the most persistent man who'd ever chased her. Finally she had agreed to see him. He was really a nice guy, and she even kind of liked him. But something was missing. She knew what love felt like; she had known love once in her life, and gotten hurt. This wasn't love. They weren't even really friends. Her best male friend was Paul, and she had never thought of him as a possible lover. With Tyrone, for some reason it just didn't quite click. Maybe it was her fault, maybe she wasn't *letting* it click. Maybe she was just not letting herself become vulnerable again. It wasn't really Tyrone's fault. But it wouldn't be fair to Tyrone to go out with him and get his expectations even higher.

Which is worse, to love someone who doesn't love you or to be pursued by someone who really wants you when you don't feel the same way? Not an easy question. Angela just knew she didn't feel comfortable right now with the second alternative. For now, she would tell him she had a headache. Maybe she'd still go out with him some other time. After all, there was no harm in going out with someone you didn't love just to have a good time. But would she have a good time, knowing he wanted so much more from her than she wanted to give? Or would she spend the whole evening on her guard? In any event, it wasn't going to happen tonight.

After talking to Tyrone, Angela poured herself a glass of Chardonnay. She opened up a book by Barbara Kingsolver, but she couldn't really get into it. She was too distracted.

The phone rang again. It was Ron Davidson.

"I don't know who else to call, Angela. But I've got to talk to someone. The guilt is killing me."

"What do you mean?"

"I sold Paul the murder weapon."

"You must not be familiar with the evidence, Ron. That gun wasn't used in the murder."

"Okay, so I got him familiar with a twenty-two caliber pistol, and he used another one just like it."

"No Ron, he didn't *do* it."

"He hated the man, Angela. From the start, Newton tormented him. And that deal with Clarence Day's removal was dirty. Newton did that to fuck with Paul as much as to get Clarence. Newton was fucking with him until the very end. I talked to Paul the day before the shooting. There was something strange about that conversation. Now I know what it is, and I feel sick."

"You're *wrong*, Ron. Paul didn't like Newton, true enough, but he didn't *kill* him. Paul wanted, more than anything else, to organize the workers at the Plant. Having Newton around gave him a focal point. In some ways, he needed someone like Newton. Sure, his life would have been easier if Newton quit or transferred or something, but Newton was also useful to Paul. He didn't do it. So you can stop feeling guilty."

Ron opened up a can of beer, his fourth of the night.

"No, Angela. Newton was really getting to Paul at the end. He wasn't enjoying the struggle, he was really down. I think after years of frustration, he finally snapped. But he was smarter than most of the guys who go postal. He did it off the job, neat and clean, with no witnesses. I don't really blame him, but I feel like shit because I contributed to it."

When they hung up, Angela finished her glass of wine. She needed to calm her nerves. Her emotions were going in twenty different directions, and the end result was a feeling of inner conflict and general uptightness. Wanting to go out with Tyrone and not wanting to, and feeling guilty about hurting his feelings. Believing Paul was innocent and feeling hurt that Ron doubted him. Worried that if Ron believed the prosecution side, her friend could be convicted. Ron could be a really damning witness. The worst kind – a reluctant witness who was a former ally on the union side of the fence. She hated to admit it, but some of what Ron said made sense. At least she understood why Ron could believe it. And they certainly hadn't come up with squat for an explanation of who else might've done it. Asking Daltry to investigate Clarence, Reggie, and the others was like grasping at straws. But she still believed Paul was innocent. Was it logic or emotion that made her feel that way? Maybe it was just faith. Faith in one of the only people in the world she truly trusted. She was still determined to do everything in her power to help the defense. But now she wasn't so confident of the outcome. You never knew what could happen in a courtroom, just like you couldn't predict the outcome of a grievance arbitration.

She poured another glass of wine.

Twenty-eight: THE CASINO

Paul got on the escalator, going up. Almost immediately, he heard the ping-ping-ping of the slot machines. When he reached the top, he was enveloped in the noise, which almost sounded melodic, and surrounded by a sea of humanity. Two days out of jail, Paul was at Detroit's brand new casino experiencing the very opposite of the isolation of a cell.

The six months Lewiston had promised turned into eight months before a hearing was held in August. All of the experienced prosecutors were busy working on another high profile murder trial. A man named Jonathan Schmitz had appeared on the Jenny Jones Show, unaware that a gay man named Scott Amadour would come on stage and reveal he had a secret crush on Schmitz. A few days later, Schmitz had murdered his secret admirer. This was tabloid stuff, and even the mainstream media were having a field day with it. The prosecutor's office didn't care what the tabloids said about all the bizarre aspects of the case, they just wanted a conviction.

That's why Andy Zellner, the newest person on the prosecution team, was left to argue against the motion releasing Paul on his own recognizance. He used all the wrong arguments. He said Paul was a dangerous criminal, and Paul was single and had no ties to the community. In short, he just repeated the arguments that had been used to deny bail originally, without addressing the legal point raised by Lewiston. The judge seemed ambivalent, but in the end he said the law was the law, and Paul was released.

When he saw his house for the first time in months, it was a welcome but strange sight. The lawn was brown. Nobody had watered it all summer. It was stuffy inside. There was a pile of mail that he didn't feel like going through right away. It was messier than he remembered. But boy oh boy, it was great to be home! That night, his mattress felt like an exquisite luxury.

The next day, Paul caught up with friends. He talked for a few hours with Angela and Joanna at the Union Office in Ferndale. It was a happy occasion, with smiles all around. Then he went out for a drink in the evening with Frank Silver, and thanked him for keeping an eye on the house all this time.

Now Paul was ready for a different kind of experience. He'd been to Las Vegas for a couple of union conventions, so he knew a little about casinos. But having one in Detroit was different.

He decided to take a look around before trying his luck at any games of chance. There was plush carpeting, a swirling pattern of red, blue, and yellow, colorful, but not too bright. Soft comfortable chairs in front of every slot machine. The slot machines were everywhere, rows of them, at all sorts of odd angles. The layout was a bit confusing; as he walked around he lost his sense of direction. There were no clocks to remind you how late it was getting and no windows to remind you of the outside world. The casino was a world unto itself. He kept having to say "excuse me" as he made his way through the crowd. Even on a weekday evening, the place was packed.

At what he thought was the northwest end, there was a small crowd watching a black female singer, accompanied by a white guitarist and bass player, and a black drummer. She was singing "Hot Stuff," an old Donna Summer disco song.

He walked around some more and almost bumped into a cocktail waitress. She was in her early twenties, with short blond hair, blue eyes, and a very pretty face, even though she wasn't smiling. She had a wonderful figure, with most of it showing. Sheer, tight leg coverings came almost up to her hips. When she turned away, he could see most of her cheeks. And her low-cut top was very revealing. Paul would have been drooling even if he hadn't been isolated from contact with women for so many months. As she started to walk away, he reached out to grab her, pulling his hand back just in time to avoid embarrassment. He slowly exhaled, regaining his composure. "Calm down, Paul," he said to himself. "Act civilized."

Paul had played blackjack in Vegas for $5 a hand, or $3 a hand when he could find a table that allowed it. Blackjack is a game in which if you play the right strategy, supposedly the odds are just about even. Paul wasn't trying to get rich. He just wanted to stay afloat, not risking too much, maybe winning a little, enjoying a game that involved a little skill, and getting a couple of free drinks.

At least, that's how it worked in Vegas. There, they give free drinks to anyone who's actively gambling, an investment that pays off for the house. But in Detroit, you pay for your drinks.

Another difference was there were no five dollar tables. The cheapest minimum was fifteen. And you had to wait in line to get a seat.

Paul wandered around some more. He passed through the Celebrity Room, where the minimum for blackjack was a hundred dollars a hand. He stood awestruck as people bet several hundred dollars a hand trying to beat the dealer. For Paul, a hundred was his limit for the entire evening. He had met people spending years in jail for stealing less money than these players threw away in ten minutes. It sure is a crazy world.

He wandered past slots with big signs that said "Wheel of Fortune" and "Monopoly." He didn't want to play the slots – he knew the odds were very much in favor of the house, and there was no skill involved. He saw other people playing video poker, but he figured that was a losing game too.

He stopped at the blackjack table, stood behind one of the players, and waited his turn. Another cocktail waitress came by, dressed just like the first one he'd seen. By now, he could react calmly to this extreme sensory stimulation, like getting adjusted to bright sunlight after seeing a movie matinee. He calmly said "no thank you" when she asked if he wanted anything to drink. Her expression was grim, businesslike. In fact, come to think of it, he hadn't seen any of the waitresses smiling. Probably a defense mechanism to discourage horny men like himself from getting out of hand.

He struck up a conversation with a woman standing next to him. Her name was Ellen. She was tall, slim, with curly dark brown hair, something like his own. She wore a summer dress, more elegant than sexy, that showed a good part of her back. She looked very attractive. And he saw she didn't have a wedding ring.

Ellen said she was a teacher in Detroit, at Pershing High School, and lived a few miles north of the school in Warren. He told her he was a clerk and union steward at the Post Office, leaving out the fact that he was out of work pending the outcome of his murder trial. They talked about their jobs. There was some talk of a possible teachers' strike, which interested Paul as a unionist, but Ellen was not that involved with the union. She would honor a picket line if a strike was called, but basically, she would roll with the punches, whatever happened. Paul and Ellen exchanged impressions of the casino patrons throwing away their money, gently mocking themselves in the process.

Paul bought Ellen a drink when the next waitress came around. He was really enjoying her company, and talking to her seemed so natural. He remembered what he liked about women was not just their anatomy, but the warmth of a woman's smile, a woman's outlook that was complimentary to a man's, and a woman's genuine friendship that was different somehow from male bonding. This conversation was so different, and so much better, than lusting after a defensive cocktail waitress. Paul realized it would be a gradual process becoming a whole person again after that dehumanizing jail experience, and this conversation was a part of the process.

After close to an hour, Ellen gave up on trying to get into the blackjack game and said she was going to play the slots a little while before she left. Paul got her phone number before she left the table. The smile she gave him as she walked away was the high point of his day.

Finally, there was an empty seat at the table and Paul got a chance to play. He placed two crisp $50 bills on the table and got back 20 chips worth five dollars apiece. He laid three of them down, the minimum, and was in the game.

At one end of the table were two black men in their mid-thirties, dressed casually in shorts and T-shirts. Paul sat between them and a pair of young Japanese guys, in their early twenties, in business attire. An unattractive white woman was at the far end. Then again, she might have been more attractive if she didn't have that sour look on her face. Evidently, she was losing. In fact, there were no smiles at the table, just grim faces.

It was odd. This was one of the few places in the city where people of all different races and nationalities came together for recreation. If people were smiling and enjoying themselves, it would be perfect. But it didn't seem that way, at least from this table.

The dealer was a slightly overweight young black woman, whose tag said she was Charlotte from Chicago. She dealt deliberately; apparently she was still learning the game. None of the players were friendly to her. When they got bad cards they blamed Charlotte; when they got a blackjack, they acted like it was because of their own skill. So it didn't look like Charlotte was enjoying herself either. But unlike everyone else at the table, she was making money.

Before he knew it, Paul was down $75. He decided if he could get back to break-even before he lost all his money, he would split. On the next hand, he had a nine and a seven, an ugly blackjack hand, and the dealer had a king showing. Even though you'll more than likely bust, the strategy card he brought with him from Vegas said the correct play was to take another card. He made the motion for another card with his index finger, and Charlotte dealt him a three. When her hole card turned out to be a seven, Paul had won back fifteen of the dollars he'd lost. Half-an-hour later, he was only down fifteen dollars on the night. The sour-faced white woman had been replaced by an eager young black woman in a Chicago Bulls T-shirt. The other players hadn't changed, and neither had their luck. Two of the other players had run out of chips and handed over a hundred apiece to get more chips. Paul got a blackjack on the next hand. Since blackjack pays 1½ times your original bet, he was now above break-even for the night by $7.50. He cashed in his chips, and slid a five dollar chip across the table as a tip for Charlotte. She smiled for the first time that evening.

Paul walked around the casino, taking everything in again. He was not going to bet any more, and was heading for the exit, but he wasn't in any hurry. He had a broad smile on his face. Having won back the $75 just added to the joy of being out of his cell and in the midst of this sea of humanity.

If he had lost his hundred, his mood might have been ugly. He would've seen the casino for what it is – a huge money-sucking operation. A way for people of all races to throw away their hard-earned cash and give it over to the rich owners. He would wonder how many people were desperately trying to win back the money they lost, only to fall further behind. How many people were giving up their rent money, their kids' school supplies, or worse, their college tuition. How many more people would become addicted to gambling. How many homes and marriages might be destroyed.

He was reminded of a joke he'd heard in Vegas. A man is playing cards, $50 a hand, and his wife comes up to the table and asks him for $20 for the slots. He says, "What, you've lost the last twenty bucks I gave you already?" She says, "Look who's talking, you've lost twelve hundred playing cards!" He says "Yeah, but at least I know what I'm doing!"

Paul knew what he was doing at the blackjack table, or at least he had the illusion that he did. He had come away spending a few pleasant hours, not losing anything, having a good time, and coming away with what amounted to a free drink. And Ellen's phone number. He felt like a winner.

Going down the escalator, Paul had the feeling that at this point in his life, his luck was turning. Maybe this was an omen. Most of the other people on the escalator with him were losers. They were trying to hide it, but you could tell. Then again, even if they had lost a few hundred bucks, they weren't facing trial for murder and a possible lifetime behind bars. You have to keep things in perspective.

Nevertheless, Paul felt great. He had to believe his trial would come out okay. For the time being, life was good. He was out of that hellhole of a jail in Pontiac. He had some time to enjoy himself before the trial, and he was savoring it. And he had the phone number of an attractive and very nice lady.

Later that night he called Ellen. He got a recording: "The number you dialed is not a working number..."

Twenty-nine: THE STRATEGY SESSION
October, 1999

A couple of days before Halloween, Paul was seated at the Union Office in Ferndale for a strategy session. His lawyer Alan Lewiston sat at the head of the table in the conference room. Paul and Angela were on his left, Joanna Carver and Ron Daltry on his right. Everyone had a legal pad in front of them; Lewiston and Daltry each had a briefcase full of material. There was a pot of coffee and some Styrofoam cups, but only Paul and Joanna were drinking.

Lewiston passed out a copy of the prosecution's witness list, and started to go through it. "Many of the names are no surprise. Vellarmo and Antonelli, the cops who first questioned Paul. Logan, the homicide investigator. The medical examiner to verify the cause of death. The ballistics expert. Then there's all the supervisors, Elliott Drummond, Red Collier, Lawrence Harris, Gwendolyn Rogers, Butch Hobson, and Shirley Jones. And of course, Stacey Kline. There could be some shills on this list. It's common practice for the prosecution to put names on the list they have no intention of using, just to keep us guessing. But some of these managers will testify about incidents between Paul and Newton, comments made, fits of anger, and so on."

Lewiston turned his gaze from one side of the table to the other. "Then there are two names that are a complete mystery: Sonia Hammond and Toni Simpson. Anyone have any ideas?"

Everybody shrugged their shoulders.

Angela suggested maybe their private investigator Ron Daltry could check into these names and at least find out who they are.

The final name was Ron Davidson. Angela related her phone conversation. She had already talked to Paul about it, but it sounded more ominous when it was reported to the group as a whole. A witness from the union, who had sold Paul the gun and heard him talk about using Newton as a target, would be quite damaging. Especially since he would come across as a sincere friend of Paul's who reluctantly reached the conclusion he was guilty.

Lewiston wanted to move on to the second part of their agenda. "We've got to attack their case. We'll start with character witnesses. Angela and Joanna will be good – I'll go over your testimony individually."

"We're going to use what's known in the trade as the SODDI defense. It stands for Some Other Dude Did It. We don't have to find the killer beyond a reasonable doubt. But we have to offer some credible alternatives – enough to create doubt that our man did it. Let's turn the floor over to Mr. Daltry."

Ron started his report by saying he hadn't turned up dramatic evidence that proved someone else had done the killing, but some of the information he gathered might be useful.

"First off, Clarence Day has no alibi, and he was never questioned by police."

"I hate to say it," said Paul, "but Clarence does have a pretty good motive."

"Second, supervisor Reggie Green lives alone with his wife. She works the three am shift at the College Park Post Office in Detroit. Reggie wasn't at work the night of the killing and has no alibi. He had plenty of opportunity to kill Newton, and the police never questioned him."

Paul scribbled notes on his pad, Lewiston interrupted Daltry.. "We're going to have to use these friendly witnesses, with a little bit of finesse. They won't want to throw suspicion on themselves. But if we can get them to testify about their hatred, or dislike, of Newton, about their history of conflicts with him, and that the police never questioned them, we've helped our case. We've shown that the police zeroed in on one person and ignored all other possible leads. In a circumstantial case, that can create doubt. We're not going to prove one of these people killed Newton, just that they hated him and had the opportunity to commit the crime.

Then we'll say, that's all they have on Paul, when it comes down to it. Good work, Ron."

"Along the same lines," Angela piped in, "we could ask Emma to testify. She's hated Newton ever since that deal with the OWCP claim. She leaves at five, so she could've made it to the Chef's Hat in time. And a woman can handle the murder weapon. If nobody questioned her, she should be on our list."

Lewiston agreed, saying the more alternative suspects, the better.

Angela continued: "I really don't think Emma did it. The incident with the claim was years ago, but we should still bring her up. And Reggie and Clarence might be more willing to help us if there's a third person, one who isn't black, sticking their neck out like they are."

Daltry then continued with the rest of his report. He had learned that Plant Manager Norm Bradford sees a prostitute once a week. She's known as "Loose Louise" and he likes to tie her up.

Lewiston liked it. "I would love to get that information in front of the jury, just to discredit the witness. Then again, Bradford might not even testify. Let's move on."

Daltry reported Newton has serious gambling debts, mostly to a bookie they call Ike. "His full name is Isaac Aaron. There are two things that distinguish him. One is he's the only person I know with a double "a" in both his first and last names. Secondly, he isn't particularly patient with people who don't pay their debts. It appears Newton owed something like five thousand dollars. I don't know that we can get my sources to testify. But people do sometimes get killed over something like this."

"Wasn't Newton in some shady financial deal?" asked the lawyer.

"Yeah, he was. A couple of years ago, he talked Elliott Drummond into starting a construction company together. Drummond and Newton basically fronted the money, and the day-to-day operation was run by Newton's son Roger.

"The company hadn't been doing well, and last September Drummond let Newton buy him out at a bargain price. Drummond thought Newton was going to sell the company at a loss if necessary to obtain the cash he needed. But two weeks later, the company landed a lucrative contract to work on one of the new casinos in Detroit."

"That must've pissed Drummond off," said Paul.

"Oh, Drummond was furious. He figured he was snookered. And they'd been having conflicts at work, too. Drummond goes along with a lot of Newton's bullshit at work, but he doesn't always like it."

"I remember Drummond was at work the day of the murder," said Angela. But it's hard to track exactly where he was shortly after 0500, or at any given moment. He doesn't punch a time clock when he moves around like us peons do. And even a weak old man like Drummond could handle a twenty-two."

Daltry finished his report with another interesting connection. Newton's son had filed a police brutality complaint against the arresting officer, Danny Vellarmo, not long before the killing.

"There's something in his work record about it now, and my friends on the force say Vellarmo was ranting and raving about Newton junior and senior when this all came down."

"Remember, Newton forced Vellarmo out over an incident the Post Office," said Paul. "We should bring that out."

"And get this," Daltry said. "Vellarmo and Antonelli have this little scam they pull towards the end of their shift. They take turns having breakfast at Denny's while they're both supposedly on patrol. Vellarmo had dropped Antonelli off about a half-hour before the murder. He could've done it himself, made it back to Denny's in five minutes to pick up his partner, and been the first to respond to the call."

"Wow!" said Angela. "This is looking better and better. But I've got one more question. Did you ever find out whether Newton's wife knew about the affair with Stacey? Like I said, a woman could handle this weapon as easily as a man."

"Boy, you keep coming back to that point. Allison Newton

has been telling people she knew nothing about Stacey. But who knows if that's true. She has no alibi for the murder, she's alone in the house that time of day."

Lewiston again commended Daltry. "That's good work Ron. Real good. I'm pretty confident that somewhere in that information you've turned up lies the real killer. But we can't prove it. All we can do is try to create a reasonable doubt at the trial."

"So what do you think our chances are?" Paul asked.

"That's hard to say. It's not an easy case for the prosecution, but there are times when people do get convicted on circumstantial evidence. It's a lot more interesting than any case I've ever handled. The media will find it interesting too. But how it's going to turn out is anybody's guess. It depends on how the evidence is presented, how the jury reacts to the witnesses, and a lot of unpredictable factors. The prosecution is going to be sweating this one out, and so will we. Between now and December seventh there are two things we have to do. Work real hard, and pray."

Thirty: DECEMBER 7th

December 7, 1999

"Going Postal – Smart." That was the theme of the news reports. The media was having a field day. They were speculating that instead of "going postal" by shooting his boss in plain view of coworkers, Paul had planned the killing and might get away with it.

The news reports weren't entirely unsympathetic. It was reported almost like a sporting event, with speculation about who was likely to win. There were interviews with managers about Paul's hot temper. There were interviews with postal employees who told horror stories about the way management treated them. Paul recognized some of these stories; others might've been invented so someone could get their name in the paper. But even these stories, which made management look awful, tended to create an impression in the reader's mind that Paul was guilty.

Paul didn't read the two major dailies. He would continue to boycott those papers as long as union members were locked out. But if the suburban papers and the television coverage he had seen were any indication, this case was going to be sensationalized to the max. In the end, neither postal workers nor postal management would look very good.

It was December 7th, 1999, and Paul was getting ready for the first day of the trial that would either make him a free man or send him to prison for many years, possibly for life. Fear wasn't the only emotion he felt, but it was the strongest. There were a lot of elements in his emotional mix as he struggled to tie his tie. There was the dread of going back to prison, of losing the chance to do anything meaningful with the rest of his life, of losing the chance to find the woman of his dreams, of submitting to brutality, and most probably rape, and the life of a caged animal. There was still the anger at Newton. Yes, he still hated this man, even after his death. He felt a stab of pain every time he thought of Ron

Davidson, the friend who was betraying him. It was even more painful because in all probability, Davidson was sincere.

On the positive side, he thought of his solid friendship with Angela, who was like a rock. Then there was Joanna Carver, his union president. And also Frank Silver, who'd promised to slip away from his job to be at the trial.

Paul's jumble of emotions were so intense that he was barely able to function. He needed the emotional equivalent of a shot of Novocain. His best approach was to try to do some simple things that he normally does by rote. He concentrated brushing his teeth. He tried thinking pleasant thoughts. He thought of Ellen at the casino and about what might have been. He thought of all the good times he'd had with Carol. He thought of what it might be like to go back on the workroom floor and organize after an acquittal. He fantasized about telling his story in open court and almost single-handedly convincing the jury. And he thought again of Angela, a truly wonderful person. Paul felt lucky to have a friend like her.

Angela had shown Paul a flier handed out at work by some radical group, protesting the "frame-up" murder charge against him. Angela liked the sentiment, but knew it was not that simple. First you had to convince people Paul didn't do it, or better yet, prove that somebody else did, before you could tell people it was a "frame-up." Sure, management steered the police towards Paul as the main suspect, but they probably believed it. And it was Angela's sense that many of Paul's coworkers thought he was guilty. They didn't completely blame him, but they didn't condone it either. Some hoped it would turn out that someone else did it. But that's a far cry from believing it was a "frame-up."

Angela could talk to Paul about the positive and negative aspects of the situation without causing anxiety. Even when they talked about the pitfalls and weaknesses of the case, it felt comforting to talk it over with her. Angela was on his side, was there for him emotionally, and he almost had the feeling that no matter what the prosecution threw at him, she wasn't going to let him lose.

But now he was alone, trying to tie his tie for the third time. Part of the problem was he hadn't worn one in more than fifteen years. Ties reminded him of management. Even on formal occasions, he wore a suit but no tie, a look that had become more fashionable in recent years. But Lewiston had insisted on a tie, so Paul had gone out and bought a tie clip and dragged a couple of old ties out of his closet.

Arriving at the courthouse in Pontiac, he was met by a mad rush of reporters with cameras and microphones. Lewiston had agreed Paul could make the following statement: "I did not kill James Newton. I was asleep at the time the murder took place. It is true that I had many conflicts with him, but I had other channels to deal with them. I believe in unionism. The truth will come out in the trial."

Paul felt a surge of confidence after he succeeded in making this simple statement without stammering, and the press seemed satisfied that he had given them an appropriate sound bite, which was all most of them wanted. A few called additional questions out as he continued to walk by them, but overall, his first encounter with the media went off without a hitch.

Lewiston didn't believe in the "No Comment" school of media relations, especially since so much of the coverage had been damaging. He wanted to go on the offensive. He was telling any reporter who would listen that Paul was a person of good character and a fighter for justice in the workplace, that Paul was innocent, and that the prosecution had no evidence to tie him to the crime. Lewiston believed this approach helped his client.

When Paul entered the courtroom his confidence disappeared. He had been in a Detroit courtroom before, as a juror. That experience had been so much different from the enjoyment of reading courtroom mystery novels or watching Court TV. The good feeling about getting some paid time off from work had given way to the realization that in his hands lay an awesome responsibility. If he and the other jurors made a mistake, they could send an innocent man to prison on a charge of criminal sexual conduct. If they made a mistake the other way, a young woman who had been abused would suffer additional emotional distress, probably much more than he could imagine. Entering the courtroom on that occasion, even when nothing was at stake for him personally, had been a sobering experience.

This time it was *his* life on the line. Every significant feature of the courtroom – the jury box (now empty), the judge's elevated chair, the two tables for prosecution and the defense, the wooden benches for spectators – all drove home to him that this is where his future would be determined. With finality. He would be free and his name would be cleared. Or he would be in a living hell for a long, long time. It would all depend on the skill of his court-appointed lawyer and the judgment of twelve strangers.

The courtroom was smaller than the one he remembered in Detroit. There was room for maybe 75 spectators, on four rows of long wooden benches with wooden backs that did not look particularly comfortable. The rows were split into two sections, and one of those sections was empty at the moment. Potential jurors would occupy that section until a panel of jurors was agreed upon by both lawyers. The first two rows of the other section were reserved for the media. No live microphones or cameras were permitted, but Paul saw artists with sketch pads (one of whom was already drawing him) and reporters with note pads. Paul's conviction, or his vindication, would be well documented.

The last two rows were for the general public, and every available inch of these benches was occupied. More people would be allowed in once the jury was selected and the other section was opened. Other than Frank Silver, Paul didn't see any friendly faces.

It was fifteen minutes until the start of the trial. Paul suddenly had a strong urge to move his bowels, and he wasn't sure if he could hold it back. He bolted from his seat, and called back to Lewiston, "I've got to use the restroom."

Thirty-one: THE ROLLER COASTER
December 7, 1999

Prosecutor Andy Zellner did not have to walk far to approach the jury for his opening statement. The prosecution table was closest to the jury box, and it was a relatively small court room.

He lectured like a college professor who could hold the attention of the class. He didn't raise his voice. He knew the jury would be interested in what he had to say, for the same reasons the news media were all over this case. And he borrowed his opening line from the media.

"This is the story of an employee 'going postal,' but doing it in a smart, planned, calculating fashion."

He went on to describe in outline form what the prosecution was going to prove. The opening statement was not the time to present evidence, but to preview what the evidence would show. More than that, it was a time to frame the issues for the jury; to start to influence jurors to interpret the testimony the way he wanted them to.

He went briefly over what the physical evidence would reveal. Newton was killed by a .22 caliber pistol, fired several times. The defendant had nitrate residue on his hands and had fired a gun recently. He had no alibi for the time of the murder. A few more sentences and Zellner wrapped up this portion; it was not the strongest part of his case.

He then went into the main themes of his presentation.

"You will hear evidence from many witnesses that Farley hated James Newton. You will see from his own writing that he was *obsessed* with James Newton. You will see that he invented a name, 'Fig Newton,' to ridicule him. You will see that the defendant wrote an article calling for Newton to be fired. Time and again, the defendant's poison pen was directed at one man – James Newton. He did not simply criticize management's policies with regard to discipline, treatment of injured employees, or what have you. It was always one man, James Newton, who was made out to be the devil in the defendant's articles."

Alan Lewiston rose to object that the prosecution was going beyond the scope of an opening statement and was actually arguing the case. The Judge sustained the objection. Zellner smiled and politely apologized. He didn't mind the objection. He had gotten this point in and the jury was thinking about it.

Zellner continued.

"There will be evidence of how much the defendant was *obsessed* with James Newton from both management and *union* sources. You will learn, for example, that when the defendant went to the gun range to practice with his .22 caliber pistol, he visualized James Newton's face as the target."

It was evident this point had an effect on the jury. Reporters were taking notes. Paul dreaded the tabloid type headlines this fact might generate.

Zellner went on to talk about the death threats the defendant had made against Newton, without going into specifics. Again, the jury took notice and the reporters scribbled furiously.

"Finally, you will hear that twenty-four hours before the murder, the defendant told another steward he was planning to call in to work the next day, even though he was not sick. You will hear that at this point in time, the defendant was frustrated, despondent, and desperate, because he felt James Newton was successfully disrupting his effectiveness as a steward. The defendant's life revolved around being a good steward. When he reported in to work, he was on a mission. In the chess match that goes on between union and management, James Newton, the man the defendant despised with such a passion, was winning. And that was something Paul Farley could not live with.

"The defendant was *obsessed* with James Newton. The defendant wanted James Newton gone. The defendant obtained what he wanted. It is up to you, ladies and gentlemen of the jury, to see to it that the defendant is held accountable for his crime. When you hear all the evidence, I trust you will agree that beyond any reasonable doubt, Paul Farley is guilty."

Paul's stomach sank as he listened to Zellner's opening statement. To the degree he could look at it from a detached point of view, he knew it was convincing. It was dramatic *and* effective. Paul started picturing himself back in a prison cell. Only this time, he might not have a cell mate who would protect him against sexual predators.

He had trouble maintaining his composure. Alan Lewiston grabbed Paul's knee firmly, a gesture the jury could not see, while he smiled and looked straight ahead. It was a reminder to stop his fidgeting and smile at the jury. Paul sat still and stared blankly at the twelve people who would decide his fate. A smile was more than he could manage.

Lewiston then rose, walked past the prosecution table, and faced the jury. He hammered away at his major theme. "The prosecution has no evidence. No witnesses will come forward to tell you they saw Paul Farley shoot James Newton. Nobody saw this, because it didn't happen. The prosecution will not even show you the gun that killed James Newton, because they don't have that either."

Lewiston's tone mocked the prosecution. He used more emotion in his voice than Zellner had, as he proceeded to hold Zellner's case up to ridicule. And he kept coming back to the same theme.

"They have no witnesses. They have no weapon. They have no case."

Lewiston's delivery was effective, in spite of his trouble with the letter "r." Apparently, years of defending clients whom he believed were guilty made him all the more effective when he believed his client was innocent. Or, he kind of believed, but wasn't really sure, which was better than many cases he handled. The truth is, he respected Paul Farley as a person with values and substance. And though he wasn't certain of Paul's innocence, he believed the prosecution had no real evidence. His opening statement was all the more convincing because he believed everything he was saying.

Lewiston held up to ridicule the evidence that Paul Farley hated James Newton.

"We're going to hear that Paul Farley raised his voice, and perhaps he cursed. We'll hear that he slammed the door. And he wrote nasty things in the union newspaper. So what? Union stewards and managers are natural adversaries, and sometimes this relationship gets heated. In Post Offices all over the country, stewards are raising their voices, slamming doors, and calling supervisors names. This is absolutely no proof of anything, other than that life goes on as usual at the United States Postal Service."

Now it was Zellner's turn to object, and the objection was sustained. Lewiston was not supposed to be arguing with Zellner's opening, he was supposed to be previewing his evidence. And, of course, the objection gained the prosecution nothing, because the point had already been made.

What was particularly effective about Lewiston's opening was the tone of ridicule. He had to counteract the shock value of Zellner's revelations about the gun range and the death threats. His theme of "so what," his confidence that the prosecution case was ridiculous, served this purpose well.

He was almost finished now.

"As Judge Richardson will instruct, the defendant is presumed innocent. He does not have to prove anything. The prosecution must prove, beyond a reasonable doubt, that the defendant committed this crime. They will prove *nothing*. They have no witnesses to the crime. They have no murder weapon. All they have is evidence that the defendant hated James Newton. As we will show, there are many other people who hated James Newton, and they are not charged with his murder.

"I know, when you hear the evidence, or the lack of evidence, you will vote to acquit this innocent man."

Paul's spirits soared. All of a sudden, the prosecution's case seemed awfully feeble.

Lewiston could sense the day had been an emotional roller coaster for his client. He put his hand on Farley's arm, leaned over, and spoke softly.

"The whole trial will be like today. First the prosecution will present their side. We'll poke some holes in their witnesses, but the overall impact will be the same as their opening statement. Things will look grim, you'll think you're going back to the slammer. Be strong through that portion of the trial, because better times will come. When we present our witnesses, it will sound like my opening. We'll start feeling better about the case. Before this is over, there will be more ups and downs than you can imagine. Just don't get too down at the low points or two enthusiastic at the bright spots. There's really no predicting the outcome, but I can tell you I'm going to put everything I've got into it."

As Paul drove away from the courthouse, he wondered how he would make it through several more days of emotional turmoil. Preferring not to stop at a bar where everyone would know his face from the TV news, he stopped at a liquor store on the way home. In solitude, he drank himself to sleep.

Thirty-two: THE PROSECUTION WITNESSES
December 9 - 10, 1999

First came the physical evidence. The medical examiner talked about the cause of death. The ballistics expert testified to the type of gun, a .22 caliber pistol (while admitting on cross it was not the same gun that was found in defendant's possession, but pointing out it was similar).

Then the first cops on the scene, Antonelli and Vellarmo, took the stand. They testified the defendant didn't answer his phone and pretended to be asleep when they came to the door.

Lewiston's cross examination of Vellarmo was brief.

"You said that Paul 'pretended to be asleep.' How do you know he was pretending?"

"He was in his pajamas. He wanted us to think he was asleep."

"But how do you know he wasn't really asleep? Was he still wearing socks? Was there some obvious sign that he was faking?"

"No, nothing like that."

Lewiston started back to the defense table, then turned around and said, "No more questions at this time." As Vellarmo stood up and started walking towards the exit, Lewiston added, "But I reserve the right to bring this witness back when the defense presents our case."

Stacey Kline testified to finding the body. She also reported trying to reach the defendant by phone and getting no answer. Her testimony was corroborated by Frank Stone from the Chef's Hat Restaurant. That made three phone calls the defendant supposedly slept through.

"You were having an affair with the victim, weren't you?" Lewiston asked Stacey, beginning his cross examination.

"We went out to breakfast."

"You did more than go out for breakfast, didn't you?"

Stacey hesitated. She looked towards Zellner, hoping he would

269

object. Zellner knew an objection would be futile. He also knew objecting would magnify the importance of the affair. Zellner didn't want the jury to think the prosecution was afraid of this testimony.

"Yes, we had an affair," Stacey admitted. Realizing where Lewiston was heading, she added. "We were *very* discrete."

"I'm sure you were. And husbands never suspect their wife of cheating on them, do they?"

Zellner leapt to his feet to object, whereupon Lewiston withdrew his question and said, "I have no more questions at this time."

Paul noticed Stacey's face turning red as she got down from the witness stand. She shot an angry look at him as she walked by.

The prosecution then turned its attention to motive. Lawrence Harris testified the defendant's hatred of James Newton was well known. He also testified the defendant considered Newton a racist and had filed an EEO complaint against him. Lewiston objected. The testimony was irrelevant, it just showed the defendant was doing his job as a steward to protect the rights of the people he represents the best way he can. The prosecution stated the next witness would tie in the relevance of this line of questioning. Judge Richardson allowed it. Before stepping down, Harris offered his opinion that Newton was not a racist and had always treated him well.

The next witness was Sonya Hammond from New Orleans. Paul had known her as Sonya Wells; that's why he didn't recognize her name on the witness list. She had remarried, and her physical appearance had changed. In ten years she had gained 25 pounds, turning a pleasingly plump figure to overweight, or maybe that was just Paul's perception, now that she was testifying against him. Her face had aged about twenty years, although she still had a pretty smile. Her hair was dyed red.

Sonya testified that she and Paul were lovers back in 1989 when Newton fired her. She testified Paul had been more upset than she was; Sonya was ready to quit and move back to New Orleans.

Paul had told her Newton was racist. Paul had also expressed the opinion Newton was firing her to get at him, since she was "Paul's girl." He had called Newton "a miserable excuse for a human being. And Paul had told Sonya "he would see to it that Newton pays for this, big time."

Lewiston was not well prepared for the cross, since he had no idea who she was. He was unable to shake her on any key points of her testimony, which had been effective and dramatic. Paul just wondered how they found her in New Orleans.

Elliott Drummond walked slowly up to the witness stand, disguising his limp as best he could. He proceeded to testify to numerous examples of Paul's hatred of Newton – cursing, slamming doors, etc. He read excerpts from the *Commentator* and *Activator*. Lewiston objected but was overruled.

Then he went on to describe two death threats. The first came when Martha Huntington had been placed in an off duty status; the second came years later during a dispute over Clarence Day's removal. While both were a little ambiguous, the fact that there were two of them indicates killing Newton was on the defendant's mind.

Drummond was an effective witness. He spoke without emotion, and he didn't appear out to get anyone. He stated that he had his own disagreements with Newton; they were both on the same management team but they were not personal friends. He seemed sincere when he talked about the death threats, and he expressed remorse that he hadn't taken them more seriously at the time.

Lewiston counterattacked:

"These so-called death threats, they weren't serious, were they?"

"It looks like they were serious. Look where we are today."

"Paul didn't state his intention to kill the victim, did he?"

"Close enough."

"Wasn't the comment about Martha Huntington's situation just a rhetorical flourish? And the gesture he made after killing the fly wasn't an explicit threat either, now was it?"

"In hindsight, I believe it was a statement of his intent."

"Did you call in the police for either of these so-called death threats?"

"No."

"Did you call the Postal Inspectors about the supposed threat?"

"No."

"Isn't there a 'Zero Tolerance' policy at the Post Office which states that any threat, even one made in jest, is to be taken seriously?"

"We did take it seriously. We issued a removal notice – I don't know how much more serious you can get."

Stung by Drummond's response, Lewiston retreated to the defense table. He picked up another legal pad and turned back towards the witness.

"Do you know of any enemies the victim had, outside of the workplace? Or anyone he owed a good deal of money?"

"Uh, no I don't."

"Anyone inside or outside of work that he fleeced in a business deal?"

Drummond was silent.

"Isn't it true that you were a business partner with the victim?"

"Objection!" Zellner was on his feet. "Where is this going?"

"You'll see in a moment, your honor," said Lewiston.

"Overruled," said the Judge.

"Didn't he con you into selling your share of the business just as he was about to land a lucrative contract?"

"Uh, that's true. But I'm still in a comfortable position financially. That business was never important to me. Mr. Newton talked me into it to begin with. I broke even, it wasn't a big deal."

"So, Newton robbing you of an opportunity to make a large profit did not upset you in the slightest."

"Objection!" called Zellner. "The witness has already answered this question!"

Lewiston nodded toward the prosecutor and declared he had no further questions."

Toni Simpson was the next witness. She had been a casual on the 110 Belt. She testified to a conversation in which she told the defendant that Stacey Kline leaves a little bit early every Wednesday. It was a small detail. But if Paul knew, or had figured out, Stacey's secret arrangement with Newton to meet for breakfast every Wednesday, it helped the prosecution's case enormously. It fit their theory that Paul had planned the murder carefully.

The last prosecution witness was Ron Davidson. This was the witness Paul feared the most. Ron testified that he and Paul were friends. Paul frequently had dinner at the house with Ron and his wife. They joked around a lot at work. They were also partners at work — fellow stewards trying to thwart the worst abuses management could dish out to employees.

To Ron, being a steward was what he did at work, but it was forgotten when he came home to his family. Paul was different. Being a steward was an important part of Paul's identity. He took his work home with him. There was a time, Ron recalled, when Paul left Ron's house on a Sunday afternoon to go to a coworker's house to get a statement for a grievance. On his off day. To Paul, fighting management abuse was a crusade. There was an intensity to him that Ron respected and feared at the same time.

From Ron's testimony it was clear that Paul hated James Newton. It started back at the beginning of Paul's steward duties. The first incident Davidson remembered was when Newton had fired a young woman Paul had been sleeping with. Newton had referred to the young lady as "Farley's whore." Paul had taken that case very personally, and the outcome left him with nothing but bitterness.

Davidson could recall one incident after another in which Newton had deliberately turned the screws on Farley, and Farley reacted with hatred and fury. Ron stated that, in his opinion, Paul was *obsessed* with Newton.

The night before the murder, Paul's mood had been morose. Newton was getting to him, making even simple union steward functions difficult. For someone as passionate as Paul was about

273

his union work, this was quite a blow. Paul said Newton doesn't deserve to be in a position of power, and "he doesn't deserve to exist."

Ron testified to selling Paul a .22 caliber pistol, the same type of gun that killed James Newton. He regretted it. He recalled that Paul joked numerous times about pretending Newton's face was on the target. He regretted not taking those remarks more seriously.

Ron's final point was that Paul stated he planned to call in sick on November 18th. And he planned to practice at the gun range on the 17th. Ron repeated Paul's words, "That target is looking more and more like Newton all the time. And I'm getting pretty good at it."

Other than getting Ron to concede that Paul hadn't actually stated he planned to kill Newton, Lewiston was unable to shake Davidson on cross. The testimony was deadly.

Paul was shaken. He didn't realize his jokes about Newton as the target had been taken so seriously. And he was surprised the conversation they had the day before the murder had made such a big impression. Had he really said that much?

Davidson didn't look at Paul as he left the courtroom.

Thirty-three: THE SURPRISE WITNESS

December 10, 1999

The trial broke for lunch after Davidson's testimony. Lewiston assumed the prosecution would rest their case when court resumed.

But the prosecution announced a surprise witness, Jacob Hamilton. There was an objection – this witness was not on the list provided in advance by the prosecution. A conference in chambers followed, and then Big Jake, Paul's cell mate, took the stand.

Lewiston was grim. He asked Paul, "Did you tell your cell mate anything that might come back to hurt you?"

"No, of course not."

"Did you talk about the case, or about Newton?"

"I told him about Newton's character and obnoxious style. I talked about how Newton mistreated my coworkers. I told him a lot of stories. But nothing that would hurt me. He was my friend."

"Well, your friend is about to testify against you. Maybe they promised him early release. They claim he liked you, and kept it to himself all this time, but his conscience was bothering him and he spilled his guts last night. A likely story! I'll bet they've been planning to drop this little bomb for months."

Lewiston was visibly shaken. He knew even if his client was innocent, Jake could weave a very believable tale out of the details Paul had supplied.

Jacob Hamilton began with the circumstances of his own arrest. He then testified about finding religion in prison. He read the Bible and prayed on a daily basis. He never initiated violence and broke up fights when he could, but it was also well known he could defend himself if necessary.

He told of taking Paul under his wing as a cell mate, protecting him from jailhouse predators. The jurors paid close attention to this big, imposing presence on the stand. They could easily imagine how comforting it would be to have this man on your side if you were in jail.

He then testified of the many conversations they'd had in jail about the Post Office. Objections that this was hearsay testimony were overruled, the prosecutor arguing this testimony went to the defendant's state of mind. Jake described in detail the circumstances surrounding Clarence Day's removal and Paul's fury at the unfair treatment. He described this incident in even more detail than Paul remembered giving him in their conversations. He was asked about the incident with the fly. He testified as follows:

"When Paul made the gesture above Mr. Newton's head, he wished Mr. Newton was dead."

Paul turned to Lewiston. "That's a lie. I never told him that."

Jake also described Paul's anguish when Sonya Wells (Hammond) was fired.

"Paul felt there was no reason to fire her. With a divorce and custody battle and her father dying of cancer, it was hard for her to concentrate. Anyone would've had trouble learning a new job under those conditions. And yet, she almost passed. She should have been given more time, like Naomi Nadeau."

Paul whispered to his attorney, "I never mentioned Naomi Nadeau's name. Somebody coached him."

Jake was asked what Paul thought Newton's reasons were for firing Sonya. Again, the defense objection to this line of questioning was overruled.

"Paul said Newton was racist. And he said Newton had called Sonya 'Farley's whore.' Paul took Sonya's firing very personally. It was a way for Newton to get back at him. Paul said he was so mad at the time that he could have killed him. And the incident has been gnawing away at him all these years."

Jake had a lot of anecdotes. Paul had compared Newton with the neighborhood bully who taught him 51 pick-up (a story Paul did remember telling Jake). Paul had described how Newton liked to "stick the knife in you and give it a twist."

Finally, Jake was asked, "Did the defendant say anything to indicate he knew who killed James Newton?"

"Yes. The defendant told me he killed Newton himself." There was a stirring in the courtroom, and the Judge pounded his gavel so Jake could continue.

"Newton had finally pushed the defendant too far. All of the frustration, built up over all these years, finally came out."

Then Jake was asked why he had taken so long to come forward. He answered that he liked Paul, he understood the pressures Paul had been under, he respected what Paul had been trying to do as a steward, and he doubted that Paul would ever kill anyone again. But in the end, Jake realized, killing is a sin, and he had to come forward to let justice take its course, even if it hurt a friend.

Paul was stunned. Lewiston was poker faced. He had seen jailhouse witnesses like this before, but none had been so effective. The testimony had been well rehearsed. Jake came across as hesitant to identify Paul as the killer, which made him all the more believable.

Lewiston asked if Jake had been offered any rewards for his testimony. Jake said all he had been offered was a "review" of his situation. When Lewiston asked if Jake had been promised early release in return for saying all these things about Paul on the stand, Jake could truthfully answer no.

All in all, it was a devastating blow to Paul's chances. He left the courtroom shaken and afraid.

Thirty-four: THE PLEA BARGAIN

December 10, 1999

When the Judge adjourned the trial for the weekend, Lewiston took Paul to a private meeting room not far from the courtroom.

"It's not too late to try for a plea bargain," he suggested. "Perhaps I can get Zellner to accept manslaughter and recommend a light sentence. You might get out in a few years."

Paul's stomach sank. Did his own lawyer think he was guilty? Or did he have no confidence in the case? But his first response to Lewiston was not an emotional, but a logical one.

"That makes no sense. Based on the evidence, it couldn't be manslaughter. Either I carefully plotted out the whole thing, like the prosecution says, knowing the rendezvous spot, using the gun range as cover for the gunshot residue test, and finally got rid of my long time nemesis, or else I didn't do it at all. It's either First Degree Murder or someone else did it. How can it be manslaughter?"

"It doesn't have to make sense. It's really a measure of the strength or weakness of the case. They've beaten us up pretty badly with their last two witnesses. But they still can't be absolutely sure of a conviction, because it's a circumstantial case. Maybe we can create some doubt. So they might take a plea bargain on a lesser charge. Besides, they probably realize that even if you got angry and killed him, you're not a hardened criminal and probably won't be a threat to kill anyone else once you're out. So they might compromise."

Seeing the look of disbelief on Paul's face, Lewiston continued:

"I'm sure your union does the same thing sometimes. A guy gets a suspension for seven days, and grieves to get it expunged with back pay. Before it goes to arbitration, management offers to expunge it, but without the back pay. The union wants to keep the guy's record clear, so you're willing to accept the offer. The guy says 'That makes no sense. If I don't deserve the suspension, why

279

can't I get back pay?' But the union thinks it has an iffy case, and clearing the record is better than nothing.

"It's the same thing here. Davidson and Big Jake did a lot of damage to you. We could easily lose and you could get life. Manslaughter would be a lot better, and the prosecution might go for it."

Paul thought back to the months of agony he'd spent in jail. It didn't take him thirty seconds to decide.

"Fight for acquittal. I've done all the jail time I can handle. I'm certainly not going back there voluntarily. Not for a few years, not for a few months. And not for something I didn't do. Because Alan, I am innocent. Big Jake is lying, and Ron Davidson is *awfully* confused. I didn't do it. It's up to you to prove it."

Lewiston had never asked Paul whether he had committed the crime. As a defense attorney, he never asked his client that question. He just examined the evidence and made the best case he could. On many occasions, his clients had protested their innocence. Sometimes he believed them, and sometimes he *wanted* to believe them. Even when he couldn't believe them, he still did his job. On this occasion, he still wasn't sure. But he knew that after the last two witnesses, his chances to win an acquittal weren't nearly as good as they had when the trial began.

Thirty-five: THE DEFENSE

December 13 - 14, 1999

On Monday morning, December 13th, the defense began presenting their case. Paul had spent Saturday with Angela and Sunday with Frank Silver. But he hadn't gotten more than two hours of sleep either night. The apparent lack of confidence his lawyer had displayed Friday evening had shaken him up. He was a nervous wreck.

Clarence Day was the first defense witness. He told the story of his removal and Newton's behavior, in some detail. Newton's rotten character came into clearer focus. Of course, this was a double-edged sword. It helped create some sympathy for whoever might have killed Newton, but it also fed the prosecution case by clarifying the motive. However, the real point, as they had planned it in the strategy session, was to show that Clarence hated Newton, which he freely admitted on the stand, and that he had no alibi for the time of the murder but had not even been questioned as a suspect.

"Can you account for your whereabouts on the morning that Newton was killed?" asked Lewiston.

Clarence admitted he had been home alone and hadn't even taken a phone call.

"Did the police interview you about the murder?"

"No, sir."

"Never asked where you were at the time of the shooting?"

Zellner rose to his feet in objection, the question had already been answered. Lewiston withdrew it, satisfied that asking it twice reinforced the fact that here was someone with a motive to kill Newton and no alibi. He winked at Paul as he sat down beside him.

Zellner tried to defuse the defense's strategy in his cross examination:

"Farley blamed Jim Newton for your removal, didn't he?"

281

"Yes."

"Farley felt Jim Newton played dirty."

"Yes."

"Farley hated Jim Newton every bit as much as you did."

"No question."

"That's all I have."

Reggie Green's testimony was similar, but with a twist. Reggie went through the motions of resisting an invitation to testify on behalf of the defense, and he had to be subpoenaed. This helped him within management circles at work by keeping up the appearance that he was part of their team. It also helped the defense because they were able to get him classified as a hostile witness, allowing Lewiston to ask leading questions.

"Newton jerked you around in terms of your work schedule, didn't he?"

"He sure did. When I left the belt to get weekends off in another area, he gave his girlfriend weekends off on the belt. Later on he took that away and made me a swing supervisor. With my seniority I didn't even have a regular area."

"When Newton suspended you, he made sure everyone knew about it?"

"Yes. And that's unusual. They don't embarrass supervisors like that. They give supervisors discipline very quietly. It's on paper, but you never miss any time. Newton suspended me and made sure the reason leaked. Or his twisted idea of the reason, he said I was falsifying, I was just making the young lady's pay right."

"Tell us about the obscene phone calls."

"The calls started after I challenged Newton for the head of the supervisors' union. The caller didn't identify himself, but I know it was him."

"Objection!" called Zellner. "The witness had no such knowledge who made the calls." The judge sustained the DA's protest.

"What was your opinion of Newton as a manager?" Lewiston continued.

"He's the worst I've ever seen."

"It's fair to say you hated the man?"

"That's an understatement."

"And you were home at the time of the murder, but you have no witness to confirm your whereabouts?"

"That's correct"

"And the police never questioned you?"

"That's correct."

Lewiston cast a questioning look at Zellner, as if the District Attorney's office had been complicit in ignoring another reasonable suspect in the case.

The third defense witness was Emma, who described the parking lot protest and her ordeal with the on-the-job injury.

"We've heard testimony that Paul was so fanatical that he took your statement off the clock. Was there more to it than that?"

"We were friends. He'd been to my house before." She hesitated, then added, "He stayed overnight sometimes."

"How did you feel about Newton?"

"I hated him. He put me through hell when I was hurt on the job. He lied. He tried to stick me with an expensive hospital bill after he made me go there. When Paul showed me the lying witness statements I couldn't believe it. I'm glad he doesn't supervise anymore, though it's a tragedy how it came about."

"Did the police question you at all?"

"No."

Lewiston cast another unforgiving look at the DA. "No further questions."

On cross, Zellner again reinforced his main theme.

"During the incident about your injury, what did the defendant say about Mr. Newton?"

"I don't remember."

"Let me remind you that you're under oath."

"He said, 'I can't tell you how much I hate that man. He enjoys making people suffer.'"

"No further questions."

Then came the character witnesses – Joanna Carver and Angela Roberts. In addition to praising Paul's honesty and dedication to unionism, Joanna challenged the prosecution focus on the "Fig Newton" quotes from the *Commentator*. She read excerpts from local postal union newspapers from Greensboro, NC, St Petersburg, FL, Des Moines, IA and Seattle, WA to show that personal attacks on bad managers are common in union publications. This testimony was admitted over Zellner's objection.

Angela corroborated Joanna's testimony about Paul's character. She talked about him in glowing terms. She also testified to an important detail. On many occasions, she had called Paul during the day and gotten his answering machine. He was in the habit of turning off the bell on his phone and letting the machine take messages when he slept. Since he worked such odd hours, this made sense. Otherwise, his sleep would be disturbed by telemarketers and other nuisance calls, not to mention well-meaning friends. In fact, Angela thought it was such a good idea that she started doing the same thing herself.

Then Lewiston led Angela down a surprising path.

"In your opinion, did the defendant want to see Mr. Newton leave?"

"No. As much as he hated Newton, he also needed him. Paul's main objective was to organize the workers at the Plant. He told me having a character like Newton around gave him a convenient target, a focus or rallying point, if you will. If it wasn't for Newton, Paul's job would have been much harder."

Remembering no such conversation, Paul was touched that Angela would invent something like that to help him at trial. But on the other hand, he wondered if it could also hurt him, by making him look cynical and calculating. He cringed when Zellner cross examined his friend.

"I have here an article entitled 'Fig Newton Must Go.' Your honor, may I approach the witness?"

"Yes you may."

"Are you familiar with this article?"

Angela mumbled, "Yes."

"Can you speak up please?"

"Yes, I'm familiar with this article."

"It calls for Mr. Newton to be removed from his position, does it not?"

"Yes it does."

"Can you name the author of the article?"

"Paul Farley."

"Yet you want us to believe the defendant liked having Mr. Newton as a boss? Give me a break. I have no further questions for this witness."

Then the defense called a surprise witness, waitress Bessie Brown from Denny's. Lewiston stated Bessie had just come forward the night before with new information, which is why the prosecution had not been informed in advance. Zellner didn't believe it, but Judge Richardson allowed it, since the prosecution had done the same thing.

Bessie testified about the daily breakfasts of Officers Antonelli and Vellarmo. She testified Antonelli was at Denny's at the time of the murder. This left Vellarmo with no alibi.

Zellner objected, saying Vellarmo was not on trial. He didn't want yet another credible suspect added to the list. Lewiston reminded Judge Worthington that he planned to recall Vellarmo as part of the defense case. Zellner's objection was overruled.

Judge Richardson recessed for the day before the defense could call Vellarmo to the stand.

On Tuesday morning, Paul made his way to the sprawling brick and concrete building that housed the courtroom. This building had seemed foreboding when the trial started a week earlier. But now, in an odd sort of way, it was part of a comfortable daily routine. He took the same combination of freeways to commute there, at the same time. He parked in the same parking lot. It was sunny and warm for December, and he felt a surge of optimism as he passed by the usual group of reporters. He gave them his daily sound bite. Today's quote was, "Today, you're going to hear my story." He gave them the thumbs up sign and went inside.

Lewiston called Danny Vellarmo to the stand. Unfortunately, Danny had used the previous evening to prepare. He knew better than to lie about Antonelli having breakfast at the time of the murder. He stated it was not uncommon on the Troy police force, it was no big deal. This testimony would not sit well with the majority of conscientious police officers, but it was the only thing he could say under the circumstances.

Lewiston cross-examined Vellarmo about the police brutality charges filed by Newton's son. But Vellarmo had been well coached. He played down his emotional reaction to it. Lewiston couldn't get him to show any anger over the incident. He said in the rough and tumble of police work complaints sometimes get filed, and you just accepted the fact that it came with the territory. Vellarmo also downplayed his reaction about the circumstances under which he left the Postal Service. He testified that actually, Newton had given him a break and he appreciated it. Lewiston knew that the witness had been very upset at the termination and angry over the brutality charge, but he couldn't elicit the response he wanted from Vellarmo on the stand.

The testimony of the gun shop owner was brief. Paul was a regular customer and he had used the shooting range on the day in question. There was no cross examination.

Finally, it was Paul's turn. They went over what he did on the day leading up to the murder. He testified about going to the gun range, which is why he tested positive for gun shot residue. He testified about going to sleep and turning the ringer off on his phone like he always does.

He also stated the gun he gave the police was the only one he ever owned. And he testified about his remarks to Davidson about using Newton as a target. It was just a harmless joke, Davidson should have known that. In fact, Davidson had joined him in the joking.

Then he went on to testify about his philosophy of unionism. He gave what amounted to a half-hour speech, broken up into segments that could be prompted by Lewiston's questions. He told the jury the most important thing to him was organizing the workers. Management was the adversary. No matter which person management puts in charge, the interests of management and the union are counterposed. It was his job to help workers defend themselves against management abuse. This is something he simply believes in. Defend the little guy against the powerful, against those who want to deprive him of a living wage, or of dignity on the job.

On the surface, the legal rationale for giving this speech was to refute the prosecution contention that Paul desperately wanted to be rid of Newton. This testimony would show Paul had a more far reaching and more noble objective, and that Newton, or whatever personality management threw at him, was not that significant. But there was an additional objective behind this testimony. The point was to impress the jury with Paul's sincerity; with his commitment to his beliefs. The idea was to get the jury to like Paul as a person, so they would want to find a reason to acquit. Then they could use the absence of witnesses, a murder weapon, and other direct evidence to form a basis for reasonable doubt.

But it didn't happen as planned. The prosecution objected repeatedly. Nearly every question was met with an objection, and when Paul started rambling on, he was interrupted with more objections. Judge Richardson played it down the middle, sustaining some objections while allowing some of the testimony. But Paul's rhythm was broken, his testimony was choppy and the content wasn't clear. Most importantly, what came across wasn't a picture of Paul as a person, the way the defense intended. What came across was simply the answers to a few specific questions whose relevance wasn't all that clear.

Paul was reminded of his presentation at the EEO hearing many years ago. He had intended, through testimony, to show a clear pattern of discrimination. But with all the objections and the disruption of his rhythm, he knew that no clear pattern emerged.

What's worse, he still had to endure cross examination. Zellner concentrated on a few areas he wanted to highlight. Newton harassed Emma when Paul was sleeping with her. Newton fired Sonya when Paul was sleeping with her. Zellner went over some of the details of Sonya's case, and started to get Paul a little riled up, which was his intention. Finally, Zellner tried to get Paul to describe the time Newton had fired him after the incident with the fly. By this time, Paul realized Zellner was trying to get him angry on the stand, and he made a concerted effort to control his temper. But in his questioning, Zellner hammered away at one theme. Wasn't there something *personal* between Newton and Farley?

Paul admitted a strong dislike for James Newton. There was really nothing else he could do. He just hoped the jury believed that this hatred had not led him to murder.

It was early afternoon when the defense rested. The Judge decided to hear closing arguments and then recess. Since the court had no trial activity on Wednesdays (one day a week was reserved for administrative matters), the jury would begin deliberations Thursday morning.

As he listened to the closing arguments, Paul was enveloped by a feeling of helplessness. Not hopelessness – he knew there was a chance for acquittal. In fact, right now, Lewiston was hammering away at the unreliability of testimony from criminals hoping for early release. Prosecutors have become very skilled at stopping just short of formalizing a deal, so a witness like Big Jake can say on the stand he is just testifying to get the truth out but he's really trying to get himself out. And he'll say whatever the prosecution wants to obtain his release.

No, it was not hopeless, the jurors seemed to be paying attention to Lewiston. The helplessness Paul felt was simply a recognition that there was nothing more he could do to influence the outcome. And he was not sure how much he had helped himself when he testified. It certainly hadn't gone the way he had pictured it.

He'd been trapped on this issue of whether he really wanted Newton removed from his MDO position. It's funny the way issues get framed in a trial and the conclusions that are drawn favoring one side or the other. It reminded him of Arbitrations he had seen, where both sides framed the issue differently than he would, placing major importance on something that seemed beside the point.

The truth was really more complicated than any of the testimony indicated. Yes, Paul believed in organizing the workers, just like he and Angela had testified. The overriding issues between labor and management transcend the individual personalities, and on one level, Newton was irrelevant. And, as Angela had indicated, there were times when having an outrageous manager like Newton helped Paul in his organizing.

Yet the glaring fact remained that Paul had really hated Newton. There was no doubt about it. He *did* want management to remove him from that position. Partly because that would be a victory in itself. And partly because Newton had been making everything difficult for him. As a steward, Paul enjoyed the simple pleasures of helping people get problems worked out. When he could help someone straighten out a pay problem, get an overtime make-up opportunity, or get a day off on annual leave, it made him feel good. And, Paul knew, helping people on these minor issues made it easier to organize them for the larger battles with management.

But in Newton's last days, Paul had been miserable and frustrated. Yes, he had hated Jim Newton. And he had wanted Newton gone more than anyone knew.

Thirty-six: THE BURGLAR

December 15, 1999

He had scouted the house thoroughly. On Wednesday morning the man of the house left for work at 5:00 AM, and nobody was home for at least an hour. Plenty of time to break in and get something of value.

There was an alarm system which would bring the police. In this Bloomfield Hills neighborhood the response time would be quick, probably within ten minutes. He would be gone by then. The trick was not to get greedy. Take some of the lady's expensive jewelry and maybe a VCR or a computer tower that he could carry under one arm. In and out of the house one time; he wouldn't come back for seconds. That's how he would avoid getting caught.

After watching the man pull out of the garage in his Lexus right on schedule and drive out of sight, he broke the glass window on the back entry door. Reaching through, he unlocked it from the inside and let himself in.

No alarm sounded. This was his lucky day. The fool forgot to set the alarm. Now he could modify his plan of action.

The television and stereo equipment would take three or four trips back to his van in the alley. The computer must be upstairs. The jewelry would also be upstairs, in the bedroom.

He went up the stairs and to the left. As he opened the bedroom door and took his first step in, a shot rang out. He collapsed on the floor, a burning pain erupting in his gut. *Damn it!* The lady wasn't supposed to be home from work yet, she worked nights!

The lady of the house hadn't killed the intruder, but she had foiled his plans with a single shot in the abdomen. A shot from a .22 caliber pistol.

Thirty-seven: THE NEW MILLENNIUM

January, 2000

Samantha Chambers stayed home on New Year's Eve rather than going partying with her sister. She was afraid the Y2K bug would shut down all the computers and cause a disaster. Afterwards, she felt foolish. Not only had she missed a good time, but she fell on the stairs at home and injured her back. Her doctor gave her a note saying no lifting more than ten pounds for a week. Had she gone out with Tawanna, she probably wouldn't need this doctor's note. And had she talked to Tawanna, she'd know the Post Office requires at least a 15 pound lifting restriction to approve light duty work.

It was now Tuesday morning, January 4th, and Samantha had been told to punch out and go home by the new MDO Veronica Robbins. Robbins until recently held an upper management position at the large Post Office on Fort Street in downtown Detroit. When Samantha asked if she could see a steward, Robbins told her she had to punch out, but if she wanted to talk to a steward on her own time, she had no problem with it.

Samantha walked gingerly down to the union office. She opened the door. The only steward inside was the one who had helped her when she had been a TE, Paul Farley.

She looked across the table at Paul and smiled. It was the first chance she'd had to talk to him since he came back to work a week ago. "I'm so glad your trial ended the way it did. I was hoping you'd be found Not Guilty, but this was even better. If the jury acquitted you on reasonable doubt, people would still wonder. There'd be a cloud of suspicion. This way, everyone knows you didn't do it, because they know who did."

"Did a lot of my coworkers think I was a murderer?"

"I don't know if I'd say that, exactly. Many people didn't know what to think. Everyone was speculating. Some said you did it, and other people had a lot of different suspects. But I never heard anyone guess it was *Harold Kline.*"

A few weeks before, Paul's ordeal had ended abruptly. Stacey Kline had called in sick that Tuesday night, leaving her car in the garage and out of sight, and surprising the burglar coming into her bedroom. Ballistics tests had determined the bullet she put in the burglar's abdomen came from the same gun that had killed James Newton. A gun her husband had bought her for protection in this type of situation. A gun her husband had used to commit murder, then quietly put back in her bed stand.

It had been Thursday, the day after the burglary, when the ballistics expert recognized the bullet removed from the burglar's abdomen as the same configuration as the bullets taken from James Newton's corpse. Jury deliberations were halted, and the jury was not told why. On Friday, Harold Kline confessed and the jury was dismissed.

The murder of James Newton had nothing to do with his abusive treatment of postal workers. It was the oldest crime in the world, murder motivated by jealousy. It really is hard to keep an affair a secret. Even as busy as he was with his job, Harold Kline noticed some of the signs. He just didn't know who was involved with his wife. That's why he'd hired an investigator – the one Stacey thought was looking into some funny business involving Harold's boss.

Prosecutor Zellner handled the situation with class. He called a press conference, along with homicide detective Logan. They explained they felt they had strong evidence, but it turned out they had the wrong man. It doesn't happen often, they said, and when it does, they want to do the right thing. The charges were dropped, and they apologized for what they had put Paul Farley through. And they credited excellent police work for rectifying the error and discovering the true killer.

The jury had come back once, before the ballistics people had reached their conclusion about the gun, early on Thursday.

Everyone in the audience thought they had reached a quick verdict. But they were just coming back to ask that Sonya Hammonds' testimony be read to them again. One juror later told a reporter they stood at 10-2 for conviction before their deliberations were halted.

Paul had come back to work right after Christmas. He'd gotten hugs from Emma Friedman and Aretha Simmons, and a big kiss from Angela. Reggie Green, the new MDO along with Veronica Robbins, shook his hand. Drummond had retired, and it wasn't clear how the new team would work out for the employees. While Green was decent and Robbins was an unfeeling hard-liner, it wasn't clear yet which one would have more clout on the tour.

Tour One had lost one steward and gained another. Ron Davidson had bid back to day shift during the trial, saying he wanted a normal lifestyle again. Probably he didn't want to face the reaction of Paul's friends on Tour One after he gave his testimony. The truth is, he felt terrible about it. The new steward on Tour One was Claudia Stinson, the former 204-B. Angela had talked her into it. Claudia had found she couldn't make things better as a manager; maybe she could do it as a steward.

Another familiar face at work was Ron Daltry. Angela had won his case at the OWCP hearing a couple of weeks before the trial. Now Ron spent his evenings sitting at the tear-up table, where he placed letters that had been torn up by the automated equipment inside a plastic wrapping, with a note of apology inside. There was enough of this work to last him eight hours a day.

After more than a year of dreading a lifetime in prison, and after hearing professional lawyers argue over his guilt or innocence, Paul was back to his job of playing lawyer and organizer at the Post Office. In front of him was the weighty issue of whether you needed to be able to lift ten pounds or fifteen pounds in order to be approved for light duty. He was loving every minute of it.

"I'll tell you what, Samantha," he said. "Go back to the doctor and get the note changed to fifteen pounds. Hopefully, you can get that done by tomorrow. Then we'll file a grievance to get you paid for today. There's really no reason you can't throw letters in a hand case with a ten pound restriction. But you should know it may take forever for your grievance to be heard at arbitration. That's why you ought to get the note changed right away. Meanwhile, you'll have one more day to rest your back, which you hopefully will be paid for some time in this millennium."

He rose from his chair, reached out his hand, and said, "It was nice to see you again, Samantha."

"It was really nice to see you."

Claudia and Angela came into the office as Samantha was leaving. "Claudia's writing an article for the Activator about turning safety issues around and using them against management. You're going to love it. And I think the workforce is ready to do something. We're going to have some fun around here."

Claudia said, "I like the new poster you put on the wall. I hope the members take its message to heart."

The poster resembled a road construction sign. The wording was "Solidarity Zone. Proceed With Respect."

Paul said, "I heard from Clarence Day. He got his old job back at Chrysler. He was involved in a walkout because it was freezing in the plant the other day. The workers shut that plant down, and they had the heat working real good the next day. And you know what? Clarence is thinking of running for a UAW steward. He might be a good one, as long as he controls his temper. A good steward should never lose his temper." Paul kept a straight face while he made this last remark. The two women just smiled.

Claudia excused herself. "I've got to hold a Step One with Lawrence Harris. He issued a Letter of Warning to a guy who's got over 700 hours of sick leave balance, just because he's had a bad few months. I can't believe that guy."

As Claudia left, the phone rang. It was Paul's supervisor in Flats, Tawanna Chambers. She said she needed him back by 0400 for dispatch. "The mail's pretty heavy today. Will that be a problem?"

It was a very weird feeling working for Tawanna. Probably for her too. Paul told her 0400 would be no problem.

Then he looked across the table at the wonderful person sitting there. Angela was really looking beautiful. He looked at her like he never had before. He loved Angela, and he had loved her for a long time. He'd never admitted it to himself, for some reason. Now he felt kind of nervous, like a teenage boy asking a girl out for the first time. "Angela, would you like to have dinner with me on Saturday, maybe take in a movie?"

A Note from the Author

As I stated in the Introduction, I was a steward in a union local that experienced two shootings (Royal Oak and Dearborn). For most of my career, I worked at a building that is part of Royal Oak – it's not the same building where the 1991 shooting occurred, but there was a high level of tension in both buildings.

After the Royal Oak shooting, my article in the union newspaper described specific examples of outrageous management behavior I had personally witnessed and suggested changes at the highest level of management:

"The bullies, sadists, and liars in management's ranks need to be disciplined or replaced. But there is another type of upper level manager who needs to change. Some of the postal bureaucrats in powerful positions are nice people. But when we bring to their attention the immoral and inhumane practices on the workroom floor, they pass the buck. They refuse to believe supervisors are really harassing the employees. Or they know, deep down, that the supervisors are lying, but they fail to take action on it. So the bullies and liars have a green light to continue. There are quite a few decent human beings in upper management who sit comfortably behind their desks and make decisions that cause considerable pain to employees they've never met."

While there was a bit of a relaxation in the atmosphere at Royal Oak, at least for a few years after the shooting, the lessons of Royal Oak were not applied generally. In 1992, Reggie Brown, a union officer at the Dearborn office, wrote an article in our local newspaper comparing the atmosphere there to a ticking time bomb. He expressed the fear that Dearborn might become the next Royal Oak.

His fear was justified. On May 6, 1993, Dearborn was the scene of another tragic postal shooting. My subsequent article again explored the root causes in terms of the mindset and behavior of

299

postal management:

"Another part of the problem is a bureaucratic mentality that can be infuriating. A couple of years ago, a labor lawyer I met at a party told me the Post Office is known for a unique brand of pettiness. I knew immediately what she meant. One example would be how they send you back to the doctor several times until your note is worded exactly the way they want it. Many readers can cite their own examples. It's not that anyone's going to get violent over a doctor's note. It's just that the combination of all the petty rules and regulations, and how they use these rules to stick it to you, is enough to make you scream."

I won't say James Newton is typical of a postal manager, but from reading union newsletters around the country I can say there are others like him. Once you have a James Newton in charge, it's not easy to get rid of him.

While none of the characters in this novel are real, some of the stories are real, or partly real. I did handle an edit grievance like the one in "The Wrong Zip." The letter from James Newton in "Blaming the Victim" was taken from a grievance file (although the issue was easily resolved with a phone call, unlike my fictional account). "Adding Insult to Injury" is also based on a real grievance file. The show of unity in "Sticker Shock" is told pretty much the way it happened. The stewards' discussion of the Royal Oak shooting in Chapter 9 is based on my memory of that tragic situation. Most of the anecdotes the stewards tell in "Jump Suits and Jump Shots" are real stories as well. I handled an EEO appeal like the one in "Going Before the Judge" and I retold that story faithfully. I should add that I've never filed a grievance for an employee I was sleeping with at the time – those characters were added for dramatic impact. "Grin and Beer It," "The Fly," and a number of other stories are simply products of my imagination.

I began writing this novel in the summer of 1998, at which time the fictional murder was in the future. I breathed a sigh of relief when November 1998 passed without incident. Since I had a full-time job in addition to editing a newspaper, work on the book proceeded slowly. After unsuccessful attempts to get it published, I pretty much gave up. I was fortunate to meet the good people at Hardball Press at a labor conference in 2012, and the project was revived.

In the time that the manuscript sat, much has changed in the postal world. The job security of postal employees is now in question, and the excellent service delivered to the public is under attack from political forces that would like to bust the unions, privatize the service, and enrich corporations that would take over the profitable aspects of mail processing and delivery. I would be remiss if I didn't say that most postal workers – in spite of complaints about some of the managers – want very much to keep their jobs. And if the forces that are out to destroy us succeed, the public will suffer along with the employees.

I believe strong labor unions are the key to solving both problems – the danger of privatization and the inhumane treatment of workers by managers in some locations. As a retiree, I intend to remain active in the labor movement, both to defend my own retirement benefits and to do my share to try to make this world a better place.

PURCHASE ORDER

Hard Ball Press
PO Box 260201
Brooklyn, NY 11226
info@hardballpress.com

Name of purchaser: _____

Street Address: _____

City, State & Zip: _____

Country: _____

Price: $15.00/book + $2.75 shipping – Total price : $17.75/book

SCHOOL & UNION VOLUME DISCOUNT PURCHASING 10 COPIES
OR MORE:

Price $10.00/book + $1.75 shipping – Total price: $11.75/book

Book Title	Number of copies	Sale Price	Shipping cost	Amount due

Add Amount due for all books: _____